THE BEND OF THE WORLD

LIVERIGHT PUBLISHING CORPORATION

A DIVISION OF W. W. NORTON & COMPANY

NEW YORK   LONDON

THE BEND OF THE WORLD

A NOVEL

Jacob Bacharach

For information about permission to reproduce selections from this book,
write to Permissions, Liveright Publishing Corporation, a division of
W. W. Norton & Company, Inc., 500 Fifth Avenue, New York, NY 10110

For information about special discounts for bulk purchases, please contact
W. W. Norton Special Sales at specialsales@wwnorton.com or 800-233-4830

Illustrations by Edith E. Newman.

Manufacturing by Courier Westford
Book design by Lovedog Studio
Production manager: Anna Oler

Library of Congress Cataloging-in-Publication Data

Bacharach, Jacob.
The bend of the world : a novel / Jacob Bacharach. — First Edition.
pages cm
ISBN 978-0-87140-682-8 (hardcover)
1. Middle-aged men—Pennsylvania—Pittsburgh—Fiction. 2. Social skills—
Fiction. 3. Friendship—Fiction. 4. Psychological fiction. I. Title.
PS3602.A335 2014
813'.6—dc23

Liveright Publishing Corporation,
500 Fifth Avenue, New York, N.Y. 10110
www.wwnorton.com

W. W. Norton & Company Ltd.
Castle House, 75/76 Wells Street, London W1T 3QT

1 2 3 4 5 6 7 8 9 0

For my brother

I. OBJECTS IN MOTION

1

It was a wet February in Pittsburgh, spring, early and without warning, and twice in one week UFOs had been spotted hovering over Mount Washington. Well, people said, that's not exactly the strangest thing you'll see on Mount Washington, which was just one of the ways that we said bullshit, but by the end of the following week there were so many eyewitnesses and cell phone pics and videos and even a sudden and suddenly popular blog called Alieyinz.com dedicated to these and other sightings around the city and the rural counties south and east that the mayor's office called a press conference To Address the Speculation. The early part of that year had been rough for the mayor. A lingering and byzantine dispute with the head of the Economic Development Council blew up when the director of the EDC publicly resigned, citing a culture of intimidation, corruption, favor-trading, and recrimination in a widely published letter. Then the papers reported that the mayor himself was under investigation for appropriating a Homeland Security grant and using the expensive new surveillance equipment to spy on his not-yet-ex-wife and her attorney. So the mayor didn't actually show up to the flying saucer press conference; his chief of staff Jonah Kantsky came instead, which was just as well, since everyone said that

Kantsky was the Svengali behind the young mayor or, since it had been pointed out that such phrasing might be a little bit anti-Semitic, that he was the Richelieu behind the child king. When the woman from Channel 4 asked him why the mayor wasn't at the presser, Kantsky said, Gail, the mayor is busy cooperating with investigators, which made the reporters laugh. Anyway, Kantsky said something to the effect of we're cooperating with DOD and DHS and the National Weather Service and the Air Force reserve wing out at the airport and all relevant state and local and federal authorities including the Pittsburgh FBI office etc. etc. etc. and I can assure you that while clearly something was seen last week there is no probative or dispositive evidence or indication that it was anything other than a meteorological phenomenon, in fact I have been convincingly assured through these consultations that it was an example of a rare phenomenon called ball lightning, the result of warm or cold air masses or vectors or something.

Then a huge bald black guy in a dark suit and a yellow yarmulke who'd been standing quietly in the back lost his shit and started screaming, You want to live in a dreamworld forever? And he had to be hauled out by a pair of police officers barely as tall as his shoulders. That effectively ended the press conference, except that a live mic caught Kantsky muttering something about a fruitcake to an aide, and the next day the story was neither the UFOs nor the outburst by the man, who turned out to be Rebbe Mustafah Elijah, the high priest and sole proprietor of a local sect called the Universal Synagogue of the Antinomian Demiurge, a weird millennial cult based out of the back room of Elijah's Africana store in East Liberty, but rather a subsequent press conference hastily arranged by City Councilwoman Mary Tremone, a presumptive mayoral challenger in next year's contest, who cited Kantsky's overheard comment as just one more indication of a heedless and uncaring administration displaying a shocking disregard for the feelings and emotional well-being of the city's LGBTQ communities, especially its youth, who faced bullying every day, and who were The Future of Our City. And so by the first week in March the whole thing became a diversity imbroglio.

Once more down the memory hole, said my buddy Johnny Robertson, waving a fry at my face over the table in our booth at the diner.

This place is shit, I said. Why do we come here?

Did you ever meet the rabbi? Johnny asked me.

Who?

Mustafah Elijah. Did I ever introduce you? No? That guy is awesome. He ate the fry. The thing is, my friend said, the thing is that there's a fourth river, you know, under the city. So if you take the aerial view of the city and you have the Allegheny and the Mon coming together at the Point to form the Ohio, if you take the Ohio and sort of extend that axis through the point and onward between the other two rivers, what you get, ta-dah, is basically the peace sign, which of course is just an inversion of a satanic symbol representing the Baphomet, which is in turn just a reproduction of an even more ancient sigil related to Ba'al worship and suchlike. So basically the Point represents a node or a nexus of intense magical convergence, an axis mundi, if you will, wherein vast telluric currents and pranic energies roil just beyond the liminal boundaries between the phenomenal and the numinous branes of existence, and obviously this whole UFO what-have-you is a manifestation of that, not some fucking ball lightning or whatever. Jesus, ball lightning? Fucking fifty years after Roswell and a century after Tunguska, and that's the best they can come up with? I was born at night, but not last night.

Uh-huh, I said.

You gonna eat the rest of those eggs, brother? Johnny asked me. Oh, and can I owe you? I'm a little short today.

2

I was halfheartedly dating a girl named Lauren Sara at the time, or she halfheartedly dating me. Ours was the sort of object in motion that, unacted-upon by an external force, remains in motion. But isn't that true of all objects, and all relationships? Johnny hated her. You're a classic gay misogynist, I told him. He objected. I don't hate all women, or even most women. Just every woman you've ever dated. Do I need to draw you the Venn diagram? The common denominator is not the vagina.

We'd met, Lauren Sara and me, the past summer in a popular bar on Penn Avenue on a day so hot and insistently humid that the sunlight turned green. It was the sort of day when thunder keeps grumbling in the distance but rain never quite seems to arrive. I'd played softball with some of the guys down at Baldy McGrady Field before a real team with real equipment and a real reservation chased us off, and I was cooling off with a beer, unsuccessfully, because even on Sunday afternoon the bar was hot and crowded. Can't they turn on the fucking air? I said to no one in particular. My friend Derek said, Hipsters hate air-conditioning. Do they? I said, and he shrugged. It seems like they would.

From behind, Lauren Sara looked like another friend of mine, and she was talking to a girl I thought I might have known, and when I went over and tapped her on the shoulder and said, Hey, and realized, when she turned around, that she was someone else, I said, Oh, sorry; I thought you were someone else.

And she sipped her whiskey through the little stirrer straw and lifted her eyes and shrugged and said, I am. She paused. Someone else. Derek, who was on his way to take a piss, heard this, and I heard him mutter, Oh Jesus Christ. I later found out that he'd dated Lauren Sara. A good time, he said, was not had by all.

So what's your name again? I asked, even though I hadn't yet asked her for her name.

Lauren Sara, she said, but someone had just then turned up the music and I leaned closer and said, Laura?

Lauren Sara, she said again. I fucking hate when people call me Laura.

Lauren Sara, I said. That's two names.

Two too many, she said.

What? I asked.

I don't know, she said. What's your name?

Peter, I said.

Can I call you Pete?

No.

She grinned, and she said, See?

We walked back to her studio. She was a graduate student at CMU, a sculptor or something, who made things or assemblages or whatever that looked like chairs to me. It had finally rained briefly and hard while we were in the bar, and the sycamores drooped over the cemetery wall. Her studio, which she shared with another artist, whom she called the Greek, was on the second floor above a closed auto body shop on Penn Avenue; you walked up a narrow concrete staircase and pushed aside a steel fire door that clanged like something in a medieval dungeon and walked into an expanse of concrete and cracked windows and piles of industrial junk.

Why do you call her the Greek? I asked.

Because, Lauren Sara answered, she's Greek.

Like Greek Greek? I said.

Like Zeus. Like ruins. Like a spinach pie. Do you smoke weed?

I watched her while she dug around for a piece or papers. She was prettier than the women I usually dated, who tended to look more like Lauren Sara's futurist constructs than like Lauren Sara: severe, planar, composed in straight lines and angles. Johnny said I only dated women who looked like little boys. You're a classic ephebophile, he said. Please, I told him. You think everyone is gay. He sighed. Not gay. Gay is an artifact of the binary twentieth century mind. What's gay? You're gay, I told him. I, Johnny said, and you have to understand that he was a big, barrel-chested beast of a man who was just

then wearing a pair of hiking boots, cargo shorts, and a Lai-
bach T-shirt, am queer. You sure are, I said.

Anyway, Lauren Sara had a round face and a body that,
if slight, could by no reasonable standard be called boyish.
She had blue eyes, but the blue was never much more than
a soft halo around big black pupils, forever dilated because
she smoked too much weed. She wore sundresses over span-
dex shorts and she rode a bike everywhere. She was in a phase
of feigned poverty; she never did introduce me to her parents,
and she was always vague about their backgrounds, but I figured out that her dad was an attorney or something and her
mom was the head or principal or director of some kind of
vaguely Catholic private school in Philly, and once during the
winter we were together, when she'd claimed to be unable to
hang out for a few days due to some pressing school projects,
I'd been driving through Shadyside and had spotted her outside of a restaurant, ducking abashedly, or so I imagined, into
the back seat of a big Mercedes with a handsome, sixtyish
couple already in the front seats.

Well, that all came later. We got a little stoned and drank
a little more warm whiskey from a bottle she snatched from
the Greek's drafting table, and she made me look at some of
her sculptures and asked what I thought about them. I said I
liked them and they looked like chairs. Cool, she said. I'd soon
discover that it was the most prevalent word in her vocabulary,
closely trailed by yeah, both of them pronounced as lilting
bisyllables, coo-ool, yeah-ah, and a doubled nod of the head
like a pigeon when it walks. Yeah, she said, they're more like
about the idea of a chair.

I laughed and said something dumb like, So I shouldn't sit on one, and she looked at me like I was a little bit nuts and said, You can totally sit on one.

What time is it? I wondered.

After lunch, Lauren Sara told me. Before dinner.

What should we do?

Do? she said, almost puzzled. She wasn't the sort of person who moved through life from plan to plan; she rarely determined through any recognizable process of deliberation what task or thought or appointment came next; it was a trait that made we want her, then annoyed me, then made me want her again in an alternating pattern from that first day until the end. I don't know, man. It might be cool to have sex and then maybe get something to eat?

Now, I wouldn't necessarily call our first attempt at lovemaking languid. Actually, I probably wouldn't call it lovemaking. But it did move at its own pace, and it also moved from moment to moment without planning or deliberation, without any sense that either of us was exactly willing it into action. We were on a plaid couch that smelled, not all that unpleasantly, like bread. At one point I realized that a radio was playing, quietly, somewhere across the room; the music had stopped and a baritone voice was asking us to please support classical radio. Then Lauren Sara lifted my face from her salty neck and held it between her hands just above her own and asked me if I was going to come. Slightly surprised—I was used to something a little more feverish—I said, No. Not yet. What about you? Are you close?

Even there, underneath me, with her hands still on my jaw,

THE BEND OF THE WORLD 11

she managed something like a shrug, and she said, Yeah, it's cool. I'm not super into orgasms.

We untangled ourselves, dried off with a stiff towel, walked back to my car, and drove to Bloomfield to get some Thai food, which we later marked by mutual consent as our first date.

3

So I was the manager of customer analytics and spend processes, which meant about as much to me as it does to you, at a company called Global Solutions, whose remarkable slogan was, Solutions for a Global World. Actually, I was one of many managers of customer analytics and spend processes, and while this bothered some of my more, uh, career-oriented colleagues, I figured it was for the best, since it meant that I didn't have to manage anything. Look, people will tell you that corporate America is an insatiable elder god, an implacable, amoral Mammon into whose gaping, bestial jaws flows the life and blood and spirit and dreams and democratic aspirations and so on and so forth of everyone and everything on this not-so-good and no-longer-so-green earth, but let me tell you, if what you really want is to read blogs all day and occasionally take the back stairs down to the largely vacant twenty-third floor to take long, private shits in a single, lockable handicapped restroom and to get paid, like, sixty-five grand for the trouble, then good God, there is no more perfect job.

No, I am serious: the office only crushes your soul if you're dumb enough to bring it to work. I saw this affliction of the soul take too many of my coworkers. They brought their souls to work with the same foolish trust that impelled them to bring snacks and a bagged lunch. Fuckers will only steal that shit from the shared refrigerator. You've been warned.

I liked my job, and it wasn't even exactly true to say I never worked; I worked, sometimes; I just wasn't working on Tuesday when Johnny called my office phone and said, Are you working? Let me read you something.

I don't know, Johnny, I said. I'm about to go into a meeting. When Johnny said, Let me read you something, it never meant, Let me read you this brief and compelling excerpt, this epigram, this interesting quotation, this passage, this page; it meant, Let me read you from here, page thirty-seven, halfway down the page, through page fifty-one; no, you know what, let me start on thirty-four, to give you the fuller context, and go through fifty-eight, which is where the chapter ends. And when he got started, you couldn't interrupt; there was no, Well, buddy, I've actually got to go; once, when we were in college, he'd called me across the country and read to me for an hour and a half from a history of the Merovingian dynasty, so impervious to my attempts to get off the line that I'd eventually just hung up on him, and he'd just called me back and kept going. Which is to say, it was best to head him off before he got started.

But he just said, What meeting? When have you ever gone to a meeting? and started reading:

Dad was military, OSS during the war. Your basic blue-blood type, too, like all the Intelligence boys back then, a Connecticuter, a standard-model Yalie Bones-

man. He came to Pittsburgh in the early 1950s to oversee a new office called Industrial Production Planning, or IPP, which was a front for the CIA.

I myself was born in 1949 and, and for much of my life, I'd have told you I had the most ordinary Pittsburgh childhood. Grew up on Linden St., went to St. Bede's and then Central Catholic, played on a lousy Little League team, gate-jumped at Forbes Field, etc. It was a hell of a city in the day, a great dynamo: the greatest fires stoked in the whole history of the world running twenty-four hours a day, seven days a week, fifty-two weeks a year, like the forge of Hephaestus.

Well, as the saying went, it was "hell with the lid off." Here is the essential point: you cannot burn that hot without releasing some manner of Luciferian energy into the ether.

And that was no accident. Pittsburgh is the one city in the world that perfectly fits the conditions of the prophesied site of the commencement of the Mayan world-end.

Now, what if I were to tell you that the Deep Government of the United States has long known this fact to be true?

I was entirely unaware of this history until 1999, even though I participated in it. My father saw to that. Were it not for certain unique abilities that I was able to conceal from him even at the height of my participation in the Project, this history would have likely remained concealed to this very day.

Through years of ritualized and chemicalized psychic abuse, based on a variety of satanic and priestly indigenous American vision practices, my father split my personality into a set of independent and mutually unaware personality forms. However, my core personality was able to conceal itself behind a subconscious wall-division subconsciously generated by certain psychic abilities, which later assisted in the reintegration of my multiple self-constructs.

What was my father working on? What was this Project?

It was manifold, but it represented over many decades a vast magical working, perhaps unmatched in all human history, a spell enacted by the fire of industry above this most metaphysically significant of landscapes, culminating in two great ritual ceremonies.

First: the linking of two long-sundered Scottish Freemasonic Illuminated Lines, those of Carnegie and Mellon, the line of World Industry and the line of Global Finance, through the merging of the Carnegie Institute of Technology and the Mellon Institute of Industrial Research in 1967—wherein my own matriculation as a freshman at the new Carnegie Mellon University was in fact the practical cover for the dark working that joined the institutional progeny of the two families and consecrated me, or, that is to say, one of my mind-division self-constructs, as the ritual child-form of that union.

Second: the completion, in 1974, of the great foun-
tain at Point State Park, the magical runic symbol at
the convergence of the three superficial and one sub-
terranean rivers, the latter brought to the surface in the
fountain itself.

Is it any wonder at all that at that very moment, with
the water aspect brought forth through those immense
pumps, the fire-aspect of industry was quenched and
went into decline?

It is no coincidence at all.

Johnny took a breath. What did I tell you? he said.

Well, I answered as I took a sip from the mug of cold coffee on my desk, that certainly does, uh, seem to bear out your
thesis.

Winston Pringle, he said.

What's a Winston Pringle?

He's an author. He's the author.

He sounds British, I said. He sounds like a wanker.

Are you wanking off over there? said Marcy, who worked in
the next cubicle.

Totally, I told her. Don't tell Karla. Karla was in HR.

Who are you talking to? asked Johnny.

Marcy, I said. The lovely occupant of Workstation six-
fourteen.

Whoa, Johnny said. They number your work-holes? That's
so satanic. Is your number six-thirteen? That number has
extreme significance in Gematria.

Johnny, I really have to go.

So you're not at six-thirteen?

No, I am. But seriously.

So this book is called *Fourth River, Fifth Dimension*. Apparently Dr. Pringle lives somewhere around here, too. I think we ought to find him. Given recent events. Recent occurrences.

We, I said.

You've got eight hours a day and a good Internet connection, Johnny said. Tell Darcy she can help.

Marcy. And I don't think she's interested in the long-sundered branches of Freemasonry or whatever. And anyway, I can't just sit here all day looking up your current crackpot fetish. I have a job. I have shit to do.

Morrison, Johnny said—alone among my friends he called me by my last name—Morrison, you're fucking nuts. By the way, do you want to be my date to the Jergen Steinman opening thing this weekend? I'm a little hard up in re: the matter of purchasing a ticket, and I figure your grandmother is one of the big Jews at the museum and can get us tickets.

Lauren Sara and I are going. I can totally get you a ticket, though.

Why is she going?

She's my girlfriend. And she's an artist. And cetera.

An artist. Misplaced affection has misplaced your critical faculties, brother. She is to an artist as Goodwill is to haute couture.

You are gay, I said.

Fuck off, Johnny said. I don't want to go anyway. Museums

are just massive institutions designed to provide scholar-backed social capital to the notion of art-as-commodity and to reify the artist as a separate caste rather than art as a fundamental human activity. I'd rather not. But seriously, the Pringle thing. Think about it.

What's the thing again? I asked, but he was already gone.

4

Did you hear? Marcy asked me later that week.

Hear what?

We're being bought out.

By we, I said, you mean Global Solutions Solutions for a Global World?

None other.

Bought out by whom?

Some European company. Danish, maybe? Pandu didn't have the details.

Pandu told you? Pandu was a math guy who did something in finance that no one understood; in particular, none of us understood why a guy that smart worked for Global Solutions. What is he, like, Hari Seldon now?

He's Hindu, I think.

No, what? No, forget it. Europeans? Are we going to get fired?

Probably, Marcy said. Or it could be worse. They might make us work.

5

This thought roiled my brain all week; I had a sweet gig, and the thought that it might be sullied by something that measured out my hours and compensation in deliverables and metrics and benchmarking and the rest of that infernal vocabulary kept me more distracted than usual. That Wednesday over dinner Lauren Sara reminded me that I was supposed to score a pair of tickets to the big art opening. I'd completely forgotten. Do you even want to go? I asked her. Whatever, she said. It's, like, cool either way. What she meant by this was something like, Fuck you, you moron, I ask you for this one thing, and. Not to say that her voice or demeanor betrayed the slightest hint of it, but you get to know a person. As surely as she'd tried to keep her own background half concealed behind a scrim of shrugs and misdirection, Lauren Sara had set about ferreting out my own relative standing on the social and economic ladder, and if there was one thing that she expected of me, one medium of exchange in our otherwise casual, anarchic relationship, it was that I get us—and her friends, and her roommates—into the good openings and parties, whenever and wherever they occurred.

So I had to call my grandmother, Nanette, to ask if she could get us into the opening reception. She answered on the first ring, but there was a horrible noise in the background, the sound of screams and machinery. Nana, I found myself shouting. It's Peter.

Who?

It's Peter!

THE BEND OF THE WORLD   19

Peter?

Nana, what's that noise?

Just a moment, just a moment. The sound faded. Peter? She was back on the line.

Jesus, Nana, I said. What was that?

Oh, some movie or other, she said.

It sounded like a slaughterhouse.

Everything is so violent these days, she replied. Honestly, who watches these things?

Well, you do, apparently.

Oh, I don't watch. I just like the noise when I'm reading.

Okay, Nana. So what's new?

What's new? she said. She was of an age and class that made her sound like a demented Hepburn. What would possibly be new?

I really just meant how are you doing?

Just terribly, but not unusually so. Have you talked to your parents lately? If you do, tell them that I'm wonderful. Tell your mother I'm in a new bloom of youth. Every damn time I tell them how I'm really doing, your mother starts taking my medical history. Needless to say, when I tell her what my own doctors say, she accuses me of lying and drug addiction. Honestly, why your father married that woman.

She's my mother, Nana.

Well, I certainly don't blame you for that, my dear. Now, what is new with you? She managed to make it sound like an accusation.

Nothing, I said. Work, the usual.

I hope you're saving.

Yes, Nana, I'm saving.

For God's sake, make sure you sock it away, or you'll wake up one day and find yourself as penurious as me.

I don't think you're penurious.

Well, I'm sorry, Peter, but there won't be one red cent for you when you die.

Uh-huh, I said. Had she misspoken? I didn't want to get into it. Listen, Nana, I said, I wonder if you could do me a favor.

I may as well, she said. After all, I'm not very long for this world.

6

On Saturday night, while I waited for Lauren Sara to arrive so that we can go to the museum to watch a Swiss-German artist reenact the aesthetics of atrocity or something, I called my mother. Strictly speaking, I got a little stoned and poured myself a few fingers of bourbon and called my mother. Don't misunderstand me. I liked my mother, loved her, even, but it was always best to talk to her with one's psychic armor on or, if that wasn't combat-ready, with a strong dose of one's psychic anesthetic.

I lived on the third floor of a converted Victorian near Friendship Avenue. The rest of the poor house, like all the other defiled old houses on my street, had long since given up its grace to cheap drywall and particleboard kitchens. An endless stream of undergraduates and itinerant hipsters and drag queens and the occasional medical residents, lured by the online promise of unbelievable (really, unbelievable) rent and a few photographs of the admittedly charming exterior as well as the wide blond floorboards and arched dormer windows that were, in fact, in my apartment alone and in no way representative of any of the others, signed leases sight unseen, arrived, and swiftly departed, paying the neat penalty of three months' rent (security deposit, first and last month) to get the fuck out of those shitholes. The third floor where I lived had been the old servant quarters, and if to nineteenth century sensibilities it had seemed appropriately plain, to our time it may as well have been a palace—real wood, real tile, built-ins with little doors of paned glass. The building was owned by Bill Morrison, a cousin to some degree or other of my dad's. Like all self-respecting minor relatives of old Pittsburgh families, he'd bought a bunch of shitty houses, long since underoccupied, fixed them up—I mean, he made them even shittier—and became a slumlord. Because the houses in my neighborhood had better-preserved exteriors than most, he could charge a modest premium, as well as running the Craigslist scam, in which I suppose I was an accomplice—at least, I knew about it and said nothing. It wasn't family loyalty. Bill was the worst, a self-styled grotesque, deliberately unbecoming, a weird WASP version of a third-rate movie gangster. He drove an immense black SUV that looked like it belonged in either a federal motorcade or a Mexican drug lord's garage; he wore shirts unbuttoned halfway down his chest and gold chains and a pinkie ring, all confounded by the fact that he was not a gangster and not a drug lord, but a pink, hairless man with tiny little hands; he reminded me of a toe.

But it was a great apartment.

So I was in the kitchen watching my squirrel jump from the overhanging branches of the big buckeye out front onto my windowsill where I left him, or her, but I thought of him as a him, little snacks. I'd called my mother's cell, but my father answered.

Dad, I said, where's Mom?

Ah, your mother, he said contemplatively, which was, along with mumbling, his main mode of speech. You know, I'm not entirely certain. And I heard him take the phone away from his mouth and yell, Suzanne? Suzanne?—or not yell, really, because he never yelled, nor really ever raised his voice at all; he just sort of mumbled her name into a middle distance, then brought the phone back to his face and said, Well, she's not answering.

Is she home?

You know, I'm not sure. She never does tell me when she's going out. Which is fine, of course. She used to tell me, and I said, Suzanne, you don't need to tell me all your comings and goings, believe me. And she said, Well, Peter, what if you need to reach me? And I said, Well, why would I need to reach you? Which she took very badly; you know how women can be. Although I suppose I can see in retrospect how, taken in a certain way, well, it could be taken in a certain way. Anyway, I guess she's not here now. How are you doing, then, kiddo?

I'm good. She's definitely there. She wouldn't leave her phone.

Now, that's a very good point. She is awfully attached to

it. They're handy pieces of technology, there's no doubt about that, but I like to forget mine from time to time.

She's a doctor, Dad. I imagine people need to get ahold of her.

Oh, they call at all hours. How's work going?

It's super-busy right now. Really busy.

You're always so busy. It must be such an interesting job. I'm sure they appreciate you.

I just try to do my part.

So many meetings. It's a wonder you get anything done.

That's just the way things work now. All companies are like that.

Well, you would know. The business world has certainly changed. Such rapid change. Very different from when I was in the trenches, so to speak. Of course, we hadn't the foggiest idea what was coming, with the computers and whatnot. Well, if I could go back, I'd certainly tell myself a thing or two. Oh, here's your mother. There was the rustling sound of a phone being handed over and the sound of my mother's voice saying something that sounded remonstrative, which was, come to think of it, *her* main mode of address.

Hello.

Hey, Mom.

I was in the garden. The fucking deer out here, really. I'm going to have to get a gun.

You have a gun.

A handgun, honey. That's for protection. I mean a shotgun.

Protection from what?

Really, sweetheart, I will not be drawn into a political debate.

I think it is perfectly appropriate that you retain your liberal views until you turn thirty, and you, likewise, can respect mine.

I'm a libertarian, and I'm already twenty-nine.

Libertarians are just liberals without student debt. We paid for everything, and so you're not interested in redistributive schemes. When you turn thirty, you'll find yourself still fiscally conservative; meanwhile, you'll find that the libertine permissiveness that attracts you to your current philosophy is less attractive than it was when you were a horny twenty-something.

Mom! Jesus.

It's a fact. If you were an anarchist or something, I'd worry, Lord knows. But a libertarian I can handle. How's work?

Busy. Super-busy.

Good. And how is Laura?

Lauren Sara. And she's fine.

Is that a thing now, having two names? Do you make your friends call you by your middle name?

My middle name is Jackson.

And?

Never mind. No. Listen, is everything okay with Nana? That's actually why I called.

Did you ask your father? What do you mean by is everything okay?

No, I didn't ask Dad. You know how he is. And I mean, I don't know, like, okay. Is she okay?

Why do you ask?

Because when I called her to get tickets to this museum thing tonight, she seemed a little off.

Off as in off her rocker or as in off the wagon?

Was she ever on the wagon? The former.

She's just a little pickled, sweetie. I wouldn't worry. She's eighty-five. She's entitled to be a little batty.

Yeah, but she was complaining about how little money she has left, which, I know, is normal, but then she said, And I'm sorry, Peter, but there won't be anything left for you after you die.

After she dies, you mean, Mom said.

No, I said. That's the thing. She distinctly said, after you die. You meaning me.

Philosophically speaking, she may be correct.

Mom.

I'm sure it's nothing to worry about. Keep me posted.

Keep you posted?

Yes, keep me posted. By the way, we have extra tickets to the opera next week. Would you like to come? You can even bring Sarah.

Now you're doing it on purpose. And she's not an opera fan. But I'll probably come.

No, she doesn't strike me as such. No hurry. Just let me know. Love you. Bye-bye.

7

I was not a libertarian. I wasn't anything, and I didn't vote or much care, but the other thing was easier to explain to my mother.

8

The museum party started at seven, so I'd told Lauren Sara six, and she clicked into the apartment in her bicycle shoes at twenty to eight. I think she was on to me. She tossed her messenger bag onto the floor with a metallic thud. Careful, I said. Jesus, what's in there?

Engine parts, she said. I need a shower.

We're so late already.

She shrugged. That's cool. I can go like this. She was in a pair of dungarees cuffed to just below the knee and a sleeveless T-shirt that read EAST END ORGANIC URBAN FARMSTEAD with a cartoon lion and a cartoon lamb both giving the peace sign.

Did you know that the peace sign is an inversion of a satanic sigil that represented Ba'al worship? I said.

Cool, she said.

Go ahead and get ready, I said. I'll wait.

She said, Cool.

I drank some more bourbon, then poured her one and brought it to her in the bathroom. She liked to drink in the shower. I used to think it was an affectation, but I was beginning to suspect that maybe she was just an alcoholic. And it may be terrible to admit it, but I didn't entirely mind. The women I'd dated before her had in common not only a certain angular aesthetic, but also attitudes of exquisite control; they weren't the sort of girls, or women, or whatever, who drank bourbon in the shower or asked questions like, Should I shave my pits? Shit, no woman I'd ever dated would have admitted to having to shave her pits. It may have been that Lauren Sara and I drifted accidentally into each other's orbit, but you could say the same about the moon and the earth, and I once read something that said the presence of that pale satellite gave us evolution in addition to the tides.

Oh yeah, she said, go check in my bag. I brought you a present.

I don't need any engine parts.

The small pocket, she said.

I went back to the kitchen, but before I picked up her bag I grabbed her cell phone and looked through her text messages. A few, from an ex, with whom she was supposedly, ahem, still friends, so be cool, be cool, were innocuous enough; one, from her friend Tom, an awful fag we'd surely see at the museum, because he worked there, referred to me as The Asshole—he'd gone to the trouble of capitalizing it. I played racquetball sometimes with Tom's boyfriend Julian at the downtown Y, and I made a mental note to imply strongly that Julian had gotten jerked off in the steam room by some twink dancer from Point Park. A text from her mom said, Check your balance. I put the phone down and checked the small pocket in her bag. Oh, Christ. A bag of mushrooms.

Psychedelics didn't agree with me. Actually, I hated them, hated the pretension that they represented some kind of contemporary shamanism, that they expanded the mind rather than just messing with it, that they made you more a part of the cosmic consciousness and not merely a butt of its ongoing and infinite joke. I hated the feeling of departing myself; it was like waking up on the departure date for a long trip, you'll pardon the expression, and realizing that you'd forgotten to pack. I hated, most of all, the weird exhibitionism of doing that sort of drug and going out in public, the artifice of it: turning yourself into a nut and then parading in front of other people and then laughing at them later for being uncool enough to have actually thought you a fucking lunatic.

No, thanks, I said to Lauren Sara when she'd showered and mostly dressed. Her feet were still bare. She came into the kitchen, where I was drinking and smoking one of the secret cigarettes I kept stashed in the freezer; she placed her hand on my neck; it was still warm from the water, and I kissed it lightly. We'd been together long enough by then for these little affections to pass into the kingdom of habit.

She took a drag of my smoke. Cool, she said. More for me.

You can't eat all of those. You'll fall through the fucking stargate.

Yeah. Totally.

So I did some as well. You know, just a few caps. A palmful. To keep it interesting.

But we hit traffic on the way to the museum. An ambulance had struck a bicyclist on the Bloomfield Bridge, and we weren't moving. To our left, beside and below the bridge, the little lit houses descended down the hillside toward the edge of the ravine, where the light abruptly stopped and the dark woods dropped down toward the railroad tracks. Cars floated by in the other direction. Oh shit, I said. I'm starting to come up.

Cool, said Lauren Sara.

They cleared the accident and we made it to Oakland, parking on a side street a few blocks from the museum near the Cathedral of Learning, or, as Johnny put it, the Phallus of Yearning, a gothic skyscraper in the middle of the University of Pittsburgh campus, as if some drunk god had grabbed the top of a squat medieval monastery and yanked it heavenward like a piece of saltwater taffy, ornate and kitschy and very slightly fascist in its fidelity-by-pastiche to an imaginary past. Ironically, the Cathedral of Learning was just across the street from the Carnegie Software Institute, a dour and actually fascist building, all outscaled marble columns still half stained from sixty years of soot and exhaust, in whose basement, according to Winston Pringle, his father and a group of German émigré scientists first succeeded, in 1949, in opening a microscopic doorway between our quantum reality and the next one over. On the green between the two was Heinz Chapel, another goofy bit of architectural homage, a near-replica of the Saint-Chapelle in Paris, although Johnny once told me that it was exactly fifty-seven paces from the cathedral to the chapel and fifty-seven paces from the chapel to the institute. Well, that makes sense, I guess, I said. Like Heinz 57. Yeah, Johnny said in a scoff. Sure. You do know that fifty-seven is the number of times the moon is mentioned in the Bible, right? Forty-seven in the Old and ten in the new. And that Ba'al was actually a moon god who served as an early model for Lucifer, and that the Heinz family were notable Satanists who built the chapel as a place to conduct black masses? Jesus fucking Christ, dude, Alumni Hall is fifty-seven paces in the *other* direction, perpendicular, and it's the old goddamn Masonic Temple. Are you that naïve? Where do you get this shit? I said. Dude, he said, didn't I lend you *Sacred*

Marks and Texture? It's Pringle's little architectural survey. With Dr. Wilhelm Zollen.

I found myself having trouble distinguishing between sounds and colors, and I found that the squares of concrete that made up the sidewalk were expanding away from me in every direction at an accelerating rate, like the universe.

Um, I said to Lauren Sara.

Be cool, she told me.

How many paces have we walked? I asked her, but she ignored me. I glanced back at the Cathedral, which was dark, but it seemed to me that either light or the sound of chanting was rising up from the steep roof of the chapel.

I feel nauseous, I told Lauren Sara.

Yeah, she said.

She was wearing a red fur coat that had belonged to my grandmother and then to Katherine, my ex. It looked like the costume of a doomed tsarina fleeing on a doomed train. Who knows where Nana had gotten it; I imagined she'd had lovers, and I imagined one of them had given it to her, because it wasn't the sort of thing that any of my rich, cheapskate relatives ever would have bought for anyone, least of all his own wife. Nana had given it to Katherine; they all thought I was going to marry Katherine; I thought I was going to marry Katherine: Katherine from Montreal, an inch taller than me, a body as carefully designed and perfectly balanced as a set of German knives, studying environmental law, crazy about fashion; well, I know, how bourgeois can you get?—how predictably of your own class and background?—how dull and how foolish, really, to pursue something that's destined to fail by its own appropriateness?

Well, very. But I did. And then, about a year and a half before I met Lauren Sara, she stomped into my apartment, and keep in mind, Katherine didn't stomp, ever, and accused me of cheating on her. Now, I had cheated on her, but I was pretty sure that she didn't really know that I'd cheated on her; I denied it so extravagantly and convincingly that I made myself cry a little bit; then she cried, not because I was crying, but because something about the fact that I'd convinced myself in that moment of the truth of my own denials confirmed for her the very thing that I was denying; then she said something embarrassing like, Wasn't I good enough for you? And I think I said, like, No, baby, I think maybe it's that you were too good for me, which was simultaneously true and the dumbest thing that I have ever said in my life, before or since. (In fact, it hadn't had a thing to do with her; I'd been drunk one night at Gooski's, and a girl with an apartment across the street had invited me up to smoke a joint after they closed, and I'd come home super-late thinking I only smelled of weed and beer and cigarettes. I'd assured myself she hadn't noticed.) Then she said something in French that I didn't quite catch. *Comment?* I said. Fuck you, she said. In English. Then she left the apartment and went down the stairs with me blubbering and apologizing to the back of her head all the way down. Then she stalked down the icy walk to her car. It was the last winter anyone could remember when it had really snowed in Pittsburgh, and the last thing she'd done before she ducked into her car and drove away was to shrug off the coat and drop it unceremoniously into the dirty snow along the curb.

We'd defriended each other, of course, and quickly passed

out of each other's electronic lives, but sometime afterward, when a change in privacy policy had left all of our everything temporarily exposed to everyone else on the whole of the Internet, I'd actually stumbled across her page: she'd never finished law school, but had gone back to biology; there were photos of her, tan, a little more muscled, dressed like a college girl, on a beach somewhere with a lot of other bright-toothed assholes, tagging birds or something, including one pic that briefly stopped my heart: Katherine smiling at some Indian guy, a huge, beautiful, almond man with the arms of a Vedic warrior and perfect long hair drawn into a tight bun on top of his head; he was smiling at her as well, and his hand was on her bare knee.

What's up, honey? said Lauren Sara.

I'm thinking about my ex, I thought.

You look great in that coat, I said.

9

Of course Tom was the first person we saw in the museum. We came up to the bright back entrance to the contemporary galleries, a stepped sculpture garden surrounded by glass and fronted by a little turnaround driveway where loud valets hustled silent, expensive cars to and from departing and arriving guests. I suppose we saw other people first, but he was the first with whom we interacted, and of course the first words out of his mouth were, Oh My God Are You Two High?

Your boyfriend fucks dudes at the Y, I answered.

What? he said.

Only a little, Lauren Sara said.

Don't worry, I said. My grandmother's a big Jew around here. An older couple on their way out overheard and gave us all a killer look.

You're really high, Lauren Sara told me.

I'm the unitary consciousness, the world matrix, I told her.

Okay, let's maybe get you a snack.

You guys are assholes, Tom told us as we headed into the party.

Assholes are like opinions, I said. Everyone's got one, and everyone's is just his opinion.

We'd missed the art, or the performance, or whatever it was; it occurred to me that I should not have said Jew in proximity, physical or temporal, to a happening or enactment or deconstruction or whatever it was by a dude whose work consisted, as I understood it, of dressing up in Nazi fetish gear and, well, doing something. On the other hand, I was a cultivated philistine; if art was just another commodity, then an original sensibility required deploring it. In any event, I wasn't in any state to enjoy a performance, less yet to enjoy not enjoying it. I need a drink, I said.

10

Someone once said that the way to enjoy a Russian novel is to treat it like a party, to stop fretting over the interminable parade of unfamiliar names and just enjoy the interaction, content in the knowledge that after a few introductions the important, recurring characters will stick. I found that advice quite useless, because I found parties to be like nothing so much as long foreign novels, interminable scenes of interactions between interchangeable personages with whom I was just familiar enough to be aware that I'd forgotten them. And at least no one in Dostoyevsky ever remembered me or knew my parents or called me Pete.

A dozen handshakes and half as many Petes and we were at the bar. I ordered a beer, figuring with the idiot logic native to all intoxicated people everywhere that the combination of high calories and low alcohol content would set me straight. Lauren Sara got a gin and tonic, which, given the state I was in, smelled like a newly disinfected bathroom.

This party sucks, I said.

We just got here.

Be that as it may.

It was your idea!

You made us miss the Nazi.

She rolled her eyes at me. He's not a Nazi. He's very important.

The one doesn't preclude the other, I said, but it sounded less clever than I'd intended it to sound.

The hall was two hundred feet long and fifty feet wide and three stories tall. We ended up at a high-top at the end farthest from the entrance. On our right, the wall of windows looked out over the courtyard and down to the entrance. The courtyard was full of stunted locust trees. There was a crowd around the bar that thinned toward the edges of the room. A

DJ was playing music that would appeal only to twenty-year-olds, and, to be fair, there were a few of those interspersed among the generally older crowd.

Lauren Sara asked me why I was always so mean to Tom, and I replied that he was a horse-faced faggot, and Lauren Sara said that just because my best friend was gay or whatever, that didn't give me the right to talk like that. I laughed; she wasn't exactly the type to take offense at a racist joke or to be bothered if you made fun of fat people, but she lived in a big, tumbledown house at the edge of Bloomfield, a graying structure on the precarious edge of a precipitous hillside, whose residents were an un-census-able menagerie of boys and girls and trannies and boyfriends and girlfriends and Differently Gendered Other Amorous Individuals and their occasional dogs and cats and reptiles and their stupid fixie bikes forever clogging the front hall and the porch, and she took offense, through some bizarre transitive property of group identification and moral sensibility, to anything that smelled like homophobia; imitate black women on the bus all you like, in other words, but don't say fag.

I didn't really have anything against Tom. I only thought he was annoying. He was Lauren Sara's age and a curatorial assistant at the museum; they'd been friends since college, having met in some art class or other; he viewed everything and everyone as inferior. He had grown a mighty tree of cultured resentment from a mustard seed of rural Pennsylvanian gay angst. A little gay boy from Wilkes-Barre, he thought the whole world was déclassé. How he ever managed to trick Julian into dating him was beyond me, Julian, who looked like an Olympic swimmer and did something vague and highly remunerative for PNC Bank—a dummy, yes, hardly more than a grown-up frat boy, but by our standards rich and by anyone's standards hot.

Lauren Sara said it was because Tom had a huge dick. I said that might be so, but given what I knew about Julian, that seemed like a sundry detail. She told me that I didn't know shit about fags and that the muscle dude was always the bottom. I later put the question to Johnny, who told me that it was the first time any woman I'd ever dated had been right about anything.

Later I'd had another beer and the effect of the mushrooms had faded to nothing more than some strange colors around the edges of my field of vision and we were talking to Tom and Julian and Tom's boss, Arlene Arnovich. Arelene was a small woman with a bob of high-gloss black hair who seemed taller than she was. She was friends, of a sort, with my grandmother. She had asked what we'd thought of Steinman's performance; I said it had been very challenging, which was something my grandmother had taught me. Never say interesting, she said. Say challenging.

Oh yeah, how so? Tom said.

It just challenged, you know, I said. It had a lot of challenging notions. Lauren Sara cracked up and had to spit some of her drink back into her cup, and Arlene smiled thinly, thinking, I suspected, that I was somehow making fun of Tom, whom she regarded with the amused and irritated expression that you see in people who own small dogs, and Julian stared after one of the caterers; Tom noticed, and clutched his arm proprietarily.

Personally, I thought it was shit. We turned.

Oh, Mark, said Arlene.

He was tall, and his girlfriend reminded me of Katherine, only more so. He had wavy black hair that swooped from his forehead and around his ears and to the nape of his neck. His nose was a little too big for his face, but it gave him a martial quality, aquiline, like a Roman. In her high, very high, heels she was of equal height, also a little birdlike, or at least very aerodynamic, her dress hardly more than a slip, her thin neck held by a strand of pearls that were so proper compared to her dress that they seemed all the more obscene. She stood like a dancer, back arched and a little splay-footed, simultaneously graceful and awkward, formal, a pose you'd praise as natural in a sculpture, but in a real human a little weird. Like him, she had long hair, although hers was drawn severely back and done up in a tight and elaborate knot in the back of her head. It was the color of corn silk, although her eyes were very dark, and when we were introduced, she held me in her gaze a little longer than necessary, until I dropped my head. Then she laughed; it wasn't audible to anyone but me; it could have been my mother laughing at something foolish I'd done when I was a little boy, which is to say: that one soft, brief sound carried the possibility of a hidden wellspring of affection, and right away I had a crush. She glanced at a thin, expensive watch on her wrist and touched her nose with the back of a long finger. He was wearing a thin black suit and a gray tie—almost the same outfit as my own, but of such obviously finer quality that the difference was more pronounced than if I'd been in a T-shirt and dirty jeans.

Arlene, Mark said. Then he glanced at us as if surprised to discover that we hadn't scattered at the sight of him. Maybe he smirked. Everyone else, he said.

They introduced themselves. Mark and Helen. He caught my eye and held it briefly with his own, and I swear I saw something flicker across it, like a nictitating membrane, like a bird of prey, like a crocodile.

So you don't like my show, Mark, said Arlene.

Mark doesn't believe in art, said Helen.

I believe in it. I just don't approve of it.

What about artists? asked Lauren Sara.

They should all be destroyed, Mark replied.

I laughed.

What's so funny? Tom said.

Nothing, I said. Well, it's from *Jurassic Park*.

Tom snorted.

What's your name? Mark asked me.

Peter.

You and I, Pete, we're definitely going to be friends. It sounded like a threat.

You disapprove of art, Arlene said, and yet here you are.

One has to observe the proper forms. This is a very important institution.

Whose very purpose you reject.

Well. He shrugged. I like the dinosaurs.

Yeah, said Lauren Sara. The dinosaurs are cool.

I'm sorry, Mark said. I didn't catch your name.

Lauren Sara.

That's two names, said Helen.

Tom was doing his best to make it clear to Arlene that he found Mark repugnant. So what would you do instead? he asked.

Instead of what?

You're in charge of the museum. What's the first thing you do?

And Mark looked at me again, winked, vertically this time, and then said to the group, so plainly and forthrightly, so casually and without hesitation that it was impossible to believe he didn't really mean it: I'd burn it to the ground.

11

Helen laughed. He was joking. We all thought, Oh, thank God. We all laughed. Mark laughed.

But look, he said, it's true, also, that I find all of this—here he gestured broadly, perhaps at Jergen Steinman, just then putting a crab cake into his mouth and bending his head to listen to something Mildred Gold, an ancient photographer whom my grandmother referred to as the Dowager Artist, was saying to him, or perhaps he meant to encompass the whole museum, the galleries and halls of sculpture, the courtyard and the café—more than a little tedious. Then he was off. The problem, he said, was that at some point artists abandoned any real attempt at crafting arresting images and sought instead to turn art itself into a kind of social and political and philosophical commentary that had theretofore been more in the realm of literature and the theater. And wasn't that really part of the problem, the comparative intellectual poverty of the so-called visual arts, including their laughable bastard brother, performance art, when you compared them to writing and theater. Anyway, look at an artist like this Steinman character, Mark said. It's all very clever, but any second-rate nonfiction normative history of the Second World War had more profound insights into the nature of fascism than some clown in a costume-shop SS outfit prancing around a museum and declaiming a bunch of puerile nonsense that he just ripped off from Adorno. I mean, Mark said, I read one of his little manifestos, and it's basically a barely literate recapitulation of the whole No Poetry After Auschwitz thing, which is hardly even interesting as an aphorism, let alone as some kind of thesis on which to base an entire performative persona. What could be more ridiculous? It would be like saying there can be no rock-and-roll after My Lai, no, I don't know, no fine dining after 9/11. What is the relationship of these things, the one to the other? The problem is that these artists, coming as they do from a fine-art academic background, studying as they did mostly in what are effectively conservatories, came up among a pack of basically undereducated art world hangers-on as well as a few scam artists whose principal interest is merely making these things into salable commodities. What they lack is any kind of analytic and philosophical framework within which they can make any kind of meaningful commentary on the you'll-pardon-the-expression way we live now, less yet a sufficient historical reach and grasp to speak meaningfully about the enormities of the twentieth century, or about neo-colonial American foreign policy, or about man's relationship to nature, or about the soul . . . the wider the focus, the more profoundly self-regarding is their work; meanwhile, even Hollywood is more insightful; the latest giant robot movie a work of infinitely greater complexity and ambition than anything you are likely to encounter in a museum; the biggest summer superhero flick more spiritually profound than anything you'll find in the New York galleries. The artifacts of contemporary culture are as fake as the Native American beadwork you buy by the road in New Mexico. The museums, he said, might as well be casinos.

12

Toward the evening's end, I found my grandmother sipping wine at a low table. She was in a wheelchair. Nana! I said. Why are you in a wheelchair?

Junior, she said, which was what she'd often call me, since my father was also Peter. I detected a subtle reproach in the nickname; our family had never had a tradition of naming sons after their fathers, and I think she disapproved of my parents for what she perceived as their egotism. Give me a kiss. I bent to kiss her cheek and sat down across from her. It's my toe, she told me, gesturing at her one elevated foot.

What's wrong with your toe?

They say it's broken, she answered in a tone of patrician skepticism that implied that they, the doctors, presumably, were putting one over on her. She was both addicted to and disbelieving of modern medicine; she availed herself of an immense network of doctors and had specialists for every part of her body; she couldn't sneeze without a consultation; but her principal joy was in doubting their diagnoses and complaining about their bills.

Well, is it broken? I asked.

I haven't the slightest idea. The X-ray was inconclusive. I've asked for an MRI. Of course they agreed. Do you know doctors are paid by the procedure? Ask your mother about it. It's the reason health care is so expensive.

I laughed and said, But would you have preferred that they refused the MRI?

They might have tried to dissuade me. I think it's a conspiracy. Do you know my ophthalmologist told me I shouldn't drive? I told him in no uncertain terms that I wouldn't be a prisoner in my own home. Now this toe business. Of course, I went to the orthopod for it. I may go to Dr. Patel, who's the podiatrist. I've always found her to be very accommodating.

Maybe you shouldn't drive if your ophthalmologist thinks your eyesight is going.

He's overly cautious. I have no trouble seeing large moving objects.

Right, but I think maybe he's more concerned about, you know, small moving objects.

She waved her ring-encumbered hand. Like what, squirrels? Kitty cats? Pigeons?

Well, children, I said.

Children, she repeated, as if hearing the word for the first time. No, I doubt it. It's not like when your father was a little boy. I don't think they're allowed out anymore, due to the

THE BEND OF THE WORLD   43

pedophiles. Nana was particularly concerned with pedophiles; for a woman of her age, she was remarkably adept with the computer, and hardly a day went by without her forwarding some link or article to me about the latest depredations of some priest or schoolteacher or coach.

Why don't you just hire a car service? I said. Then you wouldn't have to worry about it.

I could never afford it. This horrible museum has taken all of my money. I wouldn't mind if they didn't spend it on all this contemporary trash. And you know I'm not some awful old matron, either. Your grandfather and I once had lunch with Warhol. After he was famous, no less. He was trying to sell us something. Your grandfather asked why on earth we'd want a picture of a car crash, which is what it was, I think. Warhol said, Because it's going to be worth a lot of money. The two of them got on famously, but then Jack found out that he was a homosexual and backed out. I tried to tell him that all artists are homosexual, but as you know, your grandfather was very traditionally Catholic. There haven't been any good Catholic artists since the Renaissance, which is why we never accumulated a decent art collection.

Nana, you're hysterical. Wasn't Warhol Catholic? And you should meet this guy I just met. He doesn't like art, either. Anyway, I'm sure Mom and Dad would pay for the car service if you needed it.

Well, where would I go?

This was the sort of thing that infuriated my mother. Dad was either so accustomed to it or so oblivious to the behavior of others in general that he didn't notice. Nana had been

a formidably intelligent woman, much smarter than any of
the men in the family, either her Ivy League husband or his
brothers or any of their sons, but after she turned eighty, all of
her intellect seemed to turn toward an endless game of always
finding a reason to disagree with something that she herself
had just said. She may just have been bored, all the original
thoughts that she'd ever think already thought; all the conver-
sations exhausted; her friends either dead or preserved under
the Florida or Phoenix sun. She may not have known she was
doing it, although I detected an element of glee in her voice
and bearing when she pulled the trick on Mom, with whom
she'd always had an odd relationship, more like the rivalry
between sisters that between a mother and her daughter-in-
law. Not to suggest any kind of crackpot Freudianism. It was
hard to imagine that Nana worried about Mom taking Dad
away from her. Dad was so blissfully abstracted that he'd never
belonged to anyone anyway. He enjoyed wine, opera, baseball,
Yale, and the stock market in roughly descending order. He
loved us—I was sure of that—but his love was so matter-of-
fact and inevitable that it felt mostly like a product of nature
and instinct, an adaptive evolution of human sentiment that
our biology was as yet simply too primitive to explain.

Alone among my family, I thought Nana's circumlocutory
games were fun, and I usually egged her on, but Lauren Sara,
who'd drifted off for a while with Tom and a gaggle of upscale
fags, had found me, and I had to introduce her.

I'd hoped to escape the party without their meeting but
now saw how absurd that hope had been. To be fair, I'd
always tried, unsuccessfully, to keep Lauren Sara apart from

my friends and family, had always failed, and felt that they all viewed her with something like embarrassment on my behalf. That my own ridiculous, furtive behavior might have been the largest part of this reception did not, at the time, occur to me. The conclusions you'll naturally draw about my character aren't very flattering. And actually, I've exaggerated slightly. She and my father got along just fine; the few times they'd met, they'd found common topics of interest in metallurgy and materials science and welding and suchlike—Dad had trained as an engineer before becoming, ahem, a management consultant, and Lauren Sara knew her way around a shop. Johnny, of course, told me that I wasn't afraid of my family's disapproval at all, but of their approval. They loved Katherine, he told me, and you fucked that up. So obviously the whole thing is a subconscious act of superstitious, self-imposed distancing. I thought this was all rather pat. The truth was that she was just so not a Morrison. I'd taken her to one doomed dinner with my family where she'd tried to explain her current veganism to my mother, telling her she didn't eat anything with a face. Mom gave me a significant look, then offered to order her a plain cheese pizza.

Nana, I said, this is my girlfriend, Lauren Sara. Lauren Sara, this is my grandmother, Nanette.

My grandmother offered her hand and said, Lauren Sara. Isn't that two names?

My best friend when I was a kid was named Lauren, too. So she was always Lauren Nicole and I was always Lauren Sara.

Well, Nana said, that seems fully rational. Peter is named after his father. His parents toyed with the idea of calling him

PJ, but I convinced them otherwise. I said that he'd end up an unsuccessful radio sports announcer if he were to reach adulthood known only by his initials. How long have you two been seeing each other?

About six months, I said.

Seven, said Lauren Sara.

Well, be prepared, Nana said. The true tests of relationships occur at eight months, three years, and seven years. The last one is famous but less consequential, because by then you're too exhausted to care. How long did you date Katherine, Junior?

Three years, I said.

Well, there, you see. Empirical confirmation. Oh dear, here comes Mildred. I abhor her. You'd both better run off before she gets here. Don't worry, you have plenty of time. She drags herself around like a walrus with that walker. Have you seen Arlene? Good Lord, this show. You know, there was a time, before the war of course, when you could meet real, live fascists. Half your grandfather's graduating class at Yale, for God's sake. I have to suspect they'd be embarrassed by this whole charade. The Nazis deserve something more substantial than a game of dress-up, if you'd like my opinion. In any case, if you run into Arlene again, tell her that I think her show is a triumph . . . of the will.

13

Your grandmother's a trip, Lauren Sara said.

We were smoking in the courtyard. The party was winding

down. Arlene and a gaggle of curators and museum admin-
istrators and other people in important geometric glasses
had bundled Steinman off to a private dinner party. Tom and
Julian and the art fags had gone off to the same bar where
Lauren Sara and I had first met, which was a popular post-
dinner stop-off for the curators and their visiting artists
owing to its collection of works by local artists and carefully
designed tumbledown chic, and this was, not coincidentally,
why Tom and his gang had gone there; not having been invited
to the dinner, they hoped to head Steinman et al. off at the
pass, so to speak, hoping to offer up the few moments of
public sycophancy that they believed to be their natural and
inalienable right as minor vassals in the little feudal country
of Art. Julian, whose preferred topics of conversation ranged
from an expensive new squash racket to the weight savings of
the expensive new components on his expensive road bike,
would not enjoy himself, and Tom, seeing that Julian wasn't
enjoying himself, would get angry and sulk, because as he saw
it, before he'd met Julian, or Julian him, his boyfriend's life
had been a dull and effectively meaningless existence, days at
the office followed by hard workouts, tasteless expensive dinners at pricey but inferior restaurants, and the heroic intake of
beer and scotch, to be compensated for by more and harder
workouts, all of it surrounded by and fueled by and bathed
in money—Julian was no Internet millionaire or New York
finance wunderkind, but he made the sort of money that I
associated with my parents and their friends; Tom, of course,
was poor; I doubted the museum paid him more than thirty
thousand a year, if that, but he considered himself glamorous;

before him, Julian had gone to steakhouses and trashy gay house parties where everyone took off their shirts or swam naked in the pool; now he went to openings and galas and met artists and similar subspecies. These things were so self-evidently superior to Tom that he couldn't see how wasted they were on Julian, and he attributed Julian's sour moods to ungratefulness. In his version of things, his inversion of things, Tom incredibly played the role of the older, wealthier man, and Julian was the kept woman chafing against the very comforts she'd originally sought. It might have occurred to me that this said something about the way we all misapprehend our relationships, but it did not.

14

My grandmother is nuts, I said.

She seems super-rich.

Not really, I said. I guess maybe she used to be. Nobody talks about it, and I used to think there was, like, a dark secret or something. But then I figured out that after my grandfather died she gave a bunch away. Ill-advisedly, as my dad says. And then she lost a bunch in the stock market. No one ever talked about it because there wasn't anything to talk about. It's actually a very boring story.

What's a boring story?

Jesus! I yelped. Mark and Helen had appeared behind us again.

Sorry, said Helen. Mark is always sneaking up on people.

THE BEND OF THE WORLD 49

It's how we met. I was so startled that I accidentally agreed to go out with him.

Cool, said Lauren Sara.

Smokers, said Mark. I like you guys even more. Can we steal cigarettes from you? Neither of us smokes unless someone else gives us cigarettes.

We all stood for a while watching the end of the party queuing up at valet.

So what's this boring story? Mark asked.

Oh, nothing. We were talking about my grandmother.

And who's your grandmother?

It was an odd question, so I laughed, but he seemed to want an answer, so I said, No one. An old lady who may or may not have squandered her fortune.

That doesn't sound boring, said Helen.

Trust me.

I don't, said Mark. It sounds like an English novel. *The Life and Times of . . .*

He trailed off. I didn't say anything. Lauren Sara said, Nanette Morrison.

Nanette? said Helen.

That's her name, said Lauren Sara.

No shit, said Mark. We know your grandma. How about that?

How do you know my grandmother?

She bought a piece from Helen.

Oh, cool! said Lauren Sara.

A piece? I said.

Of art, Helen answered. I was an artist.

15

I have to warn you, Mark said.

Warn me?

Helen is going to stuff your girlfriend's nose full of coke.

She's not really into coke.

No offense, Mark said, but she looks a little get-along, go-along.

You might be right.

They'd gone off to the bathroom together, and I'd made some lame comment about women going to the bathroom together. Mark had asked for another cigarette. So, I said, you don't really think all artists should be shot.

He shrugged and grinned and inhaled and exhaled.

Seeing, I said, as your girlfriend is an artist.

Mark said, She's the exception that proves the rule.

It's funny that you know my grandmother.

All coincidences converge on the inevitable, he said.

I'm sorry? I said.

So what do you do, Pete? he asked as if he hadn't heard me.

Corporate shill, I said. Fake money and contracts and stuff. I work for a big company downtown, although no one's ever heard of it. What about you?

Sort of a lawyer.

What's a sort-of lawyer?

I don't practice. I'm a bit of a corporate shill myself. I used to work at a company called Dynamix.

Sounds like a breakfast cereal.

That's funny, he said. That was actually a joke around the

office. It was a consulting firm, whatever that means. Anyway, then I did some private consulting and equity stuff for a while, and now I'm working for a big Dutch NV that's gobbling up some shitty American companies for reasons that only the Übermenschen in Rotterdam comprehend.

Oh shit, I said.

He smiled—not a grin, not a smirk, not a guarded display of approval or pleasure, but an actual unmediated expression of joy. Really? He said, and then he laughed, and his laughter, too, was disturbingly genuine. Global Solutions Solutions for a Global World?

16

This, more or less, was how we ended up crushed in the back seat of Mark's little fast car on our way to what Mark called Our Club. New friendships require less bargaining than old ones, less planning, fewer points to settle and details to iron out; for instance, I'd left my car on a side street in Oakland; if it had been Tom or Derek or even Johnny (not that the issue would have come up with Johnny, who didn't have a car and did not, to the best of my knowledge, know how to drive), I'd have worried about that part—for no good reason, but nevertheless. But that evening it had seemed immaterial. The valets had brought Mark's silver teardrop around, and we were off.

We whistled down Fifth Avenue, past the university and the hospitals, a pile of immense, mismatched buildings that climbed the hillside to our right like a stepped bastard ziggurat and from whose satanic bowels there emitted a constant Luciferian thrum. Packs of students crowded across the intersections. A helicopter passed overhead. We ran a red light. Honey, Helen said, red means stop.

It was yellow.

It may have been yellow at one time.

Don't worry. If I kill someone, we're by the hospital.

Again, Helen said, a timing issue.

Beyond the hospital the road dropped in a steep S-curve toward the cantilevered highways that clung to the cliffs between the high bluff of the Hill District and the Monongahela. Across the river, lights stepped across the Flats and up the Slopes, and it struck me, not for the first, more like for the thousandth time, just what a preposterous place it was for a city, what a precarious topography. We crossed the Birmingham Bridge in a tight single lane between traffic cones. Whole lanes and great portions of the high arch and suspension cables were blocked and swathed in sheets of translucent plastic, which were illuminated from within by powerful work floodlights, revealing the silhouetted work of the tiny men within—tent caterpillars, ten million years hence, our successors.

We were on Carson Street briefly. A girl in tight pants vomited. Young men stood in gaggles outside of bars, simultaneously sinister and preposterous in their puffy jackets. I hate the South Side, I said.

Doesn't Johnny live above Margaritaville? Lauren Sara had seemed to be sleeping before she spoke, her head canted back against the seat.

Yeah, I said. I keep telling him to get out of that shithole. We should stop and say hello.

Who's Johnny? Mark asked.

My best friend.

Your only friend, said Lauren Sara, not cruelly, and anyway, I reflected, it was awfully close to being true.

We turned onto Eighteenth Street and wound our way up the Slopes. In the daylight, these were lovely neighborhoods, if a little run-down. The houses sat at odd angles to the streets, and the streets ran in switchbacks crosswise to the hills, and the whole thing was reminiscent of an Adriatic hill town, suggestive of a militarily defensible poverty, or else, not in the least because of all the little Slovak churches, of a winding stations of the cross, but there, at night, with the stands of houses suddenly replaced by bare sagging trees, with the occasional howl of a distant dog, with the old, orange streetlights buzzing and the intermittent creepy pickup truck rattling in the other direction with a slight few inches between sideview mirrors, with—was it me, or did everyone sense it?—something vague, insubstantial, and yet still threatening among the stands of weedy woods, something misty, something that, even if it didn't have the material form to drag you down into a ravine and have its murky way with you, might just have the power to compel you to wander off on your own into the weeds, well, the point I'm making is that on a strange road in a strange car with people who were, after all, still strangers to us, there was something odd about that drive, something unsettling, something that strongly suggested no good would come of it.

But then, quite suddenly, we were above the city. We'd stopped climbing several minutes before and were winding through an unfamiliar neighborhood when we burst out onto Grandview. The city, at night, was like a strange ship, like a sharp barge splitting a larger river; the black tower of the Steel Building like a crow's nest; the filaments of bridges like gangplanks, and you could almost imagine the whole thing plowing right on down the Ohio, hanging that gentle left onto the Mississippi at Cairo, and floating toward the Gulf; you could imagine waking one day to find yourself on an urban island, surrounded by water; or, anyway, I could imagine it, Atlantis, or thereabouts.

We ended up somewhere just off Grandview in a little commercial district with an Italian grocery, a storefront pharmacy advertising diabetic socks, and a few square cement-block buildings that might have been plumbers or repair shops. Mark parked along the curb across from the largest of them. Here were are, he said.

There was light coming through the glass door. There was an unilluminated sign on the wall above it. THE FRATERNAL ORDER OF THE OWLS, it read. NEST #93. And underneath, painted right onto the blocks: A "PLACE" FOR "FAMILY."

17

It was a sort of social hall, smoky and too brightly lit, the bar populated by very fat old men and very skinny young ones with a few girlfriends and wives scattered among them, the former in tight jeans and little T-shirts that squeezed their bellies and accentuated their tits, the wives in high-waisted jeans and Steelers sweatshirts and sensible hair. Everyone was drinking beer; some were backed up with watery-looking scotch; one girl with a huge purse was drinking something pink and laughing too loudly and attracting some eye-rolling. That's Alyssa, Mark said. She's a regular. She gets all tooted up, and then she gets loud.

This place is cool, said Lauren Sara.

I have to tell you, I told Mark, that when you said we were going to your club, this isn't exactly what I imagined.

You thought we were going to drink brandy in the library? I'm a proud Owl. It's an important service organization.

I glanced around. There were pool tables in the back. There was an unattended karaoke station. There were two bartenders, a pretty black-haired girl who looked no older than fifteen, and a thirtyish dude with a high-and-tight haircut and a twice-or-so-broken nose. No one was paying us the slightest attention. I feel conspicuous, I said.

Why? You think you're the first suit that ever wandered in looking for something? Go grab us a pool table. I'll get some beers. He strode toward the bar and snapped his finger toward the bartender and his voice and demeanor changed into something very nearly close to almost authentically Pittsburgh: Joey, you dick, he said.

My man, said Joey.

18

Mark and I played a game of pool while the ladies "used the restroom," so to speak, and then they returned, glassy-eyed, and a small fold of glossy paper passed between Helen and Mark when she kissed him on the cheek. Then Mark led me down a flight of stairs, but instead of going into the bathroom we walked through a blank door at the end of the hall and into a portion of unfinished basement that was filled with broken artificial Christmas trees and light-up Santa Clauses. This is the stuff of nightmares, I said. I'll never sleep again.

Sleep is a human weakness, Mark said. He'd latched the door behind us. There was a glass table with a couple of chairs near an old slop sink, and the purpose of this room, and of our visit to it, if it had not yet been obvious to me, became so. Do you know that dolphins sleep by shutting off one hemisphere of their brain at a time, so they're always active and aware? That's my goal. I'm training in that direction.

Chemically? I grinned.

By any means necessary, he answered.

You should meet my friend Johnny. He could probably tell you about sinister yogis or something who can already do it. Or a government conspiracy. CIA mind control. Military psyops. Jesus, those are serious.

Your friend sounds right up my alley. I'm into anything sinister. And as for all this, we ought to get while the getting is good. My darling Helen tends to have little mishaps in which the stuff [he drew quotation marks in the air] tends to fall into the toilet. He drew them again. I've strictly forbidden her from

THE BEND OF THE WORLD 57

purchasing any more from our friendly bartender, and since I know that's useless, I've also forbidden Shawna from selling her any.

I sniffled and handed back the bill. Shawna?

The bartendress, I should say. The Owlette. The brains of the operation.

19

The following occurred:

(1) Did cocaine. (2) Took a piss. (3) Returned to the pool table. (4) Played doubles: Mark and Helen vs. Peter and Lauren Sara. Lost. Mark and Peter vs. Helen and Lauren Sara. Lost. (5) More beers appeared. Several shots of whiskey appeared. (6) Peter and Helen vs. Mark and Lauren Sara. Won. (7) Rematch. Won again. (8) Girls wandered off again. (9) Mark said something like, Just you wait and you'll see what I was talking about. (10) Asked him what was the real story with my company. Your company? he said. Never confuse service and ownership, he told me. (11) Felt a slight pounding behind my eyes. Concluded I should not have mixed quite so carelessly. Decided another beer would do the trick. (12) Girls returned. (13) Honey, Helen said, you're not going to believe what happened. I believe everything, Mark said. I dropped the stuff in the toilet, Helen said. *Incroyable*, Mark said. I don't believe it. You're making fun of me. I'd never. Asshole. Couldn't tell if they were fighting or not. (14) Felt a thin current of hate as if near a lightning strike. (15) Got the

feeling from the placement of their bodies, however, the cant of their hips toward each other, the tilt of Mark's head toward hers, the way they drew into closer proximity as they fought or pretended to fight or flirted by means of fighting, that there was an intense and frightening physical attraction between the two, something stronger than magnetism, as in the bonds of an atomic nucleus, which, if broken, would explode. (16) Felt self-conscious staring and tried to talk to Lauren Sara. Found her tap-tap-tapping on her phone. Who ya textin'? I asked. Tom. Fuck Tom; what's up with Tom? He says there is a party in the apartment where Steinman is staying. It sounds terrible. I want to go. We just got here. No, we've been here, like, an hour, and it's boring. It's not boring. You're just staring at that fucking girl; it's boring; I'm gonna go to the party. We don't have a car. Tom said he'll pick me up. Whatever, I said. Do what you like. (17) Felt bad twenty minutes later when she left. (18) Ran out behind her and said, Listen, stay at my place tonight. Yeah. She shrugged. Okay. Cool. (19) Realized that she hadn't been half as angry as I'd imagined her to be and found myself infuriated by her nonchalance, as it suggested something inadequate about us, something not quite fully felt. (20) Went back inside. (21) Found Mark and Helen playing pool. (22) Realized how very good they both were. (23) Realized that I hadn't sunk a shot in either game that Helen and I had won. (24) Listened to them circle and taunt each other. You're always behind the eight ball, Helen said. That's funny, Mark said, coming from you. (25) Zoned out for a bit. (26) Came to and heard Helen say something like, Fuck your new friend. (27) Heard Mark say something like, Just don't talk about it on Facebook this time. (28) Saw Helen throw her cue onto the table and stalk up to the bar. (29) Tried to appear as if I hadn't been listening. Didn't fool Mark. (30) Nevertheless, Mark said, So, Global Solutions. You know I'm going to fuck you. You're going to fuck me? Not kindly, not lovingly, without compassion or quarter. That sounds terrible. Fair warning; get out while you can. Eh, if you lay me off, I can get unemployment. You don't seem like the type. I shrugged and said, All scams are essentially the same, something Johnny had once said to me in another context entirely. It seemed to impress Mark; at least, he smiled. (31) Mark said, Where'd your girlfriend go? Her friend got her; she went to a party. We bored her. She's not excitable. You stayed. You guys are more interesting, and I hate her friends. That's a recipe for disaster, Mark said; you can neither like nor dislike each other's friends; all outside affections are doomed, or else yours is. So I shouldn't have any friends? I asked. (32) He shrugged. We don't, he said.

20

The drugs, or, more accurately, the baby laxatives and other miscellaneous and sundry substances with which they'd been adulterated, had found their way to my beer- and hors d'oeuvres-soggy gut, and I had to dash to the bathroom. It was not clean. While I sat there, I felt the first nibble of conscience, the first stage whisper of what would several hours hence crescendo into the next day's regret, the sense, strange but familiar, that I could hear my own future self whispering to me across all the hours between us. Asshole, he was saying. I didn't do drugs, nor drink heavily, nor abandon my girlfriend in favor of strangers I'd only just met; well, not habitually—plainly I did do these things, when pressed, or when sufficiently tempted, or, anyway, I had done them, at least once, that night.

Conscience is a strange thing. I didn't believe that drugs or drinking heavily or staying out late were bad or morally suspect; I wasn't especially worried about Lauren Sara, who, I was sure, I would find later that evening in my bed, or who would find me there, depending only on which of us escaped our respective parties first; we might have sex, or might not; we weren't that kind of couple; I might hold her, or might not; it was warm enough that whichever of us was first into the apartment would open the windows in the bedroom; there would be the distant sounds of hospitals, which were ubiqui-tous in the city, and ambulances and late-night traffic and the strange, feral children whom we never saw, and who seemed to play only at night. In the morning, one of us would make coffee; Lauren Sara would get on her bike and ride off to do whatever it was she did when I wasn't around; I sometimes thought that she proved the crackpot science that said the world is created by observation and those things not observed at a given moment cannot with any certainty be said to exist. I would putter around the house, make more coffee, call my parents, check my email, chat with Johnny online or on the phone, consider dinner, run to the gym to play racquetball or swim a few laps once my hangover had become manageable; meet Derek or someone at a bar and have a beer and watch the

Pens for a period or two; go home early to Lauren Sara or not to Lauren Sara; sleep well, get up, and get on with it.

Nevertheless, I knew that I'd be nagged, rationally or not, in proportion to the night's excesses or out of proportion thereto, by that second self, the creature of habit and indoctrination and acculturation that lives in all of us and delights in nothing so much as picking at the scabs of our venial wounds.

When I'd emptied my bowels and small intestines and pride and dignity into the dingy toilet and cleaned myself and made it back to the bar, I found myself in the middle of an altercation. A hairy Sasquatch in a sleeveless T-shirt and a hat that read HOMESTEAD HARLEYS had Mark in a sleeper hold. I blinked. Not a Sasquatch, but a man of Sasquatchian stature. I knew I shouldn't have done those fucking mushrooms. He kept saying, Easy now, easy now. The bartender, Joey, was trying to reason with Mark. I didn't see Helen anywhere. Mark, buddy, he said. Come on. I sidled up to the girl with the bright drink; whatever she'd moved on to, it was now as blue as something out of *Star Trek*. What the fuck? I said.

Aw, no, she said, and her voice was every Pittsburgh accent blended, distilled, and evaporated into a little bouillon cube of swallowed vowels and nasal consonants. He was beatin' on his girl.

Easy now, easy now, said Bigfoot.

Mark? I said. That guy?

Naw, Billy, she said.

Who?

The dude who gawt him in the sleeper hold. Yeah, of course Mark.

Get off me. Get the fuck off me, Mark was yelling

No one else was paying much attention; they'd seen this shit before. Shawna was leaning on the bar with her chin in her hands, watching the struggle with the look of a businessman eating alone in an airport restaurant.

He hit her? I asked.

The girl shrugged. He snatched her up n'at, she said.

He snatched her up? I repeated.

Yeah. She looked at me as if we were speaking a related but mutually unintelligible language. He snatched her up.

Mark told the big man, I'm warning you.

Come on, dude, said Joey. Let's call it a night.

What did she do? I asked.

Who?

Helen. His girlfriend.

Aw, she slapped the fuck outta him and took off.

I saw Mark take a deep, three-part breath. He closed his eyes for a full second. He stopped struggling and his body went slack. He opened his eyes. He took another breath. All right, he said. Sorry. He opened his palms as much as he was able in that yeti's absurd grip. It's cool.

All right, then, said the yeti, all right. And he set Mark down.

Mark turned his head and looked straight at me. Mark, I said. The fuck?

Then I thought I saw him flash another reptilian wink. Then he wheeled around and sucker-punched the poor fat fucker right in the nose. It made a sound like someone opening a bag of chips. The bigfoot stumbled back, hand to his nose, tripped on a barstool, and sprawled on the dirty floor.

His hat fell off and sat sadly on the floor behind him. His nose might have been broken; anyway, it was bleeding. There had been a few screams as it happened, well, anyway brief yips of surprise or dismay. Joey took a step backward. Shawna now had the surprised look of a woman who never expects to be surprised. Mark straightened his tie, turned to Joey. The poor bigfoot on the floor was sitting up and gripping his damaged snout. Mark seemed about to say something; I waited for him to deliver some sort of terrifying and deadly ultimatum, but he just made a sound between a snort and a laugh and rolled his eyes and turned and walked out.

Then I somehow found the presence of mind to dash back to the pool table and grab Mark's jacket, which he'd left slung over a chair, before I scurried out after him.

21

Oh, thanks, he said. He reached into the inner breast pocket and pulled out his wallet. I thought I'd lost this. He extracted two twenties, paused, and added a third. He pushed the money into my hand. I stared at it. Listen, he said. Sorry. She gets a little crazy. I've got to go find her. She'll try to walk home and end up in a ditch. Cab's on me. Sorry for the whatnot. Listen, we'll have lunch or something next week. I owe you.

Then he walked across the street.

Then he got into his car.

Then I said, mostly to myself, But you can't get a cab on Mount Washington, but he was already pulling away.

Joey the bartender and Homestead Harley, who had a wad of brown institutional paper towel over his nose, came out onto the sidewalk. Your friend's a real piece of work, Joey said.

A real piece of shit, Bigfoot said. I think my nose is broke.

Sorry, I said. He's not my friend. I just met him.

He leave you up here? Joey said.

I shrugged. Gave me cab fare, I said.

What the fuck, Joey said. You can't get no cabs in Pittsburgh.

Yeah, I said. Whatever. I've got a friend who lives down on the South Side. I'm just going to walk to his place to crash.

Well, said Joey, you might as well tie one on for the road, since you're not driving.

Oh man, well, I'd feel a little awkward after the, uh, the whatnot.

Aw, shit, said the yeti, and he gave me a brotherly clap on the shoulder that reverberated through my spine. You can't hold nobody accountable just because his buddy's a douche. Anyways, he just caught me off guards is all.

So I had another beer, and maybe Shawna gave me a little bump for the road on my way out.

22

The Mount was a mystery to anyone who didn't live there, and although I was sure there were shorter and better routes down its face to Johnny's street, I only knew to take the McArdle Roadway, which ran crosswise to the hill from Grandview down to Carson Street on the Flats four hundred feet below. It took me a few drunken minutes to get my bearings and find my way back to Grandview; then I turned left and walked along the scenic overlook toward McArdle, the bright city across the river to my right, a half mile distant but seemingly so close that I might, with a running start, leap from here to there. I'd texted Johnny and told him I was en route; he'd replied: my r not we out late. It's a long story, I typed. U can pay for breakfast, he replied.

As I neared one of the small overlook balconies perched off the roadway, weird modern toadstools sprouted on concrete stems from the cliff below, I noted a solitary figure, and a few steps later saw that it was Helen, and I thought that Mark must not have been looking very hard, because here she was in the most obvious place you could imagine.

Helen, I said.

Oh. She only glanced at me before turning back to the view. You.

Me, I said. Are you okay?

How're you doing? How about this weather we're having? What about those Pens, think they'll win the Cup?

Yeah, I said. Sorry. Habit. Reflex. Are you cold?

I'm pissed.

I'd offer you a ride, I said.

Now she turned, and she smiled in spite of herself, the sad smile of someone who knew pretty well what was coming. I think you may be missing an important component of that offer.

True, I said. Does Mark know you're here?

No. Yes. I texted him and told him I got lost in Allentown

to flip him out. You know, delicate white woman amongst the etc. in the middle of the night. I guess I ought to tell him where I really am.

That seems wise.

Wise, she repeated. You're funny.

I've been accused of worse.

She tilted her head. Are you trying to flirt with me? she said.

I flushed. No.

You should be warned, she told me. I flirt back. She took her phone out of her purse and spent a few seconds composing a text. A moment later, it rang. She answered. Yeah, she said. I'm here. Yes. Yes. No. Yes, we seem to have bumped into each other. She covered the receiver with her hand in the old-fashioned gesture. He wants to know, she said to me, if you'll wait with me until he arrives. Yes, I said. Yes, she said, bringing the phone back to her mouth. All right. All right. Okay.

She put the phone back into her bag. She leaned on the rail and looked at the city. I let myself look at her again now that we were alone, and it seemed to me that, while Mark was slightly less than human, she looked, if you can imagine, almost too much so.

Lovely view, she said.

Struck by the incongruity, I didn't reply, but leaned on the rail beside her and looked at the skyscrapers across the way for some period of time.

Then she touched my chin with her hand, and when I turned, she looked as if she were about to kiss me, so I kissed her, meaning it to be serious but brief, getting something more than I'd anticipated in return.

Whoa, I said. Um.

Your girlfriend is very pretty, Helen said. A bit of a space cadet. You ought to pay more attention to her. She smiled. She likes you, I think. And we all need attention, one way or another. It's our worst quality as a species. We'll take what we can get.

Then Mark pulled up and hopped out of the car and strode across the grass and sidewalk to where we were standing. He looked at me, gratitude mixed with calculation, then at her, and he said, Honey, you scared the shit out of me. Jesus.

I know, she said. Punishment.

Mea culpa and so forth. Let me take you home.

You know I will.

Yes, he said.

Um, guys, I said. Because behind them, between us and the city, hovering, silent, mirrors so perfect that I could see my own face reflected even at a distance and even in the dark, were three silver disks, twenty or so feet in diameter, rounded at the edges, humming distantly, watching us, or so it seemed to me, as we watched them, before they moved, or seemed to move, at an impossible speed in a vertical line and became nonexistent somewhere above the few thinly visible clouds.

II. TERMINATION UPON THE OCCURRENCE OF CERTAIN OTHER EVENTS

1

Three days into sixth grade, a new boy sat across from me at lunch. My two best friends had both been sent to Sewickley Academy, and I felt alone as only an eleven-year-old could truly feel alone even though I'd been going to school with everyone else in Quaker Valley since kindergarten. The boy said, You're Peter Morrison. He was even skinnier than I was, with a wild tousle of brown hair like a little lapdog had perched on top of his head, and he had a slight lisp: Morrithon, he said. Yeah, I said. I did some research, he said. Did you know that your great-grandfather, William Aloysius Morrison, was a well-known Nazi sympathizer in England who was hung by his neck until he was dead for being a traitor during the war?

When I told this to my parents that evening, my mother crunched the ice in her scotch and told my dad, I told you we should have sent him to the academy.

Oh, really, Suzanne, my dad said, and he sipped his Syrah. I think this proves the other point very well. It's an awfully sophisticated imprecation for someone of Pete's age, isn't it? But, buddy, it's not true. Neither of your great-grandfathers on my side was named William, and our family hasn't lived in England for hundreds of years. Your grandmother is a Daughter of the American Revolution. Different Morrisons, I'm afraid.

You're afraid, my mother said.

Hm, said my father. Yes, I might have chosen a different way to put it.

The next day I told Johnny, My dad says that we're not related to the Nazi guy. Our family has been in America since, like, before the Revolutionary War.

Oh. His face fell. That sucks. But then it brightened. Maybe your dad is lying, he said. To protect your family from the shame. Maybe, he said, it's a conspiracy.

2

Johnny and his older brother, Ben, had moved to Leetsdale, a weedy little town just up the river from Sewickley, from Florida to live with their grandparents. Ben was sixteen. He explained, Our parents are total fuckups. They're like the biggest meth heads in Tampa. Do you know what meth is?

Yeah, I said.

What is it?

Duh, it's drugs.

You're right, Ben said. It's cocaine for white trash. Do you know what white trash is?

Yeah, I said.

What?

It's, like, I said, poor people.

We, Ben said, pointing across the bedroom at Johnny, are white trash.

Which wasn't strictly true; their grandparents' house was

small and neat, more a cottage than a real house, in a small clearing at the end of a long driveway on a woody lot surrounded by raised vegetable beds and rhododendrons, and if it lacked the acquisitive grandness of the neighborhoods in my own town of Sewickley, the inescapable tackiness of ostentation even when that ostentation is superficially elegant, it wasn't what you'd call poor. There was another building on the property, a shedlike garage that was bigger than the house itself, in which Johnny's Pappy worked on his invention, a metastasizing perpetual motion machine that looked like the vast megalopolis of an immensely advanced but tiny alien race. But I gathered that in Florida their circumstances had been reduced; actually, that was how Ben put it exactly. In Florida, he said, our circumstances were much reduced. He wore eyeliner and listened to the Smiths and sometimes affected something like an English accent. Heeth gay, Johnny told me proudly.

3

Now, at a certain point in *Fourth River, Fifth Dimension*, Winston Pringle's idyllic tale of East End childhood changes without warning to a crypto-Dickensian tale of row-house deprivation in the shadow of the Edgar Thompson Steel Works in Braddock. The digression involves a brilliant but troubled young student named Wilhelm Zollen:

> *Zollen's stepfather at the time was a member of the Order of the Moose. Most days after his shift ended at*

the mill, he'd head down to the lodge to throw a few back. A few often became a lot, and his mother would send Wilhelm to collect the old man.

One day when he was on just such an errand, he chanced upon the head of his stepdad's union, the United Steelworkers, a man by the name of Dan Stern-becker, entering the lodge with another man young Wilhelm didn't recognize. I would later learn that this sartorial fellow was none other than Dr. Martin Dopffnording, a famous German expatriate who'd worked on the Philadelphia experiment and was now a vice-chancellor of the Carnegie Institute of Technology.

Being a curious child, Zollen followed this odd duo. They were deep in conversation, and didn't notice him.

To his surprise, they did not go into the bar, but instead passed through a doorway to a small dark stairwell that he'd never noticed before. He gave them a few moments and then followed them. The stairs seemed to descend for many stories, frequently switching back on themselves. Why would a social hall have such a deep basement? he wondered.

At the base of the stairs was a small lobby with a sagging couch, a few chairs, some filing cabinets, and a receptionist desk. Beyond the desk, there was a heavy wooden door. He surmised the men had gone through the doorway, but dared not follow them, lest he be caught. Instead, he hid behind the desk.

He must have dozed off. He awoke some time later

to the sound of the men emerging from the room. They passed swiftly, speaking to each other in a language that he did not understand at the time, although subsequent studies and investigations lead me to believe that it was an Altaic derivation of middle high Atlantean.

Wilhelm dashed across the room and through the slowly closing door. The room beyond was vast and dimly lit and very cold. In it, as far as the eye could see, were row upon row of heavy wooden planters, each of which held a single, healthy evergreen.

Anyway, Wilhelm explores, leaves, finds his stepfather half delirious and drunk at the bar. He gets the man home; the mother—it's implied that she's a sort of Blanche DuBois character, lost and alone in the industrial north—remonstrates the stepfather. He strikes her. Zollen attempts to intervene. The stepfather strikes him. When he wakes, he finds himself in some sort of examination room. An orifice opens on the far wall. In walks a man whose principal identifying mark is the big signet ring on his right hand and his eerily patrician voice. Don't worry, he says. I'm a doctor.

4

Johnny said that he refused to believe that I'd seen a UFO.

I refuse to believe it, he said. You? You saw it? Of all people. Where's the justice in that?

We were at the diner on Sunday. I'd eaten a quarter of a wet BLT and pushed it away. Johnny had ordered six scrambled eggs and toast and was working his way methodically through the pile.

What can I say? I saw a goddamn UFO. Three, actually.

Spiro, Johnny called to the owner, who was near the cash register reading a newspaper. Can you believe this guy says he saw a UFO?

Spiro shrugged. Effreeone sees crazy things these days. He shrugged. Welcome to your country. He leaned back in his stool and lifted the paper. I caught the front page: Mayor Denies Gay Rumors Led to Firings at Economy Council.

So, Johnny said to me, would you say that it was mirrored, or more like quicksilver? Quicksilver? Mercury. Um, both? In other words you had a sense that the skin had a certain liquid quality, as if it had been poured? Yes, yeah. But you say you could see your reflection? Yes, clearly. Was it illuminated? My reflection? No; are you being intentionally difficult; no, the ship! Well, I guess; I mean, we could see it. Wait, we? Yes, I *told* you: me and Mark and Helen. Who are Mark and Helen? The couple we met at the museum; who formed the entire first half of the story. Did they see it, too? Yes, *like I told you.* I'm not one to get caught up in the secondary details. Now, the ship, was it illuminated—self-illuminated?—I don't know; it would have been hard to say; it reflected everything. Did you detect an aura of light around it? What sort of aura? Any sort— listen, you're the one who saw the fucker, so *describe it to me.* I would not say there was an aura. A corona? Or a corona.

A halo? You mean, like an aura? (Johnny put a hand over his face, inhaled deeply, said: Of all the people, it had to be you. It couldn't have been me.) Sorry, I said; no, no halo. Did it make a sound? Johnny asked. Not as far as I could tell. No humming, no tones? None. Vibration? I didn't feel any vibration. In other words, Johnny said, it had no visible or audible means of propulsion. Yes, I said, that would be accurate. When you looked underneath it, did you see a slight shimmering? What kind of shimmering?—sorry, sorry!—I know I'm supposed to describe it. A shimmering, Johnny said, like a heat mirage, like you'd see on a highway on a hot day. No shimmering, but I can't say I looked very closely; is shimmering important? It's strongly indicative of anti-gravity, Johnny answered. And you say, when it flew away, it tracked a precise vertical path? Precisely. And did it seem to actually *fly* away, or would you more say that it *receded*? I replied, I'm afraid I'm not entirely clear on the distinction. Johnny sighed. Do you remember *Stranger in a Strange Land*? Not especially well, no. Is that the one where he fucks his own mom? God, no, never mind. What I am asking is: Did the object appear simply to fly away, albeit on an unusual and physically impossible trajectory, or did it appear rather to fade out, as if perhaps phasing out of our plane of existence? The former, I said. It flew.

And was this—Johnny forked scrambled eggs into his mouth and chewed for a moment—was this all before, during, or after you made out with the chick?

You said you didn't . . . Fuck you. You're just making fun of me.

A little.

I didn't make out with her. She kissed me.

I do like that sort of creepy, rapey aspect to the story. It plays well with your puerile Ayn Rand philosophy. It would've been rad if she'd *taken you* right then and there.

My philosophy isn't an Ayn Rand philosophy.

Oh, please. *Libertarian*. Johnny laughed. Ridiculous. And don't try to tell me that you're an anarchist or whatever. You people are worse than Constitution fetishists. The individual. *Natural rights*. That shit makes me LOL in my pants. I happen to know that you had, and probably still have, hidden away somewhere, *every* book that Ayn Rand ever wrote. Including the books of you'll-pardon-the-expression philosophy. The trade paper versions. The ones with the crackpot Albert Speer engravings on the front.

Fuck you, Johnny. You're just mad that I saw a flying saucer and you didn't.

I am, admittedly, a little regretful, but, eh, you know what they say: miracles are wasted on believers.

Who says that? I asked.

They do, Johnny said. I don't know. Catholics, maybe. It sounds like something they'd say.

I'm Catholic, I said, and I don't remember saying that. Or hearing it. It sounds like something *you* would say.

Please, you're Catholic like I'm heterosexual. You were born to them, and they assumed you were one of them until around puberty, when suddenly they began to suspect something.

No one assumed you were a heterosexual, Johnny.

True, he said. I was born a butterfly.

5

As penance for my failing to come home the night before—
Mark and Helen had dropped me off at Johnny's, and I'd
slept on his weirdly grandmotherly couch with his fat tabbies,
Anton and LeVay—I'd told Lauren Sara that she could use my
car for the day on the condition that she be the one to bus over
and retrieve it from Oakland. The Greek had gotten a show at
a gallery downtown, and Lauren Sara was going to help her
move her paintings. Johnny and I left the diner. Johnny was
supposed to meet some people about starting a noise band,
and he said he'd walk with me as far as my apartment before
heading over to Bloomfield. As usual he was wearing shorts,
although it was only forty-five degrees and there was a chilly
drizzle. Don't you ever wear pants? I asked him. You used to
wear pants, I think.

And deprive the world of my magnificent calves? He
shrugged. Shorts are more comfortable.

Yeah, but aren't you cold?

I know that your so-called heterosexuality reacts violently
to even the thought of contemplating a masculine physique,
but I find it impossible to believe that you haven't noticed the
hirsute girth I've wrapped myself in since we were kids. I am
impervious to cold. I'm a goddamn hrimthurs.

A what? And not since we were kids. You were still skinny
in college.

True, but too hairy to be a twink, so I decided to go all-out
bear.

What's a twink? I asked.

Really, Johnny answered, you know perfectly well. I know you're terrified that people think you're a fag, as if the sad heterosexual dystopia you've left in your life's wake isn't evidence enough of a shameful sexual parochialism, but no one buys the ignorance act.

Okay, I said. Christ.

So. Let's talk about the flying saucer some more. Now, Pringle is a little, let's say, inconsistent on the issue. In *Fourth River, Fifth Dimension*, he's pretty clear that UFOs are extradimensional and that they travel back and forth from our universe and their own through a basically magical process, but then in *Fountain of Spooks*, which is the third book in the series, he implies that they come out of the hollow earth. He doesn't say much in the second book, about UFOs anyway. Your descriptions are pretty consistent with the hollow earth variety. The extradimensional ones are more like balls of light.

Ball lightning, I said.

Shut it down, Johnny said. It is very strange, though, that we're seeing both varieties in close proximity.

Yes, I said. You've definitely identified the part of this story that's very strange.

Speaking of very strange, any progress on the Where's Winston?

No, I said.

You haven't even tried. I shrugged. Not that I expected otherwise. You're such a materialist. It's depressing. Maybe your close encounter will awaken some basic human curiosity in you.

It was definitely curious. How many books did this guy write?

Well, there are five that are under his sole authorship and another two that he cowrote with someone named Dr. Wilhelm Zollen, and then there are a bunch of sort of fan-fic, self-published versions that have popped up, apparently from people who heard him speak at conventions or whatnot and became convinced that they were participants in Project Pittsburgh. I've read the first three so far.

Project Pittsburgh is the thing.

Project Pittsburgh is the everything. It's pretty awesome. You should read this stuff instead of shooting your load in bullshit liberal blog comments all day. It's sort of an all-encompassing conspiracy theory. I mean, usually you get a Nazi, a time portal, and a train full of gold, or you get aliens and Feds, or you find out that Tesla was really Rasputin or Gore Vidal's grandfather created chemtrails or AIDS was caused by sexual congress with bigfoots, but Pringle's got a real conspiracy puttanesca thing; it's all in there; he's the Whitman of wack jobs; containment has failed on the multitudes.

Well, that all sounds very elaborate. What's the upshot?

The upshot? Jesus Lord Mother of Mercy, you are becoming a corporate hack.

In a nutshell, I said.

Fuck you, Johnny said, but he could never resist; he was a pedant at heart. So basically, he said, you've got this ancient sacred geometry, sacred topography, what with the three rivers and the underground fourth river all meeting at the Point. Usual backstory. Indians knew it was holy, blah blah blah. So the Marquis Du Quesne, who's the governor-general of New France, and who also just happens to also be the grand master of the Priory of Sion, hears about this, in particular the fourth river, which is, duh, obviously, the underground stream of medieval European esotericism, immediately puts together an exhibition, kicks out the Indians, and builds Fort Duquesne. So then Adam Weishaupt, the thirty-third-degree Freemason and immortal founder of the Bavarian Illuminati, gets wind of this, and basically does the Illuminati version of Aw No She Di'in! Now, uh, well, there's basically a big digression about how Shea and Wilson stole all of Pringle's ideas about Weishaupt killing and replacing George Washington, but yeah, basically, he uses Washington, who he either *is* or *is manipulating*, and conceives the Forbes expedition, and burns down Fort Duquesne, and erects Fort Pitt, and lays the groundwork for the founding of Pittsburgh. Then etc. etc. ad infinitum, a bunch of boring shit. Then Andrew Carnegie arrives and him and Frick get involved; Frick, by the way, is linked back to the Priory of Sion via a tenuous connection to Isaac Newton; the Pinkertons at the Homestead Strike, that's all basically a blood sacrifice sort of thing, it begins this century-long magical working, which eventually gets taken over by the CIA, of course, which is where Pringle's family gets involved. It's the goddamn *Remembrances of Conspiracies Past*. Well, the point is to open up the transdimensional portal between quantum realities, allowing travel between any points in space-time and total control over the historical timeline and all that good stuff. I'm telling you, it's fucking awesome.

But only two about aliens.

Out of the first three, yeah. I mean, I think he comes back to it when he starts writing in collaboration with Wilhelm

Zollen. And they're not really aliens. They're extradimensional emissionaries; ascended beings who may already pos-
sess the power that the Project seeks. But, yeah, the second
book is called *The Testing House* and it's kind of a big digression about George Westinghouse and satanic ritual sex magic.
Sort of a one-handed reader, to be honest. Very ahem descrip-
tive, if you know what I mean.

I know what you mean.

Well, despite your general lackadaisical attitude about the
whole deal, I've put out some feelers of my own. We'll see
what pops up.

You've put out some feelers. Phoned up some old contacts.
Made some calls.

I have a not-insubstantial reputation in the Pittsburgh
demimonde.

Your dealers don't count, besides which, being a customer
isn't exactly being chairman of the board. Also besides which,
I don't see how the black guy who sells you fentanyl or whom-
ever is going to help you find the presumably white dude who
sounds like he got a little too much attention from Coach
when he was a kid if-ya-know-what-I-mean and has never
recovered. Why don't you just send him a fan letter care of his
publisher?

We were at the corner of Baum and Liberty. Ahead of us
in the middle distance the spire of East Liberty Presbyterian
poked at the woolen sky. Behind, the gray abandoned lots of
the old Pontiac dealership. We started to cross. A little gray
car zipped around the corner in order to make the light and
missed us by millimeters. That was your car, Johnny said.

Yes, I said. It was.

That wasn't your paramour in the driver seat.

No. It wasn't.

Who, pray tell?

I can only guess the Greek.

Ah, the mysterious artist-friend-roommate. Personally, I suspect them of an entirely dour and unappealing sapphism. Speaking of people we need to contrive to meet. How much booze have you stolen from her since you and Lauren Sara contracted a bad case of each other? I can't believe you don't even know what she looks like.

I guess she looks like the girl driving my car around like a maniac.

I didn't think she looked particularly Greek, but I'm not sure what a Greek woman looks like. Do they have a phenotype? I imagine they pop out as spry nonagenarians with a single hair on their chin and a single eyebrow on their forehead. We should ask Spiro about her. He knows all the Greeks. I can totally imagine what he'd say, too. Oh, Johnny, she ees artist. She never cumss to church. She ees twenty-fife and hass no babees. I wuddy, I wuddy. He's very concerned with the overall fertility of the Greek race. You know he's like whatever the Greek equivalent of a white nationalist is, right? Their party is called the Golden Dawn, apparently, which has nothing to do with the Hermetic Order. *Supposedly* has nothing to do. By the way, when are you going to get a new car?

What's wrong with my car?

Nothing in particular, but when you went all corporate on

me, I figured I'd at least get to tool around in a Bimmer as consolation for your selling out.

They don't pay me enough.

You don't have to tell me, Morrison. You sold your soul for a bag of beans. And you want to lecture me on the difference between an addict and a dealer.

I didn't say addict.

Not in so many words.

We parted ways at my apartment. There was a moving truck out front, but there was always a moving truck out front. I saw one of my Uncle Bill's cars, a little red chip like a Satanist's pinkie nail among the grimy grays of the neighborhood cars. Oh, hey, Morrison, Johnny said, can you lend me a few bucks? I need to have a beer with these guys and my sovereign debt sitch is a little precarious at the moment. Quantitatively ease a brother's burden.

I'm not a bank, I said, but I handed him one of the twenties Mark had handed to me the night before.

Maybe so, but I'm too big to fail, Johnny said, and he cackled on his way down the stairs. I texted Lauren Sara and asked her if she was letting someone else drive my car. She responded immediately; lied: no. then who almost just killed me?? I asked. me, she wrote; then, a few seconds later: only almost.

Then I texted Johnny: maybe theyre magic beans.

jack off, he responded.

I grabbed a beer and sat with the computer at the kitchen table. My squirrel regarded me through the window. Hey, squirrel, I said. He cocked his head as if he'd heard me and ran off down the roof. I wanted to look up Helen, but I didn't know her last name, and although I supposed that I could call my Nana, I didn't really want the long conversation that resulted from every call to Nana. Besides, I wasn't sure I wanted anyone to know I was interested. Then I remembered that Mark had given me his card last night, passed it deftly into my hand as I crawled out of his car with an exhortation to Call me; I could use you, which had sounded promising when he said it but hummed with ambiguity when I recalled him saying it. Mark Danner, it said. Senior Director of Special Occurrences, it said. Office of the General Counsel. Vandevoort IRCM. It bore the watermark of some sort of bizarre and vaguely Masonic implement that I would later learn was a stylized astrolabe, their logo. I googled Vandevoort IRCM and found their investor relations site. A diversified international company, it said. Combining Values with Value, it said. Empowering business to cross borders and transcend boundaries, it said. Its motto, in English anyway, was, Never Stop. Which seemed a little weirdly sexual to me, but, eh, they were Dutch, and perhaps something was lost in the translation. The French site said, *A tout de suite*, though, which wasn't quite the same thing. The German page said, *Unaufhaltsam*.

Using Mark's full name in combination with Helen and some generic art vocab, I found a few party photos in the New York social magazines; found that her last name was Witold; found that she was represented by Arnovich Galleries in Chelsea, which explained why she and Mark and Arlene had seemed to be on familiar terms. Arlene's ex-husband was

Daniel Arnovich, a bit of gossip I'd learned from my grand-mother when the museum had hired Arlene. All because of her husband, Nana said. They were still married at the time. He's thick as thieves with David [that was David Hoffman, the erstwhile chairman of the museum board], and I hear the whole thing is a ploy to get her out of New York. This was at a family dinner, and Mom had said, I never took you for a conspiracy theorist, Nanette. I believe that anything I'm not in on is a conspiracy, Nana said. At the time, I'd assumed she was referring obliquely to my mother's hints about a retire-ment home.

Well, anyway, I found a little five-hundred-word piece Helen had written for *Artforum* a couple of years ago. It said shit like:

> *What I want is for my paintings to imply a micro-cosm that could actually exist even though it may not actually exist. I want the viewers of my works to be confounded and to wonder if they are seeing the abstraction of an actual object or the concretization of an imaginary one, and I try to apply equal rigor to the creation of forms that do not exist as to the re-creation via representation of those that do.*

Not exactly Walter Pater, although I was immediately struck by its anticipatory echo of our experience the night before. I found images of her work; she painted huge can-vasses, immense, wall-sized works that implied a hybridiza-tion of abstract expressionism and a cell biology text.

Her last show was called Abstract Empiricism.

I found a few other articles about her, which were blandly flattering, but which implied that, while she'd once stood on the cusp of becoming a big deal, she was now in a serious and possibly prolonged phase of Not Doing Much.

Her Facebook page was private. We had, as yet, no mutual friends.

6

Lauren Sara asked if she could keep the car another day. I wanted to say no, but said yes. I lay around the apartment watching movies on my laptop all day, then called Johnny to see if he wanted to grab a beer, but he kept babbling incoherently into the phone, saying things like, Morphic transgraphic, Masonic melodic, tectonic Teutonic bubonic, interspersed with an unsettlingly animal bray. You're fucked up, I said. The tide, he screamed at me, is turning.

I tried Derek, whom I didn't hang out with very much anymore, and he agreed to meet me for a beer at Silky's on Liberty. How's the city? I asked him. Derek worked in the solicitor's office. Fucked, he said. Everyone knows that, I said. Yesterday council debated a resolution to amend the city's no-hunting ordinance to make it legal to shoot a bigfoot. A bigfoot? I said. A bigfoot, he said. How the fuck did that come up? Oh, council doesn't want to do anything that might result in an actual outcome, so they mostly just introduce resolutions on behalf of their constituents, and you know, only crazy people

pay attention to city government. The bigfoot thing was introduced by Jack O'Bannon, who's got Hays in his district, and
you know how many nutjobs they've got out in Hays; probably
some bigfoots, too; bigfeet. I'm surprised Tremone didn't say
that it was intimidation and discrimination against a minority
species, I told him. Ha, he said; Tremone doesn't come to
council anymore. She's in campaign mode. She decided she's
going for Gadlocki's old state senate seat. But I thought she
was going to run for mayor. Kantsky made a deal with her; he
told her she'd never make it through the primary, which was
true, and then he told her that he'd help her set up a U.S. Senate race after she served her term in Harrisburg, which is an
ingenious way to put it, because you really do serve a term in
Harrisburg; it's like prison, and no one ever escapes. So who's
going to run against the mayor? Same as every time: a couple
of asshole proggie jagoffs are going to split the East End vote
and get thoroughly bunged out of the primary with thirty percent each; the mayor'll take the blacks and the blue collars,
get forty percent, and if we're really lucky, the three remaining
Pittsburgh Republicans will draw straws to see which one gets
to hurl himself off the roof of the Duquesne Club in ritual
sacrifice to the God of the Slightly Lower Millage Rate in the
general; fuck, man, I'd say we should get rid of the government, but then I'd be out of a job.

I'm sure you'd land on your feet, I said.

Fuck that, he said. I'm perfectly happy on my ass.

Haha cheers, I said, and we moved on to our second beers.

Oh, hey, he said, you'll appreciate this. I'm assuming you
know about the whole flying saucer website thing.

Alieyinz. I hesitated; I said, Yeah, Johnny told me that it was completely awesome.

It's something. Actually, it's pretty funny. Currently blocked by the city servers, though, so I can't read it at work. Anyway, so I'm in the deputy solicitor's office the other day—have you ever met Karl? He drinks at Gooski's sometimes.

No.

Nice guy, actually. Not a moron. So we're prepping for this thing we have to do for the Fiscal Oversight Board, when Kantsky himself comes barging in, and you know, we're all basically terrified of Kantsky, who's completely nuts and completely irrationally vindictive.

Johnny says that he used to be in Mossad.

Uh, yeah, maybe if Mossad is the name of the Rodef Shalom softball team. Although, to be fair, it sounds like the sort of rumor that Kantsky would spread about himself. Anyway, he slams the door open and starts screaming, Where's DiPresta? Where *the fuck* is DiPresta? And Karl's like, Uh, the solicitor is at the municipal law conference in Dallas. He's back next week. Can we help you? And I'm like, whoa, whoa, what's this *we* business, 'cause the last thing I want is for that maniac to know who I am, so I just kind of slump down in my seat, but Kantsky doesn't care who the fuck I am. He slams this paper down on Karl's desk and Karl takes one look and sort of starts laughing but trying not to laugh, so I risk a look, and it's a screen cap from the aliens blog, and someone's pretty convincingly Photoshopped the mayor's head onto a porn shot of some twink taking a dildo up the butt and added a little gray alien dude so it looks, you know, like he's getting probed.

Oh dear.

Yeah. You should look it up, by the way. Turns out it's a fucking .gif. The dildo goes in and out, and the alien smokes a doob. So, Kantsky's all like, I want this shut down. I want this site gone. And Karl's like, Jonah, listen, political satire is protected speech. The mayor's a public official. Kantsky goes absolutely berserk; he's all like, I WILL NOT HAVE IT SUGGESTED THAT OUR MAYOR IS SOME KIND OF . . . and then he can't think of the word, because he obviously wants to say fag, but you have to be careful about that shit, so get this: he fucking says *fruitcake*, and Mary Tremone is, like, suddenly standing right behind him.

Oh shit, I said. What was she doing there?

She's still the head of the finance committee. She was meeting with me and Karl.

That's hysterical.

He couldn't even say anything. He just stared at her for a minute, and she had the hugest shit-eating grin you ever saw, and then he just walked away. Then Mary comes into the office, sees the thing on Karl's desk, and says, He doesn't look a day over twenty.

By the way, I said, trying to sound like I didn't give a shit, what's the deal with all this UFO shit?

Persistent, Derek said. That's the deal with it. We actually got a call from some producers from TLC who wanted to feature us in some kind of aliens-built-the-pyramids-and-such show.

You should've said yes, I said.

Fuck that. I referred them to Kantsky.

What if he finds out?

I'll blame it on DiPresta, the prick.

Well, what's the deal, anyway? What's the official position?

You sound like Johnny, man. The official position? Christ, Dick Markiewinsky at the Convention and Visitors' Bureau wanted to run a whole "New Area 51" campaign to attract tourists. Needless to say, that's not happening. Look, no one gives a shit. Back in the fifties a whole goddamn B-25 crashed in the Mon and no one ever found it. This is Pittsburgh, man. It's full of weird shit.

We ended up getting unconscionably drunk for a Sunday night, and Derek confessed to me that he was still pissed that I was dating Lauren Sara. You didn't even like her very much, I said. In the whole time you were together, I never met her.

She sucks you in, Derek said, but then you're embarrassed by her.

I'm not embarrassed by her.

Sure you are. She's not cooo-ooool enough for you.

You're drunk, I said.

We're friends, he said. You and me.

We're friends, I told him.

Fuck these bitches, he said.

Yeah, I said. Fuck 'em.

I gotta take a leak, he said.

After he'd been gone for ten minutes, I thought I ought to go after him to see if he was all right, and I found him sitting in the stall in the bathroom. Derek, I said. Hey, man, are you okay in there? He didn't answer. I tapped on the door. Derek?

I said. He mumbled. He grunted. I'm good, he said. I'm just going to close my eyes for a minute. Are you sure? I said. Fuck you, fruitcake, he answered. Okay, I said. I was drunk enough that it sounded like a fine plan to me. I managed, barely, to pay our tab, grabbed a few stale pretzels, and stumbled home. I fell into bed fully clothed and slept a blacked-out, anesthetized sleep until two a.m., at which point I woke with the desperate need to piss and a huge boner that made it nearly impossible. I stood unsteadily and willed it to go down; when it didn't, I did my best to force myself to pee anyway, bending at the waist and trying my best to aim for the bowl, and I made a ridiculous mess. After wiping the toilet off with wadded paper, I felt slightly soberer, so I took a shower, my still-spinning head resting on the cool tile, my back arched against the warm water, the fan humming; I had not, upon reflection, had such a weekend of excess in a long time; it occurred to me that this was the regret I'd feared and then forgotten about, and I was suddenly tired again.

When I fell back asleep, I dreamed that I woke up on an operating table in a spaceship. I wasn't bound to it by any physical restraints, but I couldn't move. The walls were reflective silver. The room was illuminated with floating globes of light like solar flares in a bad photograph. My head was free to move. I looked down and saw that I'd been drawn open like a frog in a biology class. It didn't hurt, and although I could see my own guts, I didn't feel disgust or nausea. An orifice opened in the wall and an immense man dressed like something between a fry cook and a Freemason was carried in on an ornate golden litter by four well-oiled ancient Egyptians. The litter was decorated with bas-relief images of crocodiles and pine trees. He lounged like an odalisque. They set him on the floor, but he seemed to have some difficulty getting up. They bent to help him, but he slapped away their hands prissily. No, no. I'm fine. He had a high-pitched voice, like Truman Capote but without the affectation of matinee sophistication. I just need to get a little momentum. He moved like a seal on dry land, as if he weren't in the habitat most suitable for his physiology, but he managed to rock himself into a sitting position and then haul himself to his feet. He pulled a pair of rubber gloves—not like a doctor's, like for dishwashing—from his pocket and snapped them on as he walked toward me. Don't worry, he said. I'm a doctor. What seems to be the problem? Someone's cut me open, I said; my voice was calm as if I were telling him I had a little rash. Let's have a look-see, he said. His hand nestled between my legs. Not there, I said. Now, now, he told me. I always start the exam with a little hand scan.

7

In the morning, I was so hung over that I walked out of my building and for a full minute stood gawking at the empty stretch of curb where I usually parked my car before I remembered that my girlfriend had it. It was cold but oddly humid, and I could already feel the back of my neck dampening my scarf. The sky was the same color as the sidewalk. I sighed and walked down to Liberty Avenue, where I stood on a wet corner beside the West Penn Hospital parking garage for fifteen more interminable minutes until a bus came, then discovered I didn't have exact change and shoved a five into the meter. Hey, buddy, said the driver. Yeah, yeah, I said.

The only seat left was on the side-facing bench just behind the driver between two big women who were discussing flying saucers. I'm telling you, one of them said, I'm telling you it's all just that damn mayor trying to win reelection. It's a whatchacall. It's all a goddamn distraction. Now, how's a mayor gonna make a goddamn flying saucer, Sherri? the other one asked, and you got the feeling that these two frequently had some variant of this conversation, with the latter playing the skeptical role and relishing it. Yes, it occurred to me that it was Johnny and my future, or one such possible future, two batty old men in thrift store outfits hauling around shopping bags and loud opinions on the bus. I thought about what my dad had said; what if those two old nuts could call back to us; what if they were less an extrapolation than a warning? A younger black woman across the aisle had joined the conversation and said only white people ever saw UFOs. Shit, she said, I bet if they asked them to describe the aliens, they'd be all like, a African-American man, medium build, in a hoodie. Everyone laughed. I looked at the floor.

My favorite security guard was working the main desk in my building. Hey, Rick. Happy Monday, I said. Is that what day this is? he replied. It feels like a Monday, I said as I walked toward the elevators. I don't know, Rick said. I only work here. He was as indifferent as the architecture. He had a small lexicon of workplace clichés worn through years of repetition into mantras; he had a set of about six gestures and expressions that he arranged with the infinite complexity of a Baroque composer working and reworking the same few musical figures. You and me both, I said. Yup. He chuckled. We sure got them fooled.

The Global Solutions building, which was no longer called the Global Solutions building, as our occupied square footage had declined over the last several years while a new anchor tenant, the law firm of Metzger Richards, had come into possession of most of the upper floors, was fortunately invisible in Pittsburgh's skyline. We weren't quite as tall as our neighbors, and we were a few blocks inland from the nearest river, and we'd have detracted from the city's pretty accidental outline if we'd been included in it. The building had the proportions of a shoe box turned on end, graceless and utilitarian, with horizontal rows of metal cladding between each floor's windows that made it appear squished, a spring collapsed under the weight of its own mediocrity. It had been built in the late seventies by a long-since-consumed and -digested bank, bought by a property holding company, briefly overrun by AllShip, the dot-com incarnation of Global Solutions, then partitioned out to the usual gang of lawyers and marketing firms on the make. There was a rumor that the lobby had once held a famous piece of artwork, an abstract mosaic by an artist of local origin whose name no one could ever remember, but if that had been true, the art was long gone, replaced by white walls that looked sleek until you got close enough to see that they were a hasty drywall job, and marble floors that, because they'd been improperly sealed, bore many brown spatter marks from the many spills from the many badly balanced coffees carried by the many hurried workers out of the ground-floor Starbucks.

There were thirty-three floors. Johnny thought that was highly significant, because there were thirty-three degrees of Freemasonry. I worked on twenty-five. If you add the digits, Johnny said, you get seven. Seven is a very important number.

Besides Marcy, my relatively sleepy corner of the office held Leonard, Tim, Kevin, Pandu, and the Other Peter, who obliged our need for clarity by going by Pete, although in his absence everyone reverted to calling him the Other Peter. In its internal literature and external job postings, Global Solutions emphasized its team environment. None of us knew precisely what that was, and it never seemed that we were working on the same project at the same time, but in theory, we were a Global Solutions Solve Team, and we hypothetically reported to an apoplectic thirty-seven-year-old vice president named Ted Roskopf, or, as his email signature put it, R. Theodore Roskopf, MBA, even though he was still a year away from finishing his executive MBA program. There was an unlimited supply of vice presidents at GS; they were functionaries who reported to directors who reported to senior directors who reported to senior vice presidents who reported to division directors who reported to the C-levels; they mass-produced them in the copy room or something, each imbued with glossy charts for brains and endowed with a Napoleonic desire to lay waste to the rest of Global Solutions and remake its codes and social order in their totalizing vision. Ted referred to us quite openly as My People and also referred, whenever he had the chance, to the "gray ceiling," his own coinage, apparently, meaning the gang of fifty-and-overs who held all the executive offices, and who all conspired to keep Ted from revolutionizing and revitalizing everything, everywhere. If this was a real tech company, he'd say, you wouldn't have this bullshit. I wouldn't put up with it. There seemed to be flaws in this analysis, but he was so earnest in his desire to implement impactful change or whatever that it became endearing, and even though he treated us with an attitude of feudal disdain, we felt oddly protective of him, as, I suppose, actual peasants might have once felt about their own backwater milords.

I suspected that Ted had convinced himself that he saw me as his protégé. Among our team, Marcy and Leonard were unfireable as Diversity, she being a dyke and he being black. Pandu was an Indian, which didn't count as Diversity, yet as an Indian with a heavy accent, he was suspect in Ted's estimation and unworthy of special attention. However, he was the only one of us who displayed competence or appeared to know for what reason and to what end he arrived at the office every morning. Tim was too old: the geezer of the group at something over fifty, and probably also Diversity, or at least also unfireable given the potential of Age Discrimination; Kevin was just out of school and therefore too young; the Other Peter was a mystery, a blond Californian with a surfer's drawl and an attitude of athletic disinterest so complete and imperturbable that one of us, probably Marcy, once said that he was either the Buddha or a retard.

8

Dude, the Other Peter said, you look terrible. He was putting his lunch in the refrigerator in the kitchenette, and I'd come in to find coffee.

Just a little cold, I said. I looked around. Where's the coffee machine?

Oh, man, it's cool. We got a Keurig. He pointed to a machine that looked like something out of Beverly Crusher's sick bay.

What the fuck is a Keurig?

K-cups, man. Single-serving.

Oh, I said. Yeah. The pod things. Isn't that wasteful?

Totally, he said. It produces, like, a bunch of times more plastic waste. But whatever, I don't drink coffee.

Yeah, what do you do when you're hung over?

Usually go for a swim. What about you?

I was trying to figure out the machine. Coffee, I said. Do you know how to do this?

Yup, he said, and he made me a cup of coffee.

What happened to the old machine?

I guess they all got junked. Purchasing replaced all the old machines. Didn't you read the emails?

Who reads emails from Purchasing?

You should read the emails from Purchasing, the Other Peter told me. Those ladies pretty much run shit.

Yeah, well, this coffee sucks, I said. No offense.

Wouldn't know, but I'll take your word for it. You ever drink kombucha?

My girlfriend's a fan.

It totally improves your intestinal flora.

Yeah. How is it for your liver?

Don't know, man. It's probably awesome for your liver, too.

Huh, I said.

By the way, he said, R. Theodore was looking for you.

Why?

Didn't ask.

I drank more coffee, and went to my desk, and crossed my arms and lay my head on them, and although I had every intention of staying that way for thirty seconds, no more, when thirty seconds came I decided that I could do with one more interval, and when that interval had passed, I'd fallen asleep.

I woke about an hour later; no one had noticed, or, if they had, they'd either been good enough not to disturb me, or they just didn't care, if that was even a distinction worth making. I felt better, but the bad coffee and the long weekend and perhaps the weakness of my intestinal fauna or what have you caught up to me, and I walked quickly and quietly to stairwell C, which I took down to the twenty-third floor. This was still officially a part of the Global Solutions office suite, but it had been almost entirely abandoned over the preceding five years as the Global Solutions Solutions Desk operations had been outsourced to Bangladesh and the Global Solutions TransSolve document translation program to India and the Global Solutions Brand-Solve brand management division simply and unceremoniously euthanized when its last client departed for the sharper-focused shores of a real marketing firm. Some cubicles remained, and the conference rooms remained, along with the janitor's closets and D-marks and break rooms and a few outdated copiers and something in the quiet hallways that suggested someone had recently been there, although of course no one had.

I'd surreptitiously snagged a newspaper from Leonard's desk on the way down. I found a story about Councilman O'Bannon's bigfoot-hunting measure in the B-section, written in that wry tone that tells you, reader, that you're a little too sophisticated to believe it, but you'll be amused to read it anyway. The article made a couple of references to *taking* a bigfoot, and I made a note to mention it to Johnny, who'd appreciate the double entendre, but it was the opening graf that really got me: As if the flying-saucer traffic weren't enough, Councilman Jack O'Bannon (12th District) has introduced legislation that if approved by City Council will make it entirely legal to hunt an animal that most say don't exist. Now some on Grant Street are suggesting that Pittsburgh's growing tourism industry could look to these popular tales as a potential source of dollars and new investment.

So UFOs were a thing now. It made me slightly queasy. I hadn't said anything to anyone except Johnny, but suddenly it felt as if everyone would know.

9

By the way, I never did tell anyone about that bathroom on twenty-three. I don't know why. Secrecy, in the protection and in the breach, is the currency of an office much more than money itself, the small secrets worth more than the large. Nor did I mention to anyone that week, not even to Marcy, that I'd met a sort-of lawyer who'd confirmed the rumors of an impending sale or takeover or Other Important Event by an amoebic Northern European conglomerate, and when the week passed without my seeing or hearing from Mark, whom I'd unrealistically expected to pop by my desk for lunch on Monday, I began to reconstruct my memory of my weekend around a theme of uncertainty that it had not theretofore possessed, which was reassuring.

But I did ultimately mention to Leonard that I'd seen the UFOs. It was Thursday. Back when the original sightings had been reported, he'd mentioned to me in an offhanded and unembarrassed way that he'd once seen a UFO, but—he shrugged—I was doing a lot of dope back then. I always forgot that Leonard was actually older than Tim, which probably made me a racist. He didn't look older than Tim. Leonard liked to tell stories about working at Global Solutions in the early eighties, when it was Allegheny Shipping and actually shipped things. Worked in the stockroom, he told me. You don't even know what a stockroom is.

I know what a stockroom is, I said.

Yeah, academically, he answered.

Anyway, I told Leonard that I'd seen a UFO, and he said, Did you, now? There's supposed to be some real weird shit going down this year. How do you mean? I said. Oh, you know, the whole Mayan apocalypse thing, he said. I didn't know you believed in that sort of thing, Leonard. Shit, I don't, but Elijah's got my girl into it; she's always making me watch those documentaries about ancient aliens and whatnot. Elijah,

I said. Yeah. He's got that store in East Lib. My girl's real into authentic Africana, so that's where she goes for her clothes.

Believe it or not, I said, but I think my buddy Johnny knows him.

Is your buddy into weird shit?

It's his main hobby.

Then they probably do know each other. People who are into weird shit always find each other. It's addictive behavior. Leonard was in recovery and believed deeply and zealously in everything but the anonymity. It's the same as addicts, kid, he went on. When you're an addict, you've got to find other addicts because they accept and understand your irrational behavior. To a crazy person, other crazy people are normal, and normal people are crazy. That was my main realization when I got sober. It's not the spiritual shit, or the higher power shit. That shit's important, but it's not the main shit. The main shit is when you figure out that I'm not crazy because I'm on drugs, I'm on drugs because I'm crazy. That shit is the necessary diagnosis. Until you pinpoint that shit, everything you try is treatment for the wrong disease.

10

But I wasn't worried about Johnny's addiction to weird shit; I was worried about his other proclivities. I hadn't heard from him all week other than one phone call early Wednesday morning. Silence otherwise, which was troubling, because he usually couldn't go six hours without at least texting. The call had come at three-thirty in the morning. Your phone is ringing, said Lauren Sara with her eyes closed. I reached over blindly and silenced it. It rang again. I picked it up this time to look at the screen, saw Johnny's name, and silenced it again. It rang again. Jesus Christ, I said, do you know what time it is?

Morrison, he said. Mooooorison.

Johnny, I said.

Morrison. Morrison. Lessison. Someison. Floorison, Doorison, Poorison, Goreison, Snoreison. *Bore*ison.

Johnny, I said, what do you want?

What do I want? What do I want?

Yeah, what do you want? I was awake now, my feet slung over the edge of the bed, scratching idly at a shoulder that didn't itch. It was raining, slowly and steadily, each drop against the windows the soft echo of a distant bell.

Morrison.

Fucking what? I snapped. I closed my eyes and felt the deep desire of my whole body and being to keep them that way.

Listen, he said.

I'm listening. I opened my eyes again.

Listen.

Yes. I'm listening. What?

My mind is a quantum computer.

Oh yeah?

My mind is a quantum computer.

Right. Will it still be a quantum computer during normal business hours?

A quantum hologram.

Oh, so not a computer.

Shut up. Listen. Shut up. Listen. A computer and a hologram.

Yeah, I said. Okay. What's the upshot?

The upshot? he said. The upshot? He turned the word over like a plum pit you haven't spit out yet, sucked on it as if it still had some sweetness attached. The upshot?

You sound like you could use an upshot yourself.

His voice changed. Wouldn't it be cool, he said, if we could project a quantum hologram over Heinz Field for the Super Bowl? When I say his voice changed, I mean he sounded lucid in spite of the sentiment.

I rubbed my nose. A hologram of what? I asked.

A hologram of a hologram.

Johnny, I said, I'm going to hang up. I've got to go.

Don't leave me. Don't leave me.

Yeah, I'm going to leave you. Why don't you try to get some sleep and call me when you've come down or whatever? Preferably at a more civilized hour.

Listen, Johnny said. The tide is turning.

I think you may have mentioned that to me before.

The tide is turning.

Good night, Johnny.

Don't leave me.

Good night, Johnny.

Morrison! he cried.

Yes?

I'm dead, he said.

No, Johnny, I told him. I regret to inform you that that's not the case.

Are you sure? he asked.

Not yet, I said.

Not yet, he repeated. Not yet. And then there was a pause on the other end that grew into a long silence. I could hear him breathing, and when I was sure that he'd forgotten he was still on the phone, or forgotten that he had a phone, or forgotten how a phone worked and what a phone was, I ended the call and lay back down beside my girlfriend.

Johnny, I said.

Yeah, she said to her pillow.

Totally fucked up, I said.

Yeah, she said.

I'm an alien, I said. I came in a flying saucer.

Yeah, she said.

I love you, I said.

Aw, she said. That's nice.

We should move in together.

Mm, she said. Cool. Let's talk about it later. I knew from the way she said it that we probably wouldn't. I kissed her shoulder. I think you're the most normal person I know, I told her.

She turned her head and kissed my nose. Then you are fucked, she said.

11

On the bus the following Monday, because Lauren Sara had the car again, and two dudes were loudly comparing the merits of different strains of weed while the rest of the passengers tried to ignore them. Yo what about the FGD, man? You ever hear of that? No, man, what's the FGD? That's the Federal Government Dope, man. That's the shit the Bill Clinton used to smoke. No shit? No shit. Me, I like the K2. Why's it called the K2? 'Cause that's how high it gets you, man. I turned my head. They were about my age, a black dude with dreads and a white dude in a flat-billed Pirates cap. What the fuck are you looking at? the white one said. I may have rolled my eyes. Don't roll your eyes, man, he said. I'll roll those eyes out your head. Man, shut up, said the black guy. Leave the man in peace. I turned back around. They got off at Wood Street, my stop as well. The white guy disappeared around the corner. The black guy walked up beside me and said, Hey, my man, you got three dollars you could lend me for bus fare? No, I said. You smoke weed? he asked. I shrugged. Sometimes, I said. You want to buy some? Dude, I said, really? Yeah, man. You got that corporate look about you, but I can tell you burn it down. I don't have any cash on me, I said. Go get some, he said. How do I know you've got any? I asked. How do I know it's any good? How do I know you're not just trying to rob me? Rob you? He opened his hands. Because I'm black? I've got to be honest, I said. That's one of many factors. He laughed, a hoot followed by a surprisingly girlish giggle. One of many factors, he said. I like you. Thanks, I said. It's real and it's good, he said. I'll tell you what, I told him. I'll buy it if you deliver it to my office. Where's your office? Up there. I pointed. No way, my man. How am I supposed to get in there? There's security and shit. You think they're gonna let a nigga with dreads walk up in there with a backpack—he patted his old JanSport—full of weed? Tell them you're a bike messenger, I said. Security guards don't give a fuck. I'll tell them I'm expecting you. Ask for Peter Morrison at Global Solutions. That's you? That's me. I'm gonna charge extra, man, for delivery. How much? Seventy an eighth. That seems a little steep. Delivery, he said, pronouncing each syllable emphatically. Right, I said. Come by around nine-thirty. You're a weird dude, he told me. If you knew my friends, I said, you wouldn't think so.

12

Hey, Rick. Happy Monday, I said. Is that what day this is? he replied. It feels like a Monday, I said. I wouldn't know, Rick said. I only work here. You and me both, I said. Maybe one of us, he said. Hey, Rick, I said. I'm expecting a package around nine-thirty. Just send him up. Sounds suspicious, Rick said. Drug deal, I told him. Haha, he said. I'll keep him away from the dogs. This place is buttoned up tight, I said. Oh yeah, said Rick. We're a regular fucking Alcatraz.

13

I deleted some emails and agreed to some meetings and checked out the latest affronts to liberty on the Reason site and saw that one of their writers had picked up the story of the mayor and Marissagate, so-named for his estranged wife, in which the Growing Trend of Important Public Officials utilizing the tools and technologies of the Surveillance State for personal ends was flogged around the track for a few laps. Then Ted stopped by my desk and asked if I'd come to his office, and when I did he said, Close the door, and I said, Ted, are you firing me? and he said, Hell, no, you're my main man around here, Pete. Okay, I said.

He tossed his jacket on the back of his chair and we sat down. He was a car nut, and his office was full of framed pictures of exotic Italian cars and signed portraits of drivers; I always thought it looked like a ten-year-old boy's bedroom.

Pete, he said.

Yes, I said.

You're buddies with the Other Pete, right?

I wouldn't say buddies.

You get along, though. He doesn't suspect you of anything.

Suspect me? I said.

You know what I mean.

I didn't know what he meant, but I nodded.

I think he's trying to make a move.

A move?

Has he said anything to you?

Last week he told me that I should try interval training if I wanted to improve my resting heart rate.

What?

No. He hasn't said anything about making a move.

I heard his name up on twenty-six last week.

Maybe they're talking about me, I joked.

He frowned. No, they're talking about the Other Pete.

What are they saying?

He threw up his hands. He looked simultaneously older and younger than thirty-seven. He had good hair and a broad, dumb face and an air of clumsy athleticism that reminded me of a certain type of lawn-mowing dad—not my own, obviously—a certain type of clunking suburban prosperity that both my poor friends in the city and my family in their rich old Ohio River town viewed with varying kinds but equal degrees of contempt. He was aggressively conventional, and I felt that I ought to hate him, but I liked him, the dummy; for all the injustices that sustained his life, America's wars and overseas empire, the depredations of business and the inequalities of income, the immiseration of the world's poor, the destruction of the environment, the extraction of resources, the heedless burning of carbon fuels, the poisons in the water, the collapse of global fisheries—for all these things, which in large and small ways undergirded his four bedrooms in Treesdale and his elementary-school-teacher wife and their daughter and their OBX vacations, I found myself sometimes hoping that none of this would change; that it would all roll on as it was then rolling on, in order that he not be thrown into a different and unfamiliar world in which he couldn't have exactly what he had and therefore wouldn't be able to be happy, or to sustain, at least, that facsimile of happiness that so often passes for the real and original thing.

Well, anyway, I asked him what they were saying about the Other Peter, and he said, It's nothing specific, but I just get the feeling that he's trying to leapfrog. These kids, he said— he often referred to these kids, as if he and I were the same age looking down on the twenty-somethings coming up after us, and in this particular case I was pretty sure that the Other Peter was actually a few years older than me—these kids have no respect. You know, they've all been told they're special. Trophies for everything. Everyone gets a prize. And they just expect everything to be handed to them without having to work for it.

Helicopter parents, I said, because the best way to converse with Ted was to pull a current, topical phrase out of the air and toss it into the air whenever he paused.

Exactly, he said. My dad, boy. You didn't get any of that from him.

You have to pay your dues, I said.

Of course, on the other side, there's the gray ceiling. These guys have been here forever, and they're never going to change. They don't want the new ideas. Do it our way, don't rock the boat.

It is what it is.

Exactly, he said. Exactly.

I didn't imagine that there could be a plot between the oldsters in the executive suites and the Other Peter; even in the abstract, taking Ted's beliefs about the old and the young employees at face value, it made no sense; but Ted lived, I knew, in a world of self-created anxiety about his status; he'd risen, I gathered, very fast at first and then stalled. Most of the other vice presidents were in their mid-thirties. He felt his few years on them acutely. I promised that I would keep him posted.

Yeah, he said. That'd be great. Keep me posted. Keep your ear to the pavement.

I said I would keep an eye out.

By the way, Pete, he said. Someone told me you've been seen palling around with that dickhead Mark Danner. You oughta watch that guy.

I will, I said.

He's not a team player.

Then there was a knock on the door and one of the administrative assistants poked her head in and said I had a visitor. I headed back to my desk. It was twenty after nine. You're early, I said as I turned the corner into my cubicle.

You were expecting me? Mark said. He was sitting in my chair. He was wearing a pale gray suit and there was a VISITOR tag on the lapel.

Yeah. No. I was expecting someone else.

I like your area, Mark said. No photos, no tchotchkes, no indication of a human presence.

I like to keep my life and my work separate.

Hm, he said.

I find it hard to believe that your office is full of mementos.

I don't have an office. My office is my immediate surroundings, wherever and whatever they happen to be. I'm a starship fitted out for distant voyages of exploration, armed when necessary.

That's an interesting turn of phrase.

I thought you'd like that. So. He gestured to my spare chair, and I saw, despite the smirk, despite the mockery, what he meant about his office, because I felt immediately as if I were the visitor instead of him. So, he said, what Global Solutions have you come up with today?

I don't really come up with the solutions, I said. I'm more of a licensing agreements and contracts kind of guy.

A fake lawyer, Mark said.

That's a fair description. I'm probably cheaper than a real one.

Lawyers are pretty cheap these days. You'd be surprised.

You're a lawyer, I said, and I don't imagine you're especially cheap.

I'm a recovering lawyer. The first step is admitting that you're powerless to control your professional degree.

So what are you doing here? I asked. I don't suppose you dropped by just to say hello.

No, he said. I had some early meetings, and I have some late meetings, and I figured I'd find your oar down in the slave galley to see how hard they make you row.

I hardly break a sweat. It's very civilized.

You know what I like about you, Pete? he asked. I raised an eyebrow. Anyone else, he said, would pretend to be murdering himself to complete a hundred and ninety hours of work in a seventy-hour week. I like your nonchalance. I think you were serious about that unemployment thing.

Completely, I said.

Too bad, he told me. I have other plans for you. I've been bandying you about upstairs. Preparing the way.

That sounds ominous.

It is. How's your girlfriend?

She's well. She mentioned you the other night.

Oh yeah?

Just in passing. Whatever happened to your new friend, I

believe, was how she put it. I told her I thought you'd already forgotten me. How's Helen?

He glanced at his watch. Probably sober, he said. You made quite the impression on her. I tried to find some hint as to his meaning in his face, but he was inscrutable. She asked me to spare you. She said, Leave the poor boy alone and don't get him caught up in your schemes and conspiracies.

Tell her I owe her one.

Oh no. She'd take it seriously, and then at some future point she'd actually try to extract the favor. Better let it dangle. You can owe me instead. We should all hang out again, however. She thinks we need more friends.

I remember you said you didn't have friends.

He smiled thinly. Did I? he said. I say such interesting things.

Just then my other visitor arrived. Shit, I thought. De-livery, he said, singsong. Hey, I said. Who's this? Mark said. I'm the bike messenger, he answered. Your shoes are wrong, Mark said. Shit, I said. Mark glanced between us; his eyes did that thing, that sideways wink, that high-speed scan of the circumstances. He bore his canines and grinned. Peter Morrison, he said. At work, no less. You dog.

14

We stopped at the newsstand on Liberty and Mark bought rolling papers and tobacco, because Mark said he only ever smoked spliffs, and then we walked down to the Point and got stoned sitting on the wide steps between the fountain and the rivers. This was the point of mystical convergence, the weak spot between worlds where Winston Pringle's byzantine Project was supposed to break through the opalescent barrier dividing one second from the preceding and subsequent seconds, one world of potentiality from the next. Right now it was under construction, the whole sprawling bowl and the stocky pump houses cordoned off by temporary chain-link. There was one forlorn backhoe, and a couple of workmen in hard hats leaned against it as if they had nothing else to do in the world. Johnny would have said the superficial renovation was just a cover for the real construction deep underground, but to me it seemed like the typical Pittsburgh construction project, itself an exercise in a more mundane sort of time manipulation, the hours stretched to days, the days to months. I thought I remembered reading somewhere that the work was scheduled well into 2015. How would the Mayan calendar account for all that?

There was a faint hint of life on the trees in the park and on the trees across the water on the bluff of the West End Overlook—the warm, wet month just past was hurrying the living spring along. A bus crossed the West End Bridge over the Ohio. The West End Bridge always makes me think of the end of the world, I said. How so? asked Mark. He flicked our roach in a high arc; it hit the river and was gone. There were ducks in the water. The winter had been so mild that they'd never left. I don't know, I said. It looks like it should be a ruin. Well, said Mark, I guess we'll have to wait and see. Wait for what? The end of the world? I said. He shrugged and leaned back on his elbows. His jacket was across his lap. I don't think any of us is going to live to see it, I said. Hm, he said. That's the point, isn't it? No one sees the end of the world. That's what makes it the end of the world. The end of the world is like the horizon. The bend of the world, I said to that. Yeah, he smiled. Yeah. That's good. But, I said, there's more world beyond the horizon. More horizons, anyway, Mark said, which struck us both as very funny and we laughed for a minute.

Listen, I said, about the other night.

No, he said. I feel bad. I got you all caught up in the craziness with me and Helen. You got swept up in the wake. Sorry about all that.

Well, I said, to be honest, I guess I'm thinking more of the, you know, the whatever it was that we saw up there.

You seem embarrassed.

Maybe. I'm not sure how to broach the subject. Hey, nice to meet you. Had fun partying. Yeah, things got a little too wild, maybe. Oh, how about the UFOs? It's the last detail, you know?

Aren't UFOs the new thing around here? Don't you read the papers? Pittsburgh is like space invaders central.

I guess, I said.

You know what your problem is, Mark said, though not as a question. You're jaded, but it's self-imposed. How old are you, thirty?

Twenty-nine.

Close enough. Listen, how many people get to see a genuine flying saucer in their lives? Not many, which is why no one believes they're real.

As opposed to: they're just not real.

Who cares if they're real? Give credence to the incredible. He turned toward me, propped on one arm. You saw them. They exist. Whether they're real or not.

You saw them, too.

Yes.

Well, do you think they were real?

I think that's the least interesting question you could possibly ask.

You're not interested in whether those things exist or not?

Well, that's not the same thing, is it? Obviously they exist. We saw them. That doesn't mean they're real.

So they're, what, hallucinations? Illusions?

Probabilities, Mark said. When there's a ten percent chance of rain, and it rains, is the rain unreal?

I said, But you can prove it rained.

How? The rain disappears. It gets absorbed. It evaporates.

I don't know, I said. You can record it. You can collect it in a jar.

Didn't Archimedes say, Give me a jar big enough, and I will bottle a UFO?

That sounds right, I said.

So let me ask you a related question, Mark said.

Shoot.

What are you doing at Global Solutions?

How is that related?

Whatever. Pretend it isn't. The question remains.

It's my job.

Do you like it?

I don't know. Do you like yours?

I don't have a job. I am a job. I'm the mere human avatar of
something wholly inhuman.

Are you an alien?

Mark laughed and said, You have no idea. I'm a lawyer.
That's worse.

I thought you said you were a sort-of lawyer.

I'm a sort-of alien.

You know, I said, my friend Johnny doesn't believe in aliens.
He thinks the UFOs are visiting from another dimension.

That's still alien, isn't it? said Mark.

True, I said.

Anyway, you're not answering the question.

Making money, I said. Working. Getting by. Not all of us
are lucky enough to be the human avatar of something wholly
inhuman. I giggled. Some of us are just trying to pay the rent.

Now, that, Mark said, is depressing.

Let me ask *you* a question, I said.

Fair enough.

What are *you* doing at Global Solutions?

Technically, I'm not at Global Solutions.

Your Honor, I said, please instruct the witness to answer
the question.

Oh, good, Mark said. Lawyer jokes. I told you. I represent
the entity that's going to eat you. You are the giant squid,
squidling around in the depths, feeling bigger than everything
else. But Moby-Dick is heading for you. You've been pinged.
He's got you in his sonar.

You're the whale? Or the sonar?

Oh no. Just a minor tooth.

You lead a very metaphorical existence, I said.

Yeah, he said, I do. What time is it? I am literally starving.

Around eleven, I said.

Close enough for lunch. How do you feel about Thai?

15

On Friday, I got promoted. John Bates and Sylvia Georges called me upstairs, which had never happened before. He was the CFO, and she was the general counsel. If you'd have asked me, I'd have doubted they even knew who I was. We met in a conference room with a view through a gap between buildings to the Allegheny and the North Shore and the first steep rise of the North Hills. An assistant offered me coffee and water. I was such a fool that I thought they were going to fire me, as if either of them would do that themselves. There was another woman there whom I didn't recognize. This is Jennifer Swerdlow from Metzger Richards, Bates said. Peter Morrison, I said, and we shook. Bates said, You may have heard rumors that the company is for sale. Sure, I said. These are only rumors, Sylvia said. She was in her fifties and looked like she played three matches of tennis every morning. Yes, I said; absolutely. However, Bates said, they happen to be true. His shirt was open at the collar; he had a bit of a belly; you could tell he liked a drink or two. Generally true, Sylvia said. True in a limited and strictly defined sense of the word true, said Jennifer Swerdlow, who was round, though not fat; who might have been the host of a cooking show were it not for her

eyes, which suggested that you not look away if you happened
to catch them. Right, I said. Let's say instead that we're entering into a new partnership, Bates said. A deal, Sylvia said. An
arrangement, Swerdlow offered. An arrangement, I repeated.
In effect, Bates told me, an equitable merger of entities is being
set up to ease a period of transition. However, Sylvia said, the
autonomy of one of these entities may, upon the occurrence
of certain . . . other events, be terminated, in which case, the
other entity will take on a more proprietary position vis-à-vis
the prior equal partner. Okay, I said. It seems, Bates said, that
you're acquainted with one of the principal movers in the other
entity. He asked for you, Swerdlow said, by name. She picked at
one of her nails. She sounded neither pleased nor displeased. I
didn't say anything. Our feeling, Sylvia said, is that, given this
existing relationship, and given this person's clear confidence
in your abilities and, moreover, in your discretion in re: the
matter at hand, you could very adequately serve as an ongoing liaison until such time as those other events occur. You're
talking about Mark Danner, I said, from Vandevoort. We're
talking in the abstract, said Swerdlow. Right, I said. Well, in
the abstract, what happens to me after, uh, the occurrence of
these other events? Assuming any of these events occur, said
Sylvia, and assuming you take part in them as we've just laid
it out for you, you would be, along with the group of us man-
aging the transition, insulated from any potential negative out-
comes that might accrue to less directly involved employees.
Insured, Bates said. Indemnified, Swerdlow said, with emphasis. So this is a promotion, I said. For me. It's a transition, said
Sylvia. What about Ted? I asked. Who? said Bates. Ted, Sylvia

told him. That veep I mentioned to you. The forty-year-old? Bates said. Yes, she said. Oh. Bates shrugged. He's your boss? he asked me. Yeah, I said. Currently. Fuck him, said Bates. He's a zombie. He's a nice guy, I said. He's a zombie, and you're still human. It doesn't matter what he was. Keep the shotgun handy. Swerdlow stood up. Are we good here? she asked. I've got another thing. Sylvia looked at me. Are we good here? she asked. Then I did something I didn't know I had it in me to do. How much? I said. What? said Bates. How much money? I said. For me, I mean. Oh. He looked at Sylvia, who shrugged. How's a buck ten? A what ten? I couldn't believe it. Sylvia laughed. Obviously sufficient, she said. Great, said Bates. He took my hand in his meaty paw. Welcome aboard. If you say anything to anyone before we tell you, I'll chop your fucking head off. Karla will call you on Monday to get all the HR shit ironed out. They left me in the conference room alone.

16

I called Lauren Sara and said, Let's have dinner tonight. I can't, she said. I've got Patra's opening. Who? I said. My roommate, she said. Which one? No, she said. Not at the house. At my studio. Skip it, I said. I can't, she said. I promised. Plus, I'm hanging out with Tom, who's still mad at you, by the way. A woman scorned, I said. What? she asked. Nothing, I said. She said, How about tomorrow night? I've got the opera, I told her. Well, after, she said. We can get a drink. Aren't you going with your parents? You'll need one.

That's true, I said, and it was agreed.

I tried Johnny and he still wasn't answering. I tried Julian, suggested we play a few games of racquetball and have a beer. Love to, he said, but I have to go to some art thing with Tom. He said Lauren Sara was going to be there. You're not going? I don't do art things, I said, when I can help it. Lauren Sara doesn't mind? No, I told him, she prefers it that way. Your girlfriend is a miracle, he told me. Then I'm fucked, I said. I called Derek. I've got to meet someone later, he said, but I'd have a beer. We met at the Thunderbird on Butler Street, where a bluegrass band played a distracted set against the din of a lot of assholes who didn't care. Someone even turned on the jukebox at one point, until the bartender noticed and pulled the plug.

What's new in the private sector? Derek asked me.

I am, I said. Promotion.

No way. Let me buy you a shot.

I will indeed.

How the hell did you get promoted? I always figured you and Johnny just IM'd all day.

I know all the right people.

So it was an inside job? He caught the bartender. Two Maker's, he said.

A conspiracy, I said.

Well, congrats. The shots arrived. We raised them. Yinz and yourn, Derek said. Cheers, I said. We touched the glasses to the bar and then drank. So, he said, what's the new job?

No idea.

Sounds like your old job.

Exactly, I said.

I'm ashamed in the shadow of your ambition.

You're ambitious. You went to law school.

Law school is the opposite of ambition. Also, I think if they offered me a promotion, I'd turn it down.

I wouldn't call it an offer, exactly. It was phrased more like an ultimatum.

Well, cheers nevertheless. When did all this happen?

Just today. You're the first person I've told. Of course, you're the only other person I know with a real job.

Lies and deceptions. You take that back.

No offense.

None taken. Hey, on an unrelated note, have you heard from your buddy Johnny?

Not exactly, I said. Why?

Well, he called me the other day. I was at work, so I just let it go to voice mail, and he left me this cryptic message where he just said, The tide is turning.

Yeah, I've heard that one.

What the fuck?

You know Johnny.

Yeah, well, he sounded as if he was phoning in from the fifth dimension. He forgot to hang up, so I have this message with him telling me that the tide is turning and then heavy breathing for another five minutes.

I've gotten similar calls. I opened my palms and raised my eyebrows. What can you do?

Nothing much. But the reason that I ask is that that website, you know, the Alieyinz site, hasn't been updated for a
couple of weeks, and obviously Johnny is on his annual chemical pilgrimage, and somehow I wondered.

Oh, Jesus Christ, I said. Of course. Of course it's his site.
That fucking asshole.

Really? He told you.

No, I'm an idiot. It never occurred to me before. But it's
totally obvious, isn't it? I mean, who else?

Yeah. And the thing is, I heard from my buddy over in the
DA's office that Kantsky's really been shaking the police tree
on that whole thing I told you about, the picture and all.

Fuck. Is he in trouble?

Probably not for the website. I mean, I suppose Kantsky
could ruin his future political career. He laughed. Otherwise,
there's not really anything they can do about the Photoshop-
ping. But what with Johnny's other, uh, habits and behaviors,
let's say, there's always the chance that they could get him for
something unrelated and nail him to the wall in an act of vin-
dictiveness. I mean, you remember when they busted Ron Javronski's kid for selling coke.

Who?

Javronski? He was the head of the Health Department
and was going to run in the Eighth District against the may-
or's buddy Joe Tallon, but then his kid got busted for minor
possession and Kantsky somehow got it bumped up to intent
to distribute. Poor guy hadn't even officially announced his
candidacy yet. His kid pled out and got probation and time

served for the couple of weeks that they kept him in county, but everyone said the plea deal was contingent on the dad dropping out of the race he hadn't even entered yet. Then they fired him, the fucks.

Christ, I said. How do you work with these people?

Hey, whaddaya want, a bunch of Republicans? Good God, those people don't believe in evolution! We laughed. But seriously, if you talk to him, just tell him to watch his ass. The whole thing will blow over when someone else looks at the mayor the wrong way, but until then, Photoshop of the Mayor Getting Diddled by a Little Gray Man is on the agenda. Your Government in Action.

17

As a sidebar, this is a persistent theme in the collected works of Winston Pringle; the narrative tended to dilate around minor disputes between obscure named officials. You kept waiting for the wormhole to open and the ancient evil to pop out, tentacles flailing, and instead you got:

Major Bradley, who was in charge of Project logistics, approached me one evening in the canteen. He reproached me for going above his head to Colonel Nelson regarding my concerns about the environmental impacts of the chemical processing units.

I had long believed that the major resented my

presence as a civilian. Also, these guys were visibly upset at the privileges I garnered through my family connections.

I suggested that we resolve our differences by approaching a joint liaison officer with a background in mediation and arbitration, but Bradley worried that this could compromise the deep classification of the Project. "Perhaps someone already involved," I offered, but he wouldn't hear of it. Both of us ultimately wrote up separate incident reports detailing . . .

It goes on in that vein for a while. They could've been talking about Global Solutions, although, to be fair, at the end of that particular chapter they actually instantiate a yeti out of the interdimensional ether. It rampages through the compound before Pringle figures out how to incapacitate it using a quantum something or other. Then Major Bradley, the hothead, draws his sidearm and shoots the poor creature between the eyes.

18

Because Lauren Sara had to borrow the car on Saturday, I was late to pre-opera dinner with my parents at the Duquesne Club. I told you I needed the car by six, I said. It's only ten after, she said; it's cool. What were you doing, anyway? I asked. I was helping Hegemonica get ready for her show tonight. Whatahwhoica? I said. Who's that? My roommate, she said. Patra? I said. The Greek? No, she said. My room-mate roommate. Corey. Hegemonica is his drag name. Hege-monica, I said. Hegemonica Preshun, she told me.

She asked if she could use my Internet; then she was going to his show; then we'd meet up when I got back from the opera. Yeah, yeah, I said, and I ran down the stairs and sped downtown.

The club was on Sixth Avenue, just around the corner from the theater in a square stone building that was meant to recall a London club but which managed to look merely institu-tional. I mean, mental institutional. Incidentally, my offices were just up the street. It had been founded back in the 1870s by exactly whom you'd expect, and the front hall still bore a prominent and terrible oil portrait of Andrew Carnegie gaz-ing down in beneficent disdain. The captains of industry still belonged, although they tended toward the lunchtime hours, and the membership had long since declined in aristocratic quality so now any asshole with an MD or a buck-fifty paycheck from a bank could join. And did. Johnny was fascinated by the place and had once pestered me into sneaking him in so that he could seek out the Masonic initiation chamber in the basement. I told him I was pretty sure the kitchen was in the basement, but he insisted. It involved several trips to the thrift store to find a suit and tie sufficient to his dimensions, but eventually we did go. Fearing repercussions, I'd confessed the whole plan to my father. I'd expected him to try to dissuade me, or forbid me. Lord knows what I was thinking, because my father wasn't the sort of man who forbade things. He laughed and said delight-ful several times, then insisted on taking us to dinner himself.

While he engaged the waiter in a colloquy about Italian vari-
etals, Johnny and I slipped down a service stairs to the basement, where we found the kitchen. Of course, Johnny pointed
to the floor. Black and white tile! he exclaimed. Didn't I tell
you? It's a goddamn Masonic temple. It's part of the sacred
geometry and architectural symbology of the whole underground stream! Johnny, I said. It's linoleum. Nevertheless, he
said, and he grinned and grinned for the rest of the night. I
was too embarrassed tonight to valet my little car at the club,
and parking made me even later. I took the steps to the front
door two at a time, but the host stopped me before I could
dash past him and indicated with a subservience calculated to
indicate his social superiority that I'd be required to wear a tie.
I'm wearing a tie, I snapped, but then realized that, although
I'd picked one out, I'd forgotten to put it on, having got too
caught up in anticipating Lauren Sara's lateness to remember.
Oh, Jesus Christ, I said. Really?

I'm sorry, sir. The host shrugged. He wore a tuxedo and his
black hair was combed and pomaded in an old-fashioned slick
away from his forehead. He was chubby. He looked like a cartoon killer whale. I should not, I decided, have smoked some
more of that weed while I waited for Lauren Sara. He gave
me a paisley tie that looked like it had been salvaged from the
costume of a college glee club. Really? I said. I'm sorry, sir,
he said. We used to have more, but people always forget to
return them. Whatever, I said, and I tied it in the mirror above
the foyer fireplace and then found my parents at a table in the
Laurel Room.

Peter, Dad said, we wondered if you'd make it.

Traffic, I said.

I didn't notice any, said Mom.

Well, Suzanne, we did come from the other direction, Dad said. Would you like a drink? He motioned for the waiter.

What are you having? I asked.

Gin and tonic, my mother told me.

My father had a bowl of red wine. I'm having this very interesting Petite Sirah, he said.

I'll have Syrah also, I told the waiter.

Actually, my dad said, it's not Syrah; it's Durif. The name is rather misleading. Of course, Durif actually *is* related to Syrah, a cross, I believe, between Syrah and Peloursin.

The waiter looked at me as if this might change my mind.

It's fine, I said.

Very good, he said.

We'll just have a bottle, Dad told him. You'll have a glass, won't you, Suzanne?

When was the last time you saw me drink red wine? she asked.

Yes, that's very true. You've never cared for the tannins. Well—he patted my shoulder and winked across the table— I'm sure Peter and I will manage, won't we?

The wine arrived. My mother ordered a scotch. My dad asked my mom what she was going to order. You always ask me what I'm ordering, she said, and then you order the same thing.

You're a good orderer, he said. Left to my own devices, I always make the wrong decision.

The filet, she said. Just like every time. It's the only thing they don't routinely fuck up. I snickered. She looked at me. Peter, she said, where on earth did you get that tie?

You don't like it? I said.

You look like a game show host.

The front desk, I said.

Ah. She drank the rest of her G&T and switched to her new drink. I told you we should have gone to the Carlton, she told my father.

Did you? he replied. I do like their wine list.

So I have some news, I said.

Oh dear, my mother said.

Suzanne, said Dad.

I got promoted, I told them.

Thank God, Mom said. I thought you were going to tell us you were getting married.

Married? I said. It sounded as improbable as encountering extraterrestrials, except of course that I had, perhaps, encountered extraterrestrials, and people my age did get married, quite often, in fact, and it occurred to me without warning, as if the whole world had briefly slammed on its brakes and sent my body surging against the restraint of the present moment in time, that I would be thirty in July.

Congratulations, buddy, my dad said. That's great. What's the new job?

It's, well—I considered my phrase book of management mumbo-jumbo—it's a new position, I said. So it's going to be a collaborative development process that's going to involve my input as well as a lot of the senior staff group. It's pretty cool, actually; I basically get to design my own job.

Hm, my mother said. Like when you designed your own major? I'd flirted with this option in college, a tantalizing prospect that involved movies and books and trips abroad, which had amused my dad and infuriated my mother, who'd suggested that I might also design my own funding mechanism for tuition, which in turn sent me scuttling back to econ. In retrospect, it made no difference; economics was a far more elaborate fake than anything an undergraduate could ever come up with on his own; it inhabited a world of Tolkienian depth and ingenuity, a mythic creation with its own gods and greater and lesser spirits and heroes and conflicts and magic: a monument of imaginative world-building, albeit a little embarrassing as an adult enthusiasm. Fortunately I could tell the difference between a supply function and an indifference curve about as readily as I could tell the difference between a wizard and a wood-elf.

No, Mom, I said. Not like that. And I got a raise.

Well, now, that's more like it, she said. She smiled. You can pay for dinner.

Now, Suzanne, we need to make our minimum, Dad said.

I was kidding, she told him.

On occasion, sweetheart, it's a little hard to tell.

Seriously, honey, we're very proud of you, Mom said, and she patted my hand across the table. Keep me in the loop.

We all ordered the filet, which arrived too soon and at mysteriously different temperatures. Mine sat in a pool of its own blood; Mom's was medium. My father touched his gingerly with his fork. It seems, he said, a bit crisp.

Send it back, I said.

Well, he told me, they can't exactly *un*cook it, I suppose. And he tucked in methodically. I glanced toward my mother. Don't look at me, she said. I never send anything back. Why give them the opportunity to compound what they've already fucked up? Give me yours; take mine. I don't mind blood.

We exchanged. Well, I said, you're a surgeon, after all.

I'm not a cow surgeon, she said.

During the meal, the conversation turned to my grandmother. I hear you ran into Nanette at the museum, Mom said.

Yeah. You didn't tell me that she'd broken her toe.

She broke her toe? My father was surprised.

She didn't break her toe, Mom said. I looked at it, remember. She just bruised it.

She was in a wheelchair, I told them.

Oh, good Lord, Mom said. She stared at my father. Peter, honestly, we have to do something.

That seems a bit precipitous, don't you think?

We've been talking about it for years. It's the very opposite of precipitous.

I'll talk to her, Dad said.

If she's in a wheelchair, Mom said, then she's doc-shopping again. You know how I feel about all this. How many Dr. Feelgoods does one aging matriarch need?

Believe it or not, I said, she seemed fine, despite the wheelchair.

She was very pleased to see you, my dad said, although she did say that you never call unless you need something.

It's hard to get off the phone with her.

Honestly, Mom said.

I never noticed, my father said. He was finishing his steak. He poured himself more wine. I find that as long as I have something to work on or read, then I don't mind that she goes on a bit. What did you talk about, buddy?

Her toe and her failing eyesight. And pedophiles.

Hm, yes, Dad said. I remember when you were in preschool, she was very concerned about the satanist day cares in California. Do you remember, Suzanne?

Yes. I remember.

She wouldn't believe that it was all a hoax.

She still doesn't believe that it was all a hoax, Mom said.

I laughed. That's why she always loved Johnny, I told them. They both believe in everything.

How is your friend Johnny? Mom asked. I can't remember the last time I saw him. No, that's not true. It was at your uncle's Christmas party a few years ago. He and your father were embroiled in a conversation about concentration camps all night long.

He's very knowledgeable about the Eastern Front, my dad said.

Yes, Mom said, but at Christmas?

He's good, I told them.

Before we left to walk to the theater, I excused myself and went to the restroom. The club still used bathroom attendants, and I struggled mightily to pee into the marble urinal while a little old man who looked like a turtle in a tuxedo stared at my back. I managed to dribble something out. I washed my hands. He handed me a towel, then collected it in a little basket. Keep an eye out, he said as I turned to leave.

I'm sorry? I said.

Have a nice evening sir, he said.

I stepped into the hall. The whole place seemed a little down on its heels of late. If those captains of industry and politics had once run a good portion of the world, or at least the Commonwealth of Pennsylvania, out of these rooms, anymore it looked like an overgrand B&B, flocked and dusty and a few decades out of date. But what was odd was that I thought I saw my mother at the far end of the corridor, grasping the hands of the fat maître d' in a weird, cross-armed handshake. It was dim, and they were far away. They saw me looking and swished through a door. I should not have smoked that weed, I thought. I went back downstairs and found my parents, both of them, at the table. So, I said. Yes, said my mother. Let's, Dad said.

19

But Johnny was not good at all, and during a witch's sabbath scene whose staging was what I imagined a drag show by Hegemonica Preshun would look like, my phone vibrated in my pocket, which, when surreptitiously checked, presented a text from Derek: hey call me asap re jonhy. So I slipped out of the auditorium and through the lobby and lit a cigarette under the marquee.

Hey, Derek answered. I'm glad you called so quick. Listen. Johnny got picked up by the cops.

Oh shit.

Don't freak out.

I'm freaking out a little. They arrested him?

No. It's nothing like that. Forget what we talked about. Nobody knows about any of that. He's not in jail. He's at Presby.

The hospital? Oh Jesus.

It's okay. I don't know that much, but he's okay. High and paranoid, but okay. Mine was the last number called on his phone, and apparently he's got me listed as Brother Derek, so they thought I was actually his brother. They called me from the hospital and sort of gave me the rundown.

Which is what?

Well, they're not sure exactly what he's on. Some kind of dissociative, or dissociatives. So apparently he went down to the museum dressed in some kind of Nazi costume and was pacing around the sculpture garden telling people that the tide was turning. You may remember that turn of phrase.

Fuck.

Yeah. Anyway, the guards called the cops, but no one wanted to press charges, and the cops didn't want to throw some highed-up wack job in county, so they took him to the hospital. I figured maybe you'd know how to get in touch with his family.

Yeah, I said. Well, his parents are down in Florida and they're completely estranged, and his brother died years ago, and so did his grandparents.

Does he have insurance?

Does he seem like he'd have insurance?

Point taken.

Oy, I said. I'd better go over there.

Are you sure?

Yeah. I'm wearing a suit. I look like an upstanding citizen. If someone has to talk to cops and doctors, it might as well be me.

Let me know if you need anything?

I will, I said. Thanks for calling me.

Sure, he said. What are friends for but to deliver bad news?

20

There were two police at the hospital, Officers Bild and Granson, the former thin, black, and wearing dark shades; the latter large, white, and with the suggestion of muscle below his fat that implied a former military man. After they clarified our relationship—No, not a relative, a friend; he hasn't got any family; we grew up together—Bild said, We aren't going to charge him. He resisted arrest a little, but I think your buddy must've been strung out for a few days now, because once we snatched him up, he pretty much collapsed.

Yeah, I said. I'm sorry about the inconvenience.

That ain't your fault, sir, said Granson.

True, I said.

We do have to file a report, though, said Bild. And we'll need you to sign saying we released him into your custody.

Isn't he in the hospital's custody?

Technically? Bild said.

You know what, I said. I don't care. Yes, I'll sign.

I signed their report.

I really am sorry, I said. He can be a handful.

He was docile enough once we got him in the squad car, said Granson. The cop laughed. He told me I looked like Volstagg.

Who? I said.

That's what I said, Granson told me. Apparently he's a fat guy in comic books.

He's Thor's friend, Bild said. He laughed, too. My kid's into comics. He asked me what I thought about them putting a black guy in the *Thor*.

Oh man, I said. I'm really, really sorry.

No, Bild said, and he patted my shoulder. Don't worry about it. He didn't mean nothing by it. I told him I didn't give it a lot of thought, and he told me that if America can put a black man in the White House, Kenneth Branagh can put a black man in Asgard.

21

They'd sedated Johnny, and I fell asleep in a chair beside a nurses' station down the hall from his room. I dreamed of Helen. We were standing in a familiar round room, featureless but for the pale luminescence of the walls. There was a sound like the sound of the hospitals in Oakland, although, it occurred to me, it might also be an engine. If he dies, she said, we're in the hospital. A timing issue, I said. I've heard that before, she said. Is it true, I asked her, that you were the youngest artist-in-residence ever at artPace? Because even in my dreams, apparently, I'd been Googling the shit out of her. Everything is true, she said. I've heard that before, I told her.

V'ayn kal hadash tachat ha'shamesh, she said. Huh? I said. Shh, she said, and she touched my face with her hand.

I woke up. A nurse had her hand on my shoulder. Hon, she said. Your friend is awake.

What time is it?

About five.

In the morning?

Yeah, sweetie. It's the morning.

He was in a private room, a single IV dripping into his arm. He was staring into the middle distance, but when he saw me, his eyes focused on my face, and when they did, when he smiled, although I'd resolved to be angry, to be firm, to ask him just what the fuck he thought he was doing, I found that I had tears in my eyes. How did they get there? I touched them away with the back of my hand. You fucker, I said.

Hey, he said. His voice sounded like an engine with a bad starter. He smiled. His lips were cracked. Nice tie, he said.

III. WITCHY-POO

1

By the middle of March the city had forgotten about flying saucers; Mary Tremone had reneged on her deal with Kantsky and announced her intention to contest the mayoral primary; the head of the local Blue Cross/Blue Shield turned up drunk and belligerent at the home of his wife's lover and proceeded to smash all of the first-floor windows with a tire iron before the cops arrived. The *Trib* had done a person-of-interest interview with Helen Witold, a New York artist who now called Pittsburgh home. What's your biggest phobia? Reptiles. Favorite food? Bad coffee, embarrassingly. Artist? Hogarth, or Rothko. One thing you can't live without? A mirror. I'd pretty much decided that whatever I'd seen that night on Mount Washington had largely been the effect of too much drinking and an ill-advised cocktail of drugs. Lauren Sara was still pissed at me for blowing her off after the opera. It had been an emergency, I'd argued, but she'd only grudgingly accepted. Not for the first time in my life, I felt that I'd serially overindulged and let myself be caught in the undertow of my best friend's weirdness. And all I wanted was to swim parallel to the shore until the outrushing current released me and let the waves bear me back onto the sand. But it's hard, you know, to do what you know you're supposed to do when it would be so easy to float away.

2

When we were about fourteen—I could pretend to remember exactly, but memory is the most statistical of all our senses and sentiments; that is to say, the greater the specificity, the lesser the confidence level—my father acquired, for reasons that remain mysterious to me, one of the early Sony Handycams. He may have brought it to the beach that year, but I doubt it. It sat in his study, perpetually charging for a few months, before Johnny noticed it and decided that we should make a movie.

We dutifully set out to write a script, but discovered that writing scripts was boring, and decided that we would rely on improvisation within the confines of the hazy story we'd talked out. Johnny had two classic, full-head rubber masks: Tor Johnson and a gorilla. I don't know where he got them; they weren't relics of Halloweens past or anything like that; he dug them out of a closetful of his and his brother Ben's old toys and kid's books, but the masks were too big and too real to realistically date from that earlier epoch of childhood. Ben had gone off to college that year or the year before and couldn't be consulted. We suspected they might have belonged to Johnny's Pap, who was an indiscriminate collector of odd things, although not, to our knowledge, of costumes.

In any case, we had these two masks, and that seemed sufficient for a movie, and we knew that the movie would be called *Hunting for Headless* and would follow a man on his quest for a deranged mutant killer named Headless. In retrospect it's hard to say exactly what we were thinking: Headless, as a character, was defined by nothing so much as the fact that he was a rubber Tor Johnson head; he was the opposite of headless; but that sort of error of logic and continuity didn't really trouble us at the time.

We needed only a forest and at least one other member in our cast and crew, so we recruited our friend Billy Drake, who'd overheard us planning principal photography in the cafeteria and bought his way into the picture with the promise of extensive camping gear and expertise. All that remained was to convince my parents to let me go, which I did by eliding the fact that, while Johnny's Pap was going to drive us up to the mountains, near Ligonier, he was only planning to drop us off. My parents had met Pap a few times, and since he dipped and spoke with a southwestern PA accent and wore a camouflage army jacket, I suppose they assumed he was an outdoorsman and a hunter and all that. It's worth mentioning that my mother was originally from Cambria County and should have known better, but college and medical school and marriage to my father and self-will had almost entirely eradicated her Appalachian good sense, and she and my dad both thought Pap was 100 percent authentic. He was 100 percent authentic, all right, just not authentically what they thought he was. I don't think he'd touched a gun since Korea, and the closest he came to camping was falling asleep in his shed while working late on his invention.

Nevertheless, Pap took the essentially anarchic view of childhood that still prevailed in the woodier parts of the state, beyond its enclaves of money and urbanity. He saw nothing wrong with dropping us off on a state route roadside somewhere on Chestnut Ridge. We had some maps, and he told us to meet him at the Main Square in Ligonier at eleven the next morning. He also told us that the state had been reintroducing mountain lions into the woods around. They don't like fire, apparently, he told us, and they smell like piss. He was hunched over the wheel of his old Bronco. Johnny rode shotgun.

What kind of piss? I asked. Time around Pap was a license to swear and talk a language that was thoroughly discouraged in my home.

How the hell should I know what kind of piss? he said. Panther piss. I don't imagine you get a lot of other animals pissing on a panther.

He also told us to keep an eye out for any bigfoots. Billy laughed, and Pappy said, What's so goddamn funny? and Billy said, There's no such thing as bigfoot.

I've seen bigfoots as surely as you see me right now. They used to get in my trash when me and Mona lived down in Fayette County back when I worked for the coke company. Rootin around in there and making a mess. Plus I've done extensive research on the subject. They are highly prevalent in this area. They smell like rotten eggs, and sometimes—he raised an eye to the rearview mirror—they will attempt to mate with a human female. His eye wandered toward Billy, who had long blond hair and the features of a Grecian youth. So keep an eye out, hot dogs, Pappy said.

Billy had claimed to know of a bat cave in the area. His family, like mine, was from the rich part of Sewickley, and they had a cottage in Ligonier. This cottage had six bedrooms, but never mind. In his telling, he knew the wild terrain of the area like back of his hand; he'd actually used that cliché, which should have been a clue to the truth. Close your eyes and describe the back of your hand. The closest you'll get is that it looks like a hand. We tromped around in the woods for a while, with Johnny occasionally pulling out the camera to shoot randomly through the trees. What the fuck are you doing? I asked him. Establishing shots, he told me. This was before Steadicam and all that. I told him that shooting while we walked was stupid. It's going to look like shit, I said. It's going to be all shaky.

Don't worry, he told me. I have a very steady camera hand.

We never found the cave, but we eventually found a little rock outcrop beside a small creek that seemed a promising spot to set up camp. Billy's tent, which belonged on the side of Everest, proved too complicated for us to set up, so we left it in a heap of struts and blue fabric. Johnny had snuck a couple of bottles of whiskey into his bag, and Billy had something that he said was weed. The weed was doubtful, but the Jack Daniel's was real, and after taking a few slugs each, we filmed some scenes. Headless (me), running through the woods. Johnny, dressed in camouflage, examining broken twigs and footprints. This creature, he said, this monster must be stopped before it rapes again.

What do you mean, rapes? I asked him between shots. I thought he was a murderer. We had already filmed several scenes of me killing Billy with, I thought, professional-level conviction.

He rapes before he kills, Johnny said. Like in *Deliverance*.

I'd never seen *Deliverance*, but it was the sort of movie that every teenage boy had heard about. Johnny had seen everything, because of Ben.

That's stupid, I said. That's fucking dumb. Why would he even want to have sex with a person? He's not even supposed to be human.

Bigfoots haves sex with people according to Johnny's crazy granddad, Billy said.

Shut up, Billy, Johnny told him. If bigfoot rapes anyone, it's going to be you.

Whatever, Billy said.

The climactic scene was supposed to be a clifftop fight between Headless and Johnny, with both ultimately plunging to their doom. Billy, who'd been stuck on camera duty but for his death scenes, got pissed that he wasn't getting more screen time. You'll get producer credit, Johnny told him.

Fuck you, Johnny. I want to be *in* the movie.

There's no role for you, Johnny said. What would you even do?

I don't know. Maybe I could, like, put on the ape mask and become the hunter's sidekick.

That's fucking stupid. He doesn't have a sidekick.

Then I could be, like, a wise forest creature who helps the hunter track down Headless.

We could do that, I said, mostly because I was getting sick of the movie. Also, guys, it's getting dark, and we should get back to the camp and build a fire before it does.

First of all, you're not going to play Targivad, the Wise

THE BEND OF THE WORLD 147

Monkey of the Forest, or whatever, Johnny said. And second of all, Morrison, don't worry. I have excellent night vision.

Targivad, I said. Where'd you come up with that?

Or *whatever*, Johnny said.

But we did go back. We managed to get a fire started. We managed to burn some hot dogs. Why did your Pap call us hot dogs? I asked Johnny.

I don't know, Johnny said. He's Pap.

We got drunk.

I threw up in the creek.

I was in my sleeping bag.

My head was spinning.

I remember drifting in and out of sleep; I remember the stars moving overheard through the trees; I remember that I'd worried that I'd be scared sleeping out in the woods like that, which I'd never done before, but I wasn't scared; it was as if I could feel myself, many years later, remembering that I hadn't been scared; I could hear everything in that immense darkness; I heard rustling and whispering; I heard Billy say, No, man, come on; I heard Billy say, Well, okay, I guess; I slept; I woke. We walked back to the state road and down to Ligonier, where we sat in the pretty square. Pap picked us up at eleven and took us to a diner before we drove back to the city. He looked me in the eyes and said, You look like you tied one on last night, hot dog.

What? I said.

He tipped his thumb toward his mouth and made a clicking sound. You'd better have some coffee, he said.

Coffee is gross, I told him.

He chuckled. Lots of things seem gross at first. Try it. Which I did, and I found, to my surprise, that the bitterness was pleasant even in my dry mouth.

I realized after he'd dropped me off at home that Johnny and Billy hadn't spoken, hadn't even looked at each other, for that entire day.

3

Another Monday. As had been promised, I'd received a call from Karla and gone off to Human Resources, a Strasbourg in Global Solutions' medieval landscape, a free city at the cross-roads of all the trade routes, with its own weird culture and amalgam language. I hadn't been in HR since I'd first been hired. My colleagues, those who used their health plans and considered their retirements, were up here all the time filling out mysterious forms and pestering about reimbursements or withholdings or the rising cost of a monthly parking pass in the basement garage, but I thought the place was a bit spooky, full of hushed, confidential voices and bowls of candy and women who came and left the office in white tennis shoes.

Karla was the director of HR and by reputation a bitter, distrustful harpy who spent her hours nursing an evil resentment at not being considered a part of senior staff despite running her own department. I suspected this was more a reflection of the way my coworkers imagined that they would have felt in her position, because I sort of liked her. She wore her hair in an extraordinary crown of tiny braids, and her neck and wrists bore an impressive overabundance of bracelets and necklaces. You probably don't remember me, I said. Peter Morrison.

Oh, you, she said. She waved her hand and her bracelets clanked. Come on in, Mystery Man.

She had me sign a series of forms. I asked her if I should read them. They all say keep your mouth shut and do what you're told, she said. Also, they teach you the secret handshake, the passwords, and how to operate the decoder ring. Really? I said. No, she told me, but they do say that you're an at-will employee and that either you or Global Solutions, its others, owners, licensees, assignees, and subsidiaries can, at any point, without cause or notice, terminate the agreement.

Termination upon the occurrence of certain other events, I said, principally to myself.

What? No, she said. There are no events. It *means* keep your mouth shut and do what you're told, or they'll fire your ass. Now sign this. It's your status update form.

It listed my new title as Associate Director, Special Planning and Projects.

What's an associate director? I said. Do we have those?

We do now, I guess. I try to tell them that the paperwork is a pain. We get audited, and they want to know where these titles come from. I tell them, don't ask me, I only work here.

The salary is wrong, I said. I'd read down the form. It said eighty-five.

You're damn right it's wrong. A thirty percent raise? We're supposed to be on a one percent annual right now.

No, I said. I mean, they told me a bigger number.

I'm sure they did. Was it Bates? That fool is supposed to be the chief *financial* officer, but I swear to Jesus he only understands one, two, and many. Every time he offers someone a promotion, he says one thing, and then he tells me something else. Let me be straight with you: the lower number is always the right number, so you can go upstairs and ask him if you want, or you can just sign off and I'll get the raise into your next paycheck. Makes no difference to me.

I should just sign off, then.

Yes, she said. You should.

On the way out the door, she called me back. Hey, Mystery Man, she said.

Yeah?

I've seen this company go through one bullshit IPO and two private equity sales, she said. Bool-shit, she pronounced it, for emphasis. Let me give you some advice. Getting noticed is never the right strategy.

We're not getting sold, I said.

She laughed. Nice try, she said. Maybe they won't fire your ass after all. But please. I was born at night, but not last night.

4

Still, I had no idea what my new job was. That in itself was no big change. I contemplated calling Bates or Sylvia Georges, but they were not the sort of people that my sort of employee just phoned or emailed on a Monday morning. Instead, I called Mark. I had his business card, after all, and it listed a phone number. His voice said, Hi, you've reached Mark Danner. I'll be traveling abroad this week and will return on April first. I'm available by email, or leave me a message, and I'll call you back. I tried to write him an email, but I discovered that I didn't know what I wanted to ask him. So I went back to doing what I'd been doing, which wasn't much, and I figured that at some point, someone would tell me what it was that I was supposed to do instead.

I did bump into Leonard that week. Disconcertingly, I was down on twenty-three. I'd just come out of the restroom, heedlessly, since no one was ever around down there, and I nearly ran into him. He'd been texting or otherwise reading something on his phone. We both regarded each other suspiciously for a moment. Finally I said, Leonard. What? he said. You think you're the only dude who's ever gotta pinch one out at work? Jesus, I said with a laugh. Listen, he said, tell me straight up: Did they can you? Can me? I said. No, why? You got called upstairs. Marcy said they canned you. She said you got the nastygram this morning. Marcy's full of shit. Shit, man, I know that. So you're good? I'm good, I said.

He seemed relieved, and it gratified me. I liked Leonard. By the way, he said, I told my girl about your little close encounter.

Oh, man, I said. Really? I told you not to say anything.

Man, a successful relationship don't have secrets.

Seriously?

She told me to tell you don't worry. The UFOs, they got nothing to do with the end of the world. They're a CMU thing.

Like the university?

Yeah, military, man. Psyops. Intelligence shit.

Well, that's reassuring, sort of, I said.

Is it? I guess so. Personally, I'd take the goddamn aliens over the goddamn Nazis.

Nazis? I said.

Yeah, who do you think designed that shit? It was all back in the fifties or whatever, after the war. Some CIA dude and this German scientist they brought over to work at Carnegie Tech. I thought you were supposed to be into all this.

My friend is, I said.

Yeah, he said. Your *friend*. Whatever, my man. And then, whistling, he went into the bathroom and turned the latch in the door.

5

I'd also been visiting Johnny in the hospital, trying to piece together his little chemical walkabout. I mentioned the three a.m. phone call; I mentioned that he may have called Derek as well. Well, what had happened is that Johnny had reread *Fourth River, Fifth Dimension*. The psychic adept, it said in chapter fourteen,

has long been viewed by many cultures and societies as possessing the unique ability to see the future. There is a notion of time that dominates in our technologically advanced civilization. It imagines time in geographic terms. Thus the psychic has, in effect, sharper eyesight than the rest of us. In fact, time's higher dimensionality cannot be visualized in three-dimensional terms, and the psychic does not see into the future so much as he momentarily substitutes it for his present. Scientifically speaking, psychics are able to transform their internal time equation, thereby deriving different time-point-slopes from various points along the time curve. Truly understanding these functions requires highly advanced mathematics that we will not delve into here. Suffice it to say that the psychic "dials in" on different times through a calculitic-arithmetical process in the mind-computer. He or she is quite literally able to remember the future and convey it via quantum tunneling into the past, creating what an electrical expert would call a Feedback Loop. Technical details, for those so inclined, are included in Appendix C.

The Project sought to enhance these abilities via chemical-cortical stimulation. Many supposedly primitive peoples (e.g., Aboriginal Dream Time) have a far more sophisticated understanding of the nature of the personal time index and have used traditional shamanic techniques and rituals to transcend present-index and participate in the holistic continuum of the time function. These techniques and rituals often involve a chemical component. Contemporary science has synthesized some of these miracle molecules, for instance DMT, the so-called "death particle," as well as creating powerful dissociative anesthetics such as Ketamine.

While prior Top Secret experimentation (viz. MKUltra) focused on the mind-control effects of the so-called classical hallucinogens ("serotonergic psychedelics"), the Project sought to tie mind control to time control via the recombinant properties of the tryptamines and the NMDA receptor antagonist family.

You got the sense, reading these books, that there was just an insufficient amount of truth in the world, that the neat parsing of probability and possibility down to the merely actual was just such a drag that the author had to admit every strand of improbable and impossible narrative to the tale as a hedge against the disappointing thinness and paucity of the real reality.

So you never quite got a hold on what they were trying to accomplish, really; or, you got the feeling that they were trying to accomplish everything—a new age or the end of the world or something in between. But there was a curiously self-effacing quality to the story, too. All these secret agents and psychics and UFOlogists leveraging their vast, secret power toward some odd end that, at last, had nothing to do with them at all.

6

Well, Johnny reasoned, I just happen to have some MXE, and I've got plenty of dextromethorphan hydrobromide cough syrup. Might as well give it a shot.

7

Johnny's strategy was to ride the methoxetamine through a few stages of mild dissociation before augmenting it with enough Robitussin to achieve the fourth plateau and to see where that left him vis-à-vis his personal time index, but the first intramuscular dose of MXE caused him to miscalculate the second dose, and he forgot the precise nature and exact goal of his psychonautical voyage and ended up doing what he usually did when he was fucked up, which was to sit at his computer in his underwear, drink beer, and play *Panzer General II.*

It seemed to him that he needed to keep injecting the anesthetics to ease the pain of improperly healed battle wounds, the many scars of many past campaigns.

And, although the Allied advances on the Western Front appeared like they would overwhelm his positions, he found himself walking along a snowy wooded path with the Führer and Keitel and a number of senior aides. The boughs of the fir trees drooped under the weight of the snow. The sunlight was distant and gray. Keitel tried to tell the Reichskanzler that it was necessary to regroup and retrench. The Allies had no stomach for prolonged combat, but they had superior armor. And what do you think, Generaloberst? Hitler asked Johnny. *Mein Führer*, Johnny said, clasping his hands behind his back, I have allies in England who are awaiting my word. Upon receiving my orders, they will mount a crushing civil uprising that will cripple the will of the Anglo-Americans. Yes, said Hitler, soon England will be ours. Um, excuse me, said Keitel, did you order this pizza? Your neighbor downstairs let me in. Tell that Jew Mussolini he's next, said Johnny. He motioned to one of his aides. Give Keitel his money, he said. The aide, a chunky young officer who moved, nevertheless, with a certain feline grace through the snow, handed Keitel a crumpled ten and some ones. The Führer knelt in the snow and picked up a stone. *Mein Gott!* he cried. Do you see this? Do you know what this is? Yes, Johnny said. Yes, *mein Führer*! It is the Fist of Odin. Call your allies, said Hitler. The tide is turning. So Johnny called his fascist allies in London. Herr Morrison, he said. The line was poor, but serviceable. Morrison, the tide is turning. Hm, said Morrison, that insufferable British prick, I think I've heard that before. The fist of Odin! Johnny cried. Yeah, said Morrison. Bloody jolly goody well. I've got to toodle off and Winston my boot in the Pringle lift. THE TIDE IS TURNING! Johnny called, but the line was cut, and the enemy was advancing.

The walls were collapsing. The Generaloberstabsarzt came into his quarters with a syringe. Generaloberst, he said, this is prepared for you, should it come to that. Death with honor, Johnny said, and he stuck the needle into his ass cheek. The Generaloberstabsarzt, a heavy man, almost as fat as Göring, stroked Johnny's cheek as he fell back onto his bed. He touched his chest, and then set his hand on Johnny's thigh. How about a hand scan? he said.

Okay, said Johnny.

Relax, the surgeon said. I'm a doctor.

Am I dead? Johnny asked him.

For the time being, the doctor told him.

My throat hurts, he said.

Here, said the doctor. Try some of this cough syrup.

When he woke up, he was in his apartment. The ceiling fan whose blades were stained black at the leading edges from all those passages through the dusty air went around. He was on the couch. Anton was curled on his chest. There were several used syringes on the coffee table, some beers, an empty bottle of Robitussin DM. Squiggles went round and round on his computer screen on the desk across the room. Oh God, he said. A steady, dull pain thudded rhythmically in his head. No, not a pain. The door. He pulled on a T-shirt and answered it. A being—not a man, precisely, but not *not* a man, either, taller somehow and more birdlike, a high peaked chest that stuck far out in front of the rest of its body, a suggestion of wings, though it had no wings, the suggestion of another eye on its face, though there was no extra eye. He—he seemed like a he, anyway—was wearing a white apron with Masonic insignia, or possible bloodstains, or possibly both, and he bore in his huge hands a huge white book from which emanated the smell of burning flesh.

Delivery, the creature said.

Oh God, said Johnny. Oh God, oh God, who are you?

I'm the deliveryman.

You're Calsutmoran?

Yes, the angel boomed, and he swept past Johnny into the apartment. I am Calsutmoran, a Seraph of the Lord Crown Ein Sof, borne out of the Pleroma in the flying Ophanim, bearing unto you the *Book of Judgment* and the *Book of Life*.

Oh shit, Johnny said.

Oh shit indeed, said Calsutmoran.

Did you come out of the hollow earth? Johnny asked.

Do I look like I came out of the hollow earth? trumpeted the angel.

Well, said Johnny, honestly? Kinda.

Calsutmoran tossed the book on the coffee table and sank into the couch. LeVay hopped on next to him and nuzzled his fingers. You know, Calsutmoran said, that's what I fucking hate about you people. It's the subtle racism. You think we all look alike, don't you?

Well, said Johnny.

What's with all the needles?

I've been injecting methoxetamine and ketamine.

You think I can get some of that?

You want some of my drugs?

I'm off. Why the fuck not? You got any beers? I don't need a needle, though. I only insufflate. I'm not a needles guy.

I've got beer.

Oh, and listen, I'm going to need you to make a list of who lives and who dies.

Everyone?

Yeah, sorry.

Okay.

Johnny fell asleep in the middle of the C's. When he woke, Calsutmoran was playing *Wolfenstein 3D* on his computer. Best first-person shooter ever, he said.

Yeah, Johnny, I said after he'd recounted his version of all this. I'm pretty sure that that was me. Like really.

You're Calsutmoran?

No, I said. I mean, you called me. I'm your fascist ally. Who's Calsutmoran?

You sure are, he said, and not without a measure of affection. He was due to be released the next morning. He was off the IV and eating solid food, but he was pale, paler than usual, and he seemed shrunken and dry, like an apple that's been sitting uneaten in the fruit bowl for a week too long. How did I even know how to use the phone?

I'm not sure you really did. I mean, you seemed to forget. Also, you kept rhyming. It was annoying.

Hm. I don't remember rhyming. Man. I was pretty convinced that I was actually fighting World War II. Fucking RPGs. They get into your head. I was also really convinced that Calsutmoran—the DXM angel, by the way, which you should know—came to visit me and judge me for my sins. Although that may have been the pizza guy. I'm pretty sure I kept ordering pizzas.

I'm really not familiar with Calsutmoran.

Google that shit, he said. He's like, oh, an androgynous emissary from another dimension who's often reported by people returning from a fourth-plateau dex experience. I'm pretty sure that's how I ended up at the museum.

An angel took you?

No, Morrison. Christ. I took the 54. God only knows how. I remember being really worried that the driver wouldn't take reichsmarks.

I laughed. I had to. What else would I do? Exact change, I barked. Johnny laughed, too.

Oh man, he said. When those cops came to get me, I swear

to God they were Asgardian warriors coming across the rainbow bridge on their goddamn white horses. I guess that was probably just the squad car.

I guess, I said.

Well. He shrugged and sipped at a little plastic cup of orange juice on the tray beside his bed. All's well that ends well, I guess.

And I probably should have disagreed, should have given him the you're-fucking-up-your-life route, but I just said, Yeah, and then I sat and watched TV with him until he fell asleep, mouth open, about halfway through an episode of *Ancient Aliens* on the History Channel.

8

At work, people had somehow become aware of my new role, whatever that was, and I found myself suddenly copied on a new volume of internal emails. They were mostly disputes between the Solve Teams and IT, or between finance and purchasing, and I couldn't figure out why my name kept appearing on the cc lists until I mentioned it to Mark, who'd returned from wherever he'd been traveling and seemed to spend an inordinate amount of time hanging out at my desk and taking me to lunch. They perceive your power, he told me. They see you as an avatar of the higher powers around here. When Joe Blow emails Jane Doe to tell her that his motherfucking network printer still won't scan to email, he includes your name to let her know that Others Are Being Informed.

THE BEND OF THE WORLD 161

Jesus, really? I said.

You never copied the mothership to let some dick know you mean business? Christ, Pete, what are you, like, moral or something? Self-possessed? I think I've found a gem in you. I think you understand the power of discretion.

Thanks, but I really don't feel especially powerful, I said.

Shit, son, Mark said, you're locked and loaded. What you really ought to do is start randomly responding. One-sentence emails. Has this been resolved? and that sort of thing. It will scare the shit out of everyone, and enhance your reputation as a stone-cold fucker. Huh, I said.

Set phasers on You're Fired, he said.

I've never fired anyone.

We all gotta lose our cherry sometime, Mark told me. By the way, what are you doing on Friday? Helen and I are having a little dinner thing. Bring that cute hippie of yours. What's her name?

Lauren Sara.

She's probably a vegan or some shit.

Sometimes, I said. She's currently pescatarian.

Dairy?

Yes. Usually.

Let me give you some advice. Never date a woman with dietary restrictions. Eating disorders are negotiable, especially if she's got dental. Oh, on an unrelated note, there's going to be a series of emails going around that say don't talk to the press about the merger. I've had them phrased in the most blandly unthreatening language possible, all very in the interest of easing the transition period and in order to speak in one consistent voice we ask that you refrain, etc. So of course everyone will freak the fuck out. Anyway, my point is, you should feel free to ignore this. If you should feel like anonymousing around.

I don't really talk to the press, I said. I don't think I know any press. I don't think the press is very interested in me.

He shook his head in wonder. Pete, he said.

Yes?

Never mind. You hungry? Let's go grab some lunch. How do you feel about titty bars?

Really? I said.

Christ, don't tell me you're that sophisticated. Blush has a midget. And a decent Reuben, if you can believe it. Similarly priced, too.

9

When he was sufficiently recovered from his hospital stay—surprised to find that more than a week had passed, so maybe there was something to this time travel thing after all—Johnny took the bus over to East Liberty to visit Mustafah Elijah, the One True Prophet and sole proprietor of the Universal Synagogue of the Antinomian Demiurge as well as Elijah's Afrikan Shop for the Body, Mind, and Spirit. There were a few women browsing dresses and beads in the front, and the usual dreadlocked clerk reading a *High Times* behind the jewelry case. The cover read, Federal Government Dope: the FDA's Secret Stash. The store always smelled like incense and something slightly fetid: not rotten, but a little overripe. Hey, Scooty, Johnny said. Is the rabbi around?

Scooty pointed toward the back.

Johnny went through the doorway and down the two steps into the back room, which was overflowing with tables and bookshelves full of conspiracy tracts and trade sci-fi and old VHS documentaries and newspapers and magazines and cassette tapes on every shelf and every available surface. A young white woman with tangled hair and feather earrings and a full-sleeve tattoo of tigers and birds was crouching at a low shelf paging through a glossy exposé on chemtrails. Is this shit for real? she asked Elijah. Girl, he barked, you want to live in a dream world forever?

Uncle! Johnny said.

Nephew! Elijah answered. They bumped fists. What's happening? You look skinny. For you.

I died and was reborn.

No shit? Well, that'll take it out of a man. I been going to spinning. You ought to see those Shadyside bitches when I roll up. Ahahaha. You died, huh? How'd you do that?

Powerful drugs.

Hoo, Nephew. You got to watch that shit. I keep telling you. You know what Isaiah had to say about it: Woe to those who get up early to pursue intoxicating liquor; who stay up late at night, until wine inflames them. Sounds like you got a little taste of Sheol. Your ass will end up among the Rephaim.

Aren't the Rephaim giants?

They're giants *and* they're dead motherfuckers. Anyway, you ain't so small yourself, Nephew.

Yeah, but I'm surprisingly graceful.

Shit, underwater maybe.

The white girl said, Excuse, how much is this book?

Elijah glowered at her. What's it say on the price tag?

There's no tag.

It's six dollars. With the white person discount, it's ten dollars.

Um, sorry, how much?

Ten. Dollars.

Oh, okay, that's cool. Do you take debit cards?

Elijah looked at Johnny, like, can you believe this shit? He turned back to the girl. Do I take debit cards? he said. Do I take Confederate currency? Do I invite the FBI to my house to watch me take a shit? Hey, Scooty! he called out to the front room. Do we take debit cards?

Does a nigger tan? Scooty said.

Jesus, the girl said. Sorry.

Get the fuck out of here, Elijah said. This ain't a goddamn sideshow. I'm not here to entertain your ass.

Sorry, she said again.

Take the book, Elijah said. Go on. Take it. For free. Maybe your ass will learn something.

Oh, said the girl. Are you sure?

Fuck, no, I'm not sure. Leave the book. Use the door, he said, which she did.

Jesus, Uncle, said Johnny, you're a real fucking salesman. Your customer service is top notch.

Fuck you, Nephew. I'm a model of fucking customer service. This is a customer-centric business. Your ass is always right. He glared. Johnny started laughing. Elijah held on to his frown for another second and started laughing as well. He reshelved the book. So, Nephew, what can I do you for?

Well, you know Winston Pringle?

Pittsburgh Project. Writer dude. Yeah. Why?

I need a connect.

Nephew, didn't I just tell you to lay off the goddam needle? You've got to purify your body, son.

What are you talking about? Johnny said.

What are *you* talking about?

Well, do you, like, know how I can get in touch with him? Like through his publisher or something?

Why the fuck would you go through his publisher? I told you I *know* the man.

Like, know him know him? said Johnny.

Yeah, said Elijah. Like know him know him. What the fuck, you think I mean I'm familiar with his oeuvre? You know that motherfucker's crazy, right?

Holy shit, really? Oh man. That's awesome. How do you know him?

His fat ass lives out in Wilmerding. He comes into the store sometimes. Don't like to pay for nothing neither. I'm surprised you never met him. He's a goddamn substitute teacher. You know, his real name is Wilhelm Zollen. I mean, supposedly his real name. *Doctor* Wilhelm Zollen. He *teaches chemistry*, if you know what I mean.

No. Wait, what do you mean?

What the fuck do you think I mean? The fat pervert sells drugs, my man. He's the goddamn Timothy Leary of the Mon Valley, except he's fat, insane, and a fag.

I'm a fag, said Johnny.

There's fags and there's fags, Nephew.

True enough, said Johnny.

10

After a week of waiting for the good doctor to stroll through the doors of Elijah's store, which he did, according to Elijah, no more than once or twice a year anyway, Johnny decided that he could do no worse than spend a fruitless day in the Monongahela Valley, so he bused downtown and transferred to the 69 and took the long ride through the East End and the bombed-out remains of Wilkinsburg and the fleeting prosperity on the border of Forest Hills and through Turtle Creek and over the same actual and eponymous creek into the borough of Wilmerding, population two thousand one hundred and some odd thing. According to Wikipedia, there were just over a thousand households in exactly one square kilometer. Someone, Johnny figured, must know the man.

And, mirabile dictu, as soon as Johnny stepped off the bus on Commerce Street beside the small park and next to the Allegheny Housing Authority office and below the bluff on which sat the Romanesque pile of the Westinghouse Air Brake Company headquarters, wherein, according to Winston Pringle, George Westinghouse and Nikola Tesla had performed

a series of Gnostic-Cathar sex magic rituals to divert the fire
energies of the hollow earth through the subterranean ley
lines of Allegheny County, thereby inculcating the fire element
that birthed the Satanic Industries, whose sheer Vulcanic force
weakened the liminal boundaries between this world and the
next, thus setting the stage for the Deep Government's Pittsburgh Project, through which psychically sensitive children,
including Pringle himself, were broken down via the processes
of ritual satanic-sexual abuse into subservient subpersonal-
ity psychic operators who might, one day, at the culmination
of years of research and effort, complete this greatest magical working that the world had ever known by actually dis-
sipating the barrier energies that held one reality apart from
the next and the next and the next, collapsing the Quantum
Matrix and enabling the Secret Powers of the World to pick
and choose among the infinitude of potential realities and in
doing so achieve ultimate, inexorable, and godlike power—
just there, at the bus stop, because, I imagine, Johnny must
have looked a little confused, unsure, precisely, of where to
go, an old guy smoking a cigarette in a wheelchair decorated
with American flag decals, who looked for the remaining life
of him as if he had no intention of ever leaving that spot on
the sidewalk, took one look at Johnny, spat on the pavement,
and said, Well, I guess you're here lookin for the witchy-poo.

What? Johnny said.

Yinz are always comin around looking for all that witchy-
poo. Dressed in black and all that *shit*.

I'm not dressed in black, said Johnny, who was wearing his
usual collection of browns.

You might as well be, the man said. Well, go on and ask me.

What am I supposed to ask you?

Ask me how to find the witchy-poo.

Hey, Johnny said, can you tell me how to find the witchy-poo?

Yeah. He lives up the end of Wood Street.

Winston Pringle?

I don't know his witchy-ass name. I just know he's up there at all hours, doin who knows what with all the whatchacall.

Right, said Johnny. Well, thanks.

Don't thank me, boy. I ain't do you no favors.

Thanks anyway, said Johnny.

11

He walked away from the Housing Authority and the squat forms of sixties-era Section 8 apartment blocks made of skinny glazed bricks past the Westinghouse mansion and up the hill into a neighborhood of brick and frame houses that recalled the great, gaudy, fifty-year illusion that there ever was a middle class in America, their trim having seen better days, their roofs having seen newer shingles, and as he went on, past the stained church whose front-yard marquee read GUNS, GUILT & GIFTS—the subject, perhaps, of a sermon?—as he went on, the street got steeper and greener, overhung with black walnut and weedy mulberry trees; then he was on Wood Street; it was as if he'd passed through a portal that skipped the fifty inter-vening miles and deposited him in the first, forested swells of the real Appalachia; the few houses winked in and out of the trees; their foundations were half dug into the steep hill-sides and they looked like nothing so much as dogs swimming against a brown river.

At the end of the street, a dead end, there was a gated drive-way leading into the woods. The gate looked to have been constructed of the final sales from a dozen different gone-out-of-business hardware stores. There was an old PED XING sign with a single bullet-hole on one of the posts; it had been altered with black paint so that the heads of the adult and child figure were almond-eyed aliens.

12

The gate wasn't latched. Johnny pushed it open and walked down the driveway. After a few yards, a very large dog and a very small woman of indeterminate age, somewhere between twenty and sixty, wiry and weatherworn in a pair of sensible jeans, emerged from the trees. The dog loped up to Johnny, who regarded it warily; it stuck its nose in his crotch. Stinky, the woman said; come here, you stinky-stink. The dog obeyed. Hey, Johnny said. I'm looking for Winston Pringle.

Dr. Wilhlem? she said. He's up at the house. She pointed down the drive.

Can I just go up?

It used to be a free country, she said.

Is that a yes?

It's not a no. Anyway, it's not my place. My and stinky-stinky-stinkers here were just stopping in to say hello.

That's some dog.

He's a werewolf.

Oh, really?

Not really. He's just big and stinky. Aren't you? Aren't you? Yes, you are. Yes yes you are.

Well, Johnny said. I guess I'll go up.

I guess you will, she said, and she and the dog went on down the road.

13

The house was ramshackle, a mess of asphalt shingles and rotten gutters, but still less so than Johnny had expected, given the aesthetic condition of the gate. It reminded him in an odd way of his grandparents' house; it had the same dimensions, the same roofline, a similar dormer window, and on the far edge of the property there was a large shed. There were some wrecked and useless autos and a derelict school bus without wheels in the clearing.

Pringle answered the door in an apron that read FIST THE COOK. He couldn't have weighed less than four hundred pounds, but his head and hands were delicate, suggesting a naturally small man grown huge through a dedicated program of excess. He had a rooster's jowls; he was flushed from the exertion of walking to the door, and the flush contributed to the impression that he was part poultry. Under the apron he wore jeans with an elastic waist, and he was wearing a sweatshirt despite the heat billowing out on a strong draft from inside the house.

I've been expecting you, he said. Like his head and hands, his voice was unexpectedly dainty, nasal and a little swallowed, like a birdcall run through a kazoo.

Me? said Johnny.

Pringle squinted and leaned closer. His breath smelled like peanut butter.

Oh, he said. No, not you.

Oh, said Johnny.

I thought you were someone else, said Pringle.

And Johnny, recalling unintentionally a story I'd told him, said, I am someone else.

Which must be some sort of magic phrase that unlocks the universe, because Pringle smiled—an unsettling redeployment of his lips into a sort of deflated parabola—and chuckled and made a sound like a duck that was his version of Well or Uh or Hm or *Alors*, and he said, Yes, I see that you are. Well, why don't you come inside and we'll talk about it?

Awesome, said Johnny. I'm your biggest fan.

Well then, said Pringle, maybe you can help me figure out this Internet thing.

What Internet thing? Johnny asked.

Oh, you know, said Pringle. Just the Internet. In general.

14

Then Johnny was gone, but I didn't much notice; Mark kept hauling me to meetings I didn't really understand or have any business participating in, as well as hauling me to lunchtime strip joints, which I tried to appreciate ironically, but did not. Neither did he, really; he seemed to be trying to convey something to me, some message in a language I couldn't translate; although I don't know, maybe he did like it: one afternoon he paid Sassy Cassy, who was the dwarf who worked the early weekday shift, a hundred bucks to slap him across the face. She obliged, and when he righted his head, I saw that she'd split his lip. His tongue touched the blood, and he smiled as if he liked the taste of it.

Then one night Lauren Sara and I were meeting Mark and Helen for dinner. Hey, have you heard from Johnny lately? she asked. She was in the shower, and I was shaving. It was nearly the end of July somehow; the year had only gotten hotter; it had been ninety degrees for a week and felt like Florida.

No, I said. Why do you ask?

It's like he disappeared, Lauren Sara said.

And it had been longer and deeper than his past benders. Since getting hooked up with Pringle, he'd rapidly effaced most of his online presence. We don't want our psychotronics mapped onto the Google worldmind, which is, you know, running an algorithm to simulate human consciousness, predicting to the individual level the actions of every human on earth, literally eradicating free will through the power of prediction, he told me. I thought you said he wanted you to teach him how to use the Internet, I said. How to use it, Johnny snapped; not how to be used by it. It was the last time we'd really talked, although I did receive the occasional cryptic text message. His cell phone, at least, still worked. Meeting Pringle was all he could talk about. It's all true, he told me. The

Project, everything. You have to see his research facility. We're close to a breakthrough, once we get access to the Project's files in the Westinghouse building. His research facility? I said doubtfully, and Johnny whipped out his phone and showed me some pictures he'd taken. Is that a bathtub? I said. It looks like someone's basement. It looks like a meth lab. You know, Morrison, fuck off. Whatever happened to you anyway? You see a goddamn UFO; you're a straight-up witness to the culmination of a decades-long conspiracy; you see it with your own two eyes, and you become *more* normal. It's fucking disappointing. Oh, that's disappointing? I said. I disappoint you? You put yourself in the fucking hospital and maybe almost in jail on a weeklong bender, and then, as soon as you're back on your feet, you start in with this? I'm fucking worried about you, Johnny. But as soon as I said it, I knew I shouldn't have, because his voice lost all of its hoarseness and anger and his tone went flat. I'm fine, he said. You're not fine, I said. You're far from fine. Morrison, he said, calmly and with a disconcerting lack of affect, I've seen things that would melt your mind and freeze-dry your eyes. You'd be on your knees begging for mercy. You. Don't. Even. Know.

15

His absence, however, had a surprisingly salutary effect on Lauren Sara and me. Or maybe his absence only happened to coincide with an improvement in our relationship. I suppose that without Johnny around, I felt freer to behave as he'd accused me of behaving: more normally—to behave, in any case, with greater conformity to the ordinary expectation of how a man of my age and income should behave around his girlfriend. In fact, it occurred to me that I was only just beginning to think of Lauren Sara as my girlfriend, even though we'd been seeing each other for the better part of a year.

I was working late a lot. I suddenly had work, or something very much resembling my idea of it. Not long after my promotion, Mark had reappeared in another expensive suit, still wearing a VISITOR badge, and spirited me down to the twenty-third floor, which had been filled, seemingly overnight, with the apparatus of a busy company, and I'd been there ever since. Should I say something to someone? I'd asked him. About what? he said. About, you know, moving offices or whatever. Say, he said, whatever you like. But I hadn't had anything to say, and that's what I said.

So anyway, I was working late a lot; a group of Mark-like lawyerish beings from Vandevoort, some American, some British, some Dutch, with a few other Europeans and a South American or two, rotated through the office; they all looked alike to me, as if they'd been grown in the same alien hatchery or bred from the same tub of DNA—the effect was made more unsettling by the fact that they called themselves the V's; that derived from Vandevoort, obviously, but still. They brought me personnel files, which seemed to me like it might be illegal, and asked me my opinions on such-and-such and so-and-so, and though it made me a little uncomfortable, there was no denying the allure of knowing that the Other Peter made more than Leonard or that, despite his claims to the contrary, the company was not paying for Ted's MBA. The one woman among them, a thin, beautiful, terrifying Czech named Assia, who smelled like delicate perfume and indelicate European cigarettes, would tell me to call John Boland at the *Post-Gazette* or Larry Meigel at the *Trib* to talk on background about the company's plans to move its global headquarters to Pittsburgh, about the creation of jobs, about the contribution to the local economy. Do we intend to locate the global headquarters in Pittsburgh? I asked. What the fuck does that have to do with anything? she asked. She had a slight Irish accent from doing her graduate work in Dublin. Well, I said, I'm a little uncomfortable lying to these people. Oh Christ, oh fuck me, she said. You're telling them the current truth, Mark said. I hadn't even noticed him there; I hadn't known he'd been listening. The truth is an artifact of the present. It's time that changes. He put a comforting hand on my shoulder. Assia rolled her eyes and walked away.

Mark appeared intermittently, always in those slim suits with that sticker on his breast. He was usually trailed by Global Solutions executives or trailing the tall, thin-jawed Dutch execs who came in from Rotterdam. We rarely interacted on these visits, although he'd often flash me a wink and that thin smile that bordered on a sneer without becoming one as he passed, as if he and I were the only two in on some joke or some secret; he liked to come by my office—I had my own office now—at lunchtime bearing soups and sandwiches and chat about nothing in particular as if we were old friends. Sometimes I'd return from a meeting to find him camped at my desk as if it were his own, talking into a cell phone in

Spanish or German, a laptop open in front of him. Once I found him this way in the middle of an elaborate French joke that seemed to my poor ear like it had to do with a blow job; he was flipping through a glossy publication. While I sat in my visitor's chair and waited for him to get off the phone, I picked it up and glanced at the cover. Prepare the Way, it said. It was a Vandevoort Corporate report. Underneath, the now-familiar astrolabe was printed as a pale watermark; over it, a glossy, shadowed image of two fiftyish men whose broad teeth implied prosperity piloting an expensive sailboat off a Maine-like shore and the bright corporate slogan: There for Your Business at the Turn of the Tide.

Around this time I confessed to him that I still had no idea what I was doing. What am I doing? I asked him. I know that sounds completely lame, but seriously, I'm so busy, and I have no idea doing what.

You're a real materialist, Pete, he told me.

You're not the first person to say so.

You're involved in the production of wealth.

I'm involved in answering weird questions and writing complicated emails.

Yes. It's like alchemy. It's magic. It takes hundreds of fingers typing thousands of emails to utter the spell that turns lead into gold.

That's some magic spell, I said, if it turns Global Solutions into gold.

He laughed. That's the truth, he said.

Are we going to fire people? I asked.

Oh, probably, he said.

Like, a lot of people?

The smell of burning flesh has to reach the heavens, Mark said, and they're way the fuck up there. The gods of commerce have to smell blood in the water.

You know, I said, you don't talk like any lawyer I've ever met.

I told you, Mark said, I'm not exactly what I seem. On an unrelated note, let's have dinner again. You and me and the ladies. Maybe we'll all see another flying saucer.

Sure, I said.

Great, said Mark. Thursday, then. Our place.

Okay.

Speaking of flying saucers, you know, Helen has not been the same since all that. He peered at me, and I felt as if I were being appraised from the inside out.

Huh, I said.

He blinked. Making lots of art, though, he said. Which is good. She needs a hobby. Weird stuff. She's been having dreams, she told me.

Really, I said.

Strange dreams, he said.

That seems to be going around, I replied.

Is it?

What about you? I said. Sleeping well?

Only when the frailty of this human form compels me. I prefer to be productive.

I would go home after work on the quiet nine o'clock buses. Sometimes Lauren Sara would be at the apartment watching TV or using my computer; sometimes she'd arrive shortly after me, smelling of flux and turpentine. We'd walk over to the Orient Kitchen on Baum and eat fish ball hot pots and jellyfish and fish head soup. Something made us want to eat strangely. We'd drink Tsingtaos with dinner, and then, instead of heading off to the bar or going off separately with our friends, we'd walk back to my apartment. We'd lie in bed with the window open and the fans going, and we'd watch streaming movies on a laptop perched at the foot of the bed until one or both of us fell asleep. Sometimes I'd wake up in the middle of the night and find her kissing my neck. Honey, I have to pee, I'd say. Hurry, she'd say. And I would, so that I could get back before she fell asleep again. I was not sure how any of this happened, but it did.

16

No, that's not entirely true. In addition to the whole deal with Johnny, there was the fact that Lauren Sara had noticed how often I'd been searching for Helen Witold online. You have a little crush, she told me. It didn't seem to bother her. No, I don't, I said. I'm just interested. That's a crush, she said. Is it? I said. It's cute, she told me. Yeah? I said. I didn't know that you had it in you, she said. Ouch, I said. Come here, she said. And although I'm no expert in affairs or the fascinations that lead us into them, I do know that the one thing missing from almost all the literature on infidelity is the frequent, concurrent effect it has on the principal, preexisting relationship; there must be some truth to the old saw about the rising tide and the whole harbor.

17

We'd become frequent dinner guests, actually. Mark would text me at eight p.m. on a weeknight to ask if we'd eaten yet. We usually hadn't. We'd arrive at their place around nine. It won't surprise you to learn that Mark was an excellent cook. We'd end up in their tall kitchen with its big windows looking out over the Allegheny, drinking wine and watching Mark's long-handled knife move too fast and too close to his fingers. He had the habit of chopping without looking at his hands, and I never figured out how he managed never to cut himself. His cooking reminded me of Nana's, actually. Neither of my parents was much use in the kitchen; my mother could roast a chicken with a recipe; my father could grill a steak and make a surprisingly adept omelet; but Nana, before her eyesight and coordination had really started to decline, was ingenious in the kitchen. Among the hostesses of her social set, she was the one who never hired caterers, and when I was a little boy, I can remember standing beside her in her kitchen with a piping bag, helping her to assemble hundreds of little tarts or savory pastries. Mark's cooking was rarely so dainty, but, like her, he enjoyed odd cuts and greasy little fish and offal. He was a show-off; he'd poach sweetbreads in white wine from a bottle that cost three times as much as any bottle of white wine I'd ever bought, and he seemed to be a carnivore; although he prepared beautiful vegetables and sharp salads of sorrel and frisée, he never seemed to eat them; or, maybe he ate them, but something about the *way* he ate them gave the impression that he was just pushing them around the plate. He'd served lamb at our first dinner together; he'd frenched the rack himself and just barely seared the outside. His eyes narrowly watched Lauren Sara over the rim of his wineglass as she poked the bloody meat with her knife. He'd served it on purpose. I think she knew it, and she cut a bigger piece than she had to and chewed it deliberately. Wow, she said, this is amazing. Later, he told me perhaps he'd misjudged her.

They lived in a condo in the Strip District in an old industrial building that had been converted into housing for rich people. Their neighbors were a weird mixture of young bankers and aging foundation heads who knew my grandmother. The apartment—Mark didn't like the word condo, which he said reminded him of cheap vacations on the Gulf Coast—was big and awkward; the architects or developers or whoever put the building back together hadn't been able to decide if they were lofts or not, and what walls there were seemed reluctant to be there. But the kitchen looked over the water, and the big room for living and dining looked over the Strip and past the convention center's sailboat roofs to downtown and the sun setting over the Ohio River beyond.

At that first meal, sometime between the lamb and the tarte aux pommes, Mark had begged a cigarette from Lauren Sara and the two of them went off to smoke on a balcony somewhere. Helen was wearing a light sweater cut wide and square around her neck; it showed off her collarbones. During the meal, we'd been chitchatting about work; Lauren Sara was making gentle fun of the undergrads she taught as a graduate assistant; Helen had told us about the first time she'd met Mark. It was at a bar, she said. Of course. In Brooklyn.

I know he doesn't seem like the type to go to Brooklyn. Ha! Mark said. I'm an explorer, a pioneer. Not the type, she said. I'd just come from an absolutely terrible opening. I was with a bunch of friends and we were completely drunk, and I notice this guy, all alone, at the end of the bar. I swear he hadn't been there a second ago, but now he looks like he's always been there. He's wearing a suit, so of course he doesn't belong, and he's staring at me, and I think, he either wants to fuck me or murder me, which is totally hot. So I ask my friend Beth [She looked like a Beth, Mark interrupted], Is that guy staring at me? and Beth fucking, she stumbles right over to him and is like, Are you staring at my friend? Do you *like* her? So eventually I go over, too, and then Beth disappears, and we're talking and talking, and then it's last call. And I'm like, should I go home with this guy? He's had, like, six whiskeys, and I can't believe he's not drunk. And then he says, I bet you don't even remember my name. I say, it's Mark. Then I'm like, What's mine? And he says—

Beth, said Mark.

With just the two of us, I didn't know what to say. Helen poured us both another glass. So, she said. You're working for Mark now.

Apparently, I said.

Hm, she said.

Hm? I repeated.

Keep one eye open, she said.

I will do that, I told her.

You think you will.

No, really.

I was not quite famous when we met, you know. Now I'm not famous at all.

All those museum types seem to know you, I said. You still get lots of search engine hits.

You've checked? she said.

Well, I said.

It's not the same thing. But you know, when we first started seeing each other, people would meet Mark and say, Oh, you're Helen Witold's boyfriend. I didn't know what to say, so I didn't say anything. She said, When I was a little girl, I told my dad I wanted to be a famous artist, and he said, Wouldn't you rather be rich? Can you believe that? All of the men in my life are such *dicks*.

That sounds like something my mother would say, I said.

She smiled at me. I'm boring you. Don't tell Mark I called him a dick, please.

No, I said.

I like your girlfriend.

I couldn't decide if she meant something more by it, so I said, Yeah, she's all right.

Then she stared at me like she had at the museum the first time we'd met. Her stare was unlike Mark's, who left you feeling flayed and dissected. It was less as if she were searching for something than hoping to see something she already knew she wouldn't find, and it was so sad that I had to turn fractionally away again, but it was alluring, too, and it seemed to me then, and still seems to me, that what she suffered was less an absence of love than a surfeit of want and desire. She said,

You ought to come over sometime and see what I'm working on. I'm working on some interesting pieces.

Oh? I turned back, and she was still staring.

I've been having these really vivid dreams, she said. I'm illustrating them.

And I wanted to ask, What dreams? Describe them to me, but Mark and Lauren Sara were walking back into the room, and Mark was saying, Who wants dessert?

On the way home after the second or third of these dinners, Lauren Sara had commented to me that Helen drank a lot. I said that I hadn't noticed, but I had; at least, I noticed her wineglass getting refilled more frequently than the rest of ours, and I noticed that she usually had something stronger than wine before dinner, and after. Well, we all drank a fair amount, and I wasn't really sure that I believed in addiction and alcoholism and all that anyway—I admitted to its existence, but found the categories hard to apply as practical observations about anyone I knew. I did, however, notice that despite the precision machinery of Mark-and-Helen's host-and-hostess routine, as the evenings lengthened into nights an uneasy energy crept into the room; they never fought, not in front of us, but somehow they often seemed about to. Helen would usually offer us some blow after dinner; Mark always participated, but always seemed slightly aggrieved to participate. Lauren Sara always did a bit, but that girl was immune to the allure. Coke makes me sleepy, she said. Sleepy? I was incredulous. Totally, she said. How is that even possible? I said. She said, I don't know; maybe just because it's boring.

As for me, I always felt guilty about doing it; I'd been hearing reports here and there that Johnny was in a serious hole; some of the old gang from our early twenties, whom I still ran into at the bars from time to time, had mentioned that Johnny may have propositioned them with offers of extraordinary new drugs that would send you through the wormhole and introduce you to the real Illuminati. But I don't know, said Paul Rauth, who'd actually lived with Johnny for a few years in college in a disgusting house in Garfield; I just like to get stoned, you know? What with all this, I'd resolved to stay away from drugs, but Helen was so guileless and generous about it. How could you turn her down?

18

I even asked Tom about Helen. I'd asked Julian at the gym one evening after he'd kicked my ass at racquetball, but he said he didn't know. Ask Tom, he said. Your boyfriend sucks, I told him. He laughed and slapped my shoulder and said, Fuck you, Peter. So I dropped Tom an email. Hey Tom, it said, You're the expert. What's the deal with Helen Witold?

Even though Tom hated me, I knew he wouldn't be able to resist (a) showing off his art knowledge, and (b) gossiping.

He wrote back: She used to be a big deal. Saatchi bought a couple things she did in the early 2000s which was crazy because she's American. She was supposed to be in a Whitney biennial, maybe, too. But then she did all this shitshow crap, probably after she got hooked up with whats-his-name, that asshole you work for. Also maybe she parTied a little too much? Arnovich's X still reps her in NYC, but I think she's pretty much over, or anyway, she's not making anything new.

19

But I knew that she was making something new. She'd said so. She'd never offered to show me again after that first time, and I'd never figured out how to sneak across the hall to the studio that occupied the other half of their floor. But I'd been dating an artist long enough to recognize the scent of art being made. This seemed hugely significant to me at the time. A little later, when I did actually see it, I recognized immediately that it wasn't good, although of course I said otherwise. It was the work of someone who'd fallen out of practice, who'd forgotten how to practice, or what practice is. But, as you can imagine, the smell of oil and mineral spirits filled me with intimations of mad genius, and it made me want her even more.

20

By this time, news of Global Solutions' pending acquisition by Vandevoort had been reported in the business press and the local papers, and I'd recognized, in these stories, my own words reported back as coming from high-ranking insiders and employees close to the decision-making process. It occurred to me that I was actually embroiled in a conspiracy.

Meanwhile, I'd received a series of texts from a number I didn't recognize that talked about participation by Vandevoort NV in the Holocaust in the Netherlands and in smuggling Jewish scientists to the United States as part of a trilateralist war agenda, but when I tried to call the number, I just got a message that the phone was not in service. I looked up the number online; it was registered to a pay-by-minute company. Johnny, obviously. I tried calling his regular cell, but that had been disconnected, too. Then suddenly the V's, having asked their questions, written their reports, made their blandly worded, scorched-earth recommendations, departed; the twenty-third-floor hive was gone; the offices mothballed again; the conference rooms locked. I was hauled up to the executive offices on twenty-seven and given a new office, which looked at the ass-end of an air exhaust on the building behind ours. We began firing people and suppliers.

I mean, they blend together; they were all so similar. Like, we'd haul up some poor sucker whose West Virginia company made some tiny part for some incomprehensible gadget for some massive water pump produced by some company that had at some point hired Global Solutions to get them a better deal on expensive thingamajigs. The poor guy would be balding but handsome, with a face that showed a youth spent outdoors and an adulthood of regret at having given that up. The guy would be in a nice but unimpressive suit, and I'd be sitting there with Mark and Sylvia and Swerdlow—John Bates had already been fired; it is with mixed emotions, said the email, that we say goodbye; a visionary and loyal presence at the company; moving on to new challenges and opportunities; yeah yeah; whatever; amen—or, actually, they'd be sitting there at the table, and I'd be wedged on a chair in the back, wondering what I was doing, pretending to take notes or something, and the guy, mustering his most intimidating mien, which maybe even worked with his unions back home, would say, It seems to me that you all are trying to fuck us over. No offense.

Mark would say, None taken. We're here for frank discussion. Open and honest dialogue.

Swerdlow would say, Don't worry about my delicate ears. I'm a lawyer. I've heard worse.

Sylvia would say something about changing economic realities and a mutually agreeable and fair mechanism for winding down a reorder and compensation schedule in the best interests of all the parties involved.

The guy would shake his head and say, I don't understand what's broke here. I don't see what you're trying to fix.

Mark would say, As you're probably aware, Global Solutions is entering a period of transition. We're seeing increased competition in our sector. The global economy is slowing down. The European crisis isn't helping. We need to streamline certain aspects of the business.

Do you even work for Global Solutions? the guy would ask, because Mark was still wearing that fucking VISITOR sticker.

Mr. Danner is an important part of our transition process, Swerdlow would say.

You don't work for them, either. You're just the goddamn lawyer. No offense.

None taken.

Do *any* of you work for them? the guy would say. I mean directly.

I do, Sylvia would answer. Peter does.

The secretary, the guy would say, and he'd glare at me. How's that writing hand doing? But I would never reply. Look, he'd say. Look. What're we trying to fix here? You're talking about unilaterally altering a contractual agreement. We don't see the need. We like things the way they are. You say mutual agreement, but we already agreed to all this. We hashed all this out years ago. None of you was there, so maybe none of you remembers. But I was there and I remember. What're we trying to fix? Hell, you promised us that this whole thing would make us so rich our damn janitors would retire to Hawaii, and that hasn't exactly come to pass. Like I said before, I'm not unreasonable. But you're asking for a concessionary agreement on our part. We'd go up in smoke if we agreed to this.

Well, look, Mark would say, and he'd get this bored expression, the distracted look of a priest who's said the same liturgy a thousand times before, if you'll just turn to page seven of your vendor agreement, section three-d, under the heading Termination upon the Occurrence of Certain Other Events . . .

21

That's so creepy, Lauren Sara said when I told her about one of these meetings. She'd come over. We'd intended to go out to dinner, I think, but instead we drank a bottle of Brunello that my dad had given me for some reason or other and ordered a pizza and got stoned and watched *The Big Lebowski* for the hundredth time. I remember that night in particular because it was my weed that we smoked, which was rare, and after one hit Lauren Sara looked at me and said, No way. Is this the K2? Cool. But anyway, I was telling her about one of these negotiations, or whatever they were, and she said, That's so creepy. It sounds like killing people. Like, and she did her Schwarzenegger impression, You've been terminated . . . upon the occurrence of certain other events. Your Arnold sounds like a retarded French homosexual, I told her. You're a retarded French homosexual, she said.

22

But if I began to doubt my participation in the bloodletting, it wasn't until we fired Ted. I mean, I fired him. Mark made me. It's time, he said. The caterpillar becomes the stone-cold motherfucking killer. Jesus, seriously, I said. He hired me. Come on, Mark said, just the tip. Try it. You'll like it.

I had, since my promotion, had limited contact with my old coworkers. We occasionally ran into each other in the elevators, and they treated me with a cautious politeness that made me uncomfortable but also, I'm ashamed to admit, filled at least one chamber of my heart with a vain pride, because, not knowing any better at the time, I mistook it for due deference. I was still under the impression that I wasn't doing anything; my days had a formless, timeless quality; they passed in gusts of calls and emails and presentations and meetings, but I can recall making no decisions, recording no profit, making and doing nothing of any particular note, the difference being that in retrospect I can see the purposelessness and centerlessness as adaptive features of a very particular evolution, which had rendered as vestigial the structures of authority and hierarchy and production and replaced them with something, well, vague, insubstantial, and threatening, something from which no good could arise.

I had, of course, seen people fired, or had heard of it having happened and seen its brief aftermath, but everyone who got fired expected it; they took it with the annoyed forbearance of a person who gets stuck in the rain without an umbrella even though she'd read the forecast that morning. Except, of course, for Ted. Ted had not accepted it. Ted had not accommodated himself to a world in which getting an unexpected summons to an unfamiliar office meant only one thing. Whereas I had, in the same situation, arrived assuming I'd get canned, Ted arrived expecting to be beamed up to the mothership and made a part of the crew.

But as soon as he saw me in my big chair and Mark standing like an evil consigliere behind me and some sublegal functionary with a notepad perched in the corner, his happy round face tightened and his grip tightened on his little monographed organizer. Pete, he said.

Ted, I said. Why don't you come in and have a seat? It was how I'd heard it done, so it was how I did it.

I'd rather stand, he said.

Well, all right, I said.

Sit the fuck down, said Mark, and Ted did.

I shuffled some papers. Look, Ted, I said. I want you to know how much we've valued your contribution to Global Solutions.

Oh Jesus, he said. Oh Jesus. Oh Jesus.

Ted, I said. Really. It's okay.

His head hung. Fuck, he said. Fuck fuck fuck.

Jesus Christ, said Mark. You big fucking crybaby. He hasn't even fired you yet.

Fuck fuck fuck, said Ted. I could already hear the snot in his nose. I want to tell you that I felt terribly, that I felt as if I couldn't go through with it, but I felt nothing of the kind.

Ted! I said sharply.

He looked up. Pete, he said. I didn't expect it from you.

I'm sorry, Ted, I told him, and then I shrugged and put on my best impression of that distracted look I'd seen on Mark's face a hundred times by then. I'm sorry, Ted, but it is what it is.

That night I picked up Lauren Sara and took her to dinner. We both got drunk and went back to my apartment and I may have pushed her toward the couch as if we were going to fuck then and there. Whoa, she said. Like, what's gotten into you? You remember Ted? I said. That moron I used to work for. The one who always fucking called me Pete? Yeah, she said. Totally. Well, I said, I got to fire him today. She frowned at me. She sat up. You fired him? Yeah, I said. Why would you fire him? she said. Because he was a worthless piece of shit, I said. Well, sure, I guess, Lauren Sara replied, but what's that got to do with firing the guy? It's not like anyone does anything there anyway, right? Fuck, I thought, and then we got stoned and went to sleep.

When I came in the next day, Rick at security told me all about the aftermath. How about that guy from your company? he said. What guy? I asked. The one who wouldn't leave, he told me; the guy they fired who said he wasn't going anywhere. He sighed. Poor SOB, he said. We had to go up and haul him out.

Haul him out? I repeated.

Haul him out, Rick said.

Why did you have to haul him out?

Because, like I said, they fired him, and he refused to leave.

Did you catch his name?

Ted, I'm pretty sure.

He was my old boss, I said.

What I don't get, Rick said, is why anyone would want to stay here. My boss came in and said, Rick, you're done, I'd be out the door before my seat quit spinning.

You could always just quit, I said.

And give the bastards the pleasure? No way. I intend to sit here doing nothing and taking their money.

I hope you do, Rick. You're the glue that holds this place together.

He shrugged. Beautiful day, wish you were here, he said.

21

They fired Kevin and Tim and the Other Peter.

They fired Sylvia.

They promoted Marcy, of all people, to associate director of something to do with the Internet, but she quit.

They even fired Pandu. How could you fire Pandu? I asked Mark. He was the only one worth anything.

Why would I employ one expensive Indian when there are one billion inexpensive ones?

That's kind of fucked up.

I'm kidding. But seriously, no one is worth anything, especially not due to their position in the old order.

Jesus Christ, Mark, I said. Are you going to fire everyone? Who's going to do the work?

The what? he said.

Seriously, I said.

You have to pluck the feathers, he told me, before you can roast the chicken.

The only other one they didn't fire was Leonard. Leonard, like Marcy, got promoted. Unlike her, he didn't quit. Assistant director of corporate philanthropy, he told me when we ran into each other at the Starbucks. How about that shit?

We have corporate philanthropy? I said.

He shrugged. Who knew? The European dudes are all into outdoors and the environment and green shit. We're giving a quarter million to help finish the renovation down at the Point.

Really? The fountain?

I know, right? But shit, I got a raise, so you know, it's all good.

Well, look, Leonard, I said. Keep an eye out.

Will do, chief, he said. A week later the gift to the West-

ern PA Conservancy was announced. On Friday of that same
week, they fired Leonard.

24

As my company was dismantled, my old friend Johnny had
fallen, quite by accident, into productive labor. I found out
later, of course. It was an irony, not unappreciated, that the
old model of economic productivity, in which the work of
human hands, amplified by technology, produced goods to
be exchanged for currency, positively flourished in our post-
productive age, only it did so underground. Now, as for how
we fund our little institute, Pringle had said to Johnny on his
third visit. So we sell some drugs, Johnny said. I am sure the
idea appealed to him. Drugs? said Pringle. Oh no, not drugs.
Research chemicals.

Got it, said Johnny.

I don't think this was merely a euphemism. Pringle did
refer to their customers as test subjects. I suspect that he, and
who knows, maybe Johnny, too, believed it to some degree.
If there was something gross and unsanitary in all the usual
pursuits of an entertaining or numbing or joy-enhancing or
ameliorating high, then there was something much more alien
and discomfiting in the people who sought out folks like Winston Pringle and the weird, powerful dissociatives that he was
peddling. For all the illusions of control and tolerance within
which both the most functional and the most degenerate of
alcoholics or cokeheads or junkies lived, each, in their own

way, in some small but ineradicable portion of their consciousness and conscience, knew that they were pursuing
death; knew that they were afloat on the ocean of a flat world,
over whose roaring edge was the infinite void; whereas the self-
described psychonauts, the dilettantes of higher consciousness, who bragged openly about seeking out the borders and
nature and experience of oblivion, they didn't really believe in
it—or they believed it was a thing that could be purchased, a
ticket with an open return.

25

Then one night on our way up to dinner at Mark and Hel-
en's, we ran into another couple who asked if we knew what
floor the party was on. I looked at Lauren Sara. Sorry, she
said. Really? I said. Sorry, she said. Pretend to be surprised. It
was Saturday night. The following Monday was my thirtieth
birthday. Happy birthday, old man, she said, and she kissed
me briefly on the lips, and she led me to the elevator.

26

A bar with champagne. Real champagne. Veuve. People I
knew. People I didn't know. A caterer. Waiters. Derek beside a
braided ficus talking to a girl who maybe lived at Lauren Sara's
house. Cocktail tables. All of this in the elevator lobby, before
we even got to the door of the apartment. Lauren Sara hand-

ing me a flute. Me saying I'm going to need something stronger. The bartender handing me a scotch. A bald man telling a man with a mustache that everything went to shit on the back nine. The possibility of music just audible beneath the sound of voices. Derek saying, Happy birthday, bro, as we walked past. Me asking Lauren Sara, Who's that girl he's talking to? That's Patra. The Greek? Lauren Sara giggling and saying, Shh, she doesn't know that's what we call her. A crowded doorway. People pulling cheese and pastries from the dining room table. The kitchen, brightly lit. Mark with a glass of red wine, turning from the two perfect women he was talking to. Was one of them Assia, from Vandevoort? Mark saying, The birthday boy! Someone overhearing and saying, Whose birthday? No one answering. Me shaking Mark's hand. Me saying, I hope this isn't all for me. Mark saying, Any excuse to throw a party. Someone asking, Where's the bathroom? Lauren Sara saying, I'm going to find Tom. Me spotting Julian talking to another banker. Me finishing my drink. Mark handing me a glass of red. The good stuff, he said. Me trying it. Wandering into the living room. Spotting my grandmother on a couch. Saying, Nana? What are you doing here? Nana said, Happy birthday, Junior; you don't look a day over twenty. Lauren Sara reappearing. Oh, hello Laura, Nana said. Lauren Sara rolling her eyes at me and departing immediately. Some dude telling some other dude something about nonvanilla exercise rights. Why, asked Nana, are people always talking about money? Nana—I laughed—*you* always talk about money. Only, she said, in the abstract; naming sums is déclassé. Fair enough. What's new with you? I haven't seen you in months. No, she said, not since the museum. Nothing is new with me, as you put it. Everything is quite comfortably old. I don't believe that for a minute, I said. A familiar man in a bright tie passing and saying, Hello, Nanette, and you must be Pete. Nana, after we'd exchanged pleasantries, while the man was walking away, saying with her voice pitched just loud enough for him to hear, that she had no idea, no earthly idea, who that was. Me saying, I think he used to work with Dad. Your mother and father were invited to this little soiree, Nana told me, or so they said. I don't expect they'll show up. Not their scene, I said. No, indeed, she said. Derek appearing and saying, You've got some swinging-dick friends, Peter; do you know I just saw fucking Kantsky in the library? Derek, I said, this is my grandmother; Nana, my friend Derek. Oh shit, he said. Oh, sorry. Do I appear to be quailing and blanching? Nana said, and sighed. Never get old, she said; you acquire other people's habits of assuming your own infirmity. Nana, I said, no one assumes your infirmity. They ought to, she said; I could go any day now. Turning to Derek. And who is this fucking Kantsky you mention? Jonah Kantsky, Derek said. He's the mayor's chief of staff. Ah, the young mayor, said Nana. Yes, I'd heard there was a Svengali pulling his little strings. I think Svengali was a hypnotist, I said. Yes, yes I know that, she said. Do you know that *Trilby* was the first play I ever saw on the West End? Absolutely terrible. I suppose your Cousin William thought it I'd enjoy the gothic element. Of course, I was much too young to see the original with Tree. My cousin William? I said. You mean Bill? No, no, she said, your cousin twice removed, I suppose. He was a good bit older than me. His mother was your grandfather's aunt, his father's oldest sister. She married some poor benighted minor aristocrat who needed her money. Poor thing; she didn't get much. I think your great-grandfather thought her heading back to England was a betrayal of the Revolution. Derek said, That's some family history you've got, Mr. Morrison. You have no idea, I said. Come to think of it, I have no idea.

Later, standing in the kitchen with Mark and some business types. Mark holding forth on something or other. Mark draping an arm over my shoulder and saying this guy is a real killer. Me saying I don't know if that's the case. Me saying, Hey, where's Helen, by the way? Mark saying either powdering her nose or passed out somewhere. The business dudes yuk-yukking. Mark's hand still on my shoulder, his fingers tap-tapping. Excusing myself. Running into Tom and Julian. Have you guys seen Lauren Sara? No, sorry. How about this apartment? said Julian; your buddy Mark, he said; like, whoa. Really? said Tom. I think it's awfully gaudy. A tray of wine passing. Grabbing another drink. Drinking it quickly. Walking into the library; nearly running into Kantsky walking out. Feeling him stop, assess me, move on without a word. Alone for the first time that evening. Looking at the bookshelves. The usual mix of big biographies and business shit and popular novels and some Shakespeare and a Bible and some detective fiction and a lot of heavy expensive art books and a small section of German titles and a small section of Spanish and Italian and there among the English paperbacks, catching my eye quite by chance, surprising me, frightening me a little bit, *Fourth River, Fifth Dimension*. Pulling it off the shelf. Opening it randomly. Reading:

the sexually aroused psychic was then lowered into a sensory deprivation chamber full of electrolytic fluids. Once inside, he was able to achieve full-conscious manifesting of his total priapo-orgonic field potential. Thus, the Project achieved a major breakthrough. Although not yet able to physically project ourselves into alternate quantum realities, our psychic operators were able to experience them, although they experienced them as a sort of dream. Their recollection was spotty. We began working on a recording technology that could automatically transform their visions into images on a computer screen.

One unanticipated side effect, however, was the manifestation of silver craft above the testing site. Were they advanced beings? One theory held that they were in fact future versions of the very technology we were working on. They were literally coming back into the past to ensure their own eventuality.

And herein at last the nub of it: suddenly something which had seemed at most, at worst, a hasty sketch now resolving into a more exact copy, and all those weird dreams and portents threatening to start seeming true, and if the party was already making me feel weird, dislocated, out of joint with time, now I felt all the more so. Then hearing someone come into the room and closing the book. Seeing it was Mark and saying, Interesting taste in science fiction, with a grin. Mark saying, Nonfiction. Me laughing. You sound like my friend Johnny, I said. That's your buddy with the blog? Mark said.

Me saying yes but thinking, I don't think I ever mentioned Johnny's blog. Mark saying, How's he doing? Because I'd definitely mentioned his more recent hijinks and the night at the hospital. Mark saying, We tried to invite him, actually, but we never heard back. No surprise, I said. Not well, I said. To be honest, I said, I'm worried about him. He's an addict, Mark said, and it may have been a question. Sure, I said. I guess. I mean, I don't know that I believe in addiction, exactly. All deniers are faithful at heart, Mark said. You actually remind me of him sometimes, I said. You two are equally aphoristic. Well, look, he said, having lived with an addict, let me tell you, it's for real. When did you live with an addict? I said. Seriously? he said.

Looking for Lauren Sara. Bumping into some guy I knew from Global Solutions, whose name I forgot. Promising to talk him up to Mark. Grabbing another scotch. Eating some hors d'oeuvres. Stopping to listen to someone tell a joke. Catching some people doing blow in the guest bedroom. Laughing guiltily. Getting offered a line. Saying no thanks and feeling surprised I'd said no thanks. Seeing Mark maneuvering Assia—it was definitely Assia; I could smell the tobacco across the room—toward a guest bedroom. Following. Standing by the door. Hearing her say, Holy fuck, in her weird accent. Hearing him say, Turn over. Backing away. Hurrying off. Finding Lauren Sara with the Greek in the hallway. Lauren Sara asking, Hey, honey, will you be all right for an hour or so if I take off? Patra needs a ride to the studio and then needs to get over to the South Side. Thinking, *Typical*, then thinking I only thought that because I was drunk, then thinking that didn't make it any less accurate. Saying, No problem, in a voice precisely calculated to mean the opposite. Annoyed that she ignored it. Fine, 'bye, I said. Back soon, she said. Wandering once more around the party. Seeing Nana to the elevator. You seem to have fallen in with a thoroughly self-satisfied crowd, she said. How are you getting home? I asked. I'm staying at the Renaissance, she said. I have a doctor's appointment tomorrow morning in town. What for? I asked. On Sunday? I said. I'm a good customer, she replied. Then, having sent her down, seeing Jennifer Swerdlow lumbering through the crowd with a bottle of beer and a plateful of meats, I ducked, without thinking, through the nearest door.

27

Well, what went down was that I stumbled into Helen's studio. It was the size of their whole rambling apartment, but without any walls or dividers except for a few concrete pillars here and there, the skeleton of the building itself. The walls were brick; the windows on the narrower side overlooked the river directly, while the long wall of them looked northeast along the water toward the Thirty-first Street Bridge. I mention this only to orient the room; because it was dark outside, the windows were black and mirrored. The floor was poured concrete. There were little sitting areas with the sort of thrift-store furniture that rich people like to buy, which is to say, probably not from a thrift store at all but only designed to look like it. There were a few rugs. There was a big metal drafting table with a stool and an articulated arm lamp. There was expensive track lighting, and on the two big blank walls without windows, there was the art, obsessively repeated, silvery ovals against a star field—abstracted but, to me, unmistakable. The canvases were very large. The room smelled like a recently smoked cigarette. I could hear the muffled party through the walls. I could hear the murmur of the air-conditioned air venting into the room.

Then I heard Helen say, Where's your pretty girlfriend? I turned around. She was stretched out on a couch across the room from me, her legs crossed at the ankles, her back and body propped up against some pillows, with a cheap plastic bottle of liquor in her hand. She had on a pair of cutoff jeans and a too-large, paint-stained Pittsburgh Steelers T-shirt. Several strands of her usually neat hair had escaped in the direction of her eyes. When I walked toward her, I saw a little pile—okay, not such a little pile—of powder on the glass table beside her.

She left, I said.

Seems to be a theme, she said. She wasn't slurring, but she picked her way around the words carefully, as if they were the last solid footing on a narrow ledge.

She's coming back.

Oh, is she?

She is.

Then I stood there and she sat there and neither of us said anything. It occurred to me that it was the first time I'd been alone with her since the first night we'd met. It occurred to me that I did not, in fact, know this woman. It occurred to me that I was very drunk. It occurred to me that *she* was very drunk, but nevertheless holding on to me with an amused, distant, almost dissipated smile, which reminded me so much of Mark that I imagined she'd subconsciously copied it from him. What's so funny? I asked.

Circumstances, she said.

Why didn't you come to my party? I asked.

I'm having my own party, she said. Would you like some?

Okay, I said.

Besides, she said, while I helped myself, who says it's your party?

It happens to coincide with my birthday, I told her.

Maybe it's the other way around, she told me.

My birthday predates the party, I said, and I handed her the straw.

That's one way of looking at it, she said. She pinched her nose.

I said, I like your paintings.

They're shit, she said.

No, I replied. I don't think so.

You just recognize the source material, she told me.

We've still never talked about that, I said.

She smiled again, but this time a little sadly. About the aliens? she said. No, maybe not.

To be fair, I said, they might not be aliens. They might be from another dimension.

Oh, another dimension?

Is that funny? I said. How about: another reality?

Another reality? That's funny. There's no other reality.

You don't think? I think there might be a lot of them.

I think you'll find, she said, that they're all the same reality from a different perspective.

You've given it some thought.

Believe me, Helen said, I could use another reality.

Why's that?

I'm not overly fond of this one.

Maybe you should hitch a ride, I said, and I gestured toward a painting.

Oh no. I've had enough of aliens. And other realities.

What do you mean? I asked.

Let me ask you a question, she said.

Okay, I said.

Do you like working for Mark?

I don't really work for him, technically speaking.

I wasn't technically speaking.

I don't know, I said. Sure. I guess.

You should keep an eye out, she said.

Haha, I said. Everyone keeps saying that. My best friend's grandfather used to say it.

Keep an eye out?

Yeah. He was a cool guy. He was always trying to build a perpetual motion machine in the shed.

Never worked?

No. The perpetual was always the problem.

She took a long drink. She stared past me at the paintings. I used to be so skilled, she said. I was really good.

I really don't think they're bad at all, I said. I like them.

You're sweet, she said. Shit taste, but sweet.

Um, thanks, I said.

You remind me of a boy I used to date, she told me.

That's funny, I said. You remind me of a girl I used to date.

What happened?

To the girl? She broke up with me.

Why?

Infidelity.

We're two peas in a pod, she said.

You cheated on him, too? I said.

No, she said. Not him.

28

I couldn't tell you which one of us started it, which willed it to happen, or how it came about. I can only tell you that, like the material universe itself, it was defined by the probability of it happening until it did happen; then all those caroming quanta collapsed and it was real, and, like reality, it was defined by the necessity of its own being. We did not, it turned out, need a sexually aroused psychic to choose our ideal reality; or maybe that was the joke; maybe in another room she didn't touch my hand and I didn't touch her face and it all went very differently; maybe the whole Project was an ornate description of what we did every day. And maybe we shouldn't have, but we did.

Then I went back to the party, and she went back to her drink.

29

The following Tuesday, Mark came into my office with lunch. While we were eating, I noticed him looking at me as if he were trying to make up his mind about something. What? I said.

Oh, nothing, he said.

Hey, I said, you're not wearing your badge.

My badge?

I've never seen you here without a visitor sticker.

Oh, that, he said. I'm no longer a visitor. He paused. Technically speaking, he said, and he narrowed his eyes a bit.

You're not? I said.

No, he said. You've been assimilated. It's going to be announced tomorrow, but the papers are signed and sealed.

Huh, I said. So what happens now?

We extol the virtues of the dearly departed, and then we bury the body.

Has anyone ever told you that you have a violent mind?

Pff. I abhor violence.

I saw you kick the shit out of a guy the first time we met. You paid a stripper to bust your lip.

Jus ad bellum.

I sighed and shook my head. What was the point? I asked.

Of what?

Why did you buy us? What was it for? I can't exactly see how anyone expected to make money in the deal.

I never asked. Some of us made money. You made money. I made money.

But, I said.

Look, you're trying to find a narrative where none exists. A corporation is not a person. The gods don't oblige us with motives, but they sometimes reward obedience with good fortune.

I'm not sure I'd call a corporation a god, I said.

Of course it is. Created by man and superior to him. Magnificent in its infinite amplification of his flaws and powers. The very definition of a god.

So, what, does that make us priests? I said.

No, no. Avatars. Emissaries.

Angels, I offered.

Blow, Peter, Mark said. Blow.

You've been waiting to use that one. I laughed. But it's Gabriel.

Is it? Speaking of which, and while we're on the subject of transcendent amorality, Mark said, and then I knew what was coming.

Before you say anything— I began.

I trust, he said, that a good time was had by all.

Things sort of just happened.

His smile showed his sharp teeth. He crossed his legs. His eyes flicked across me, and I felt like a mouse in the presence of a bored cat, frightened, too, by the apparent absence of anger in his predation. I think it's interesting, he said, that you find it easier to ascribe the absence of willful motive to yourself than to some big company. I'm not sure what that says about you. He shrugged. Frankly, I'm not sure what you expected to get out of it. Other than the obvious, of course, for which there were plenty of other drunken whores at the party.

He said it flippantly, and although I had no right to be, it made me angry. I said, I'm not sure I was trying to get anything out of it.

Well, that I really can't understand.

Well, and I'm not defending myself, but it's not like it was some transaction.

Of course it was. What do you fail to understand about its fundamentally transactional nature? You had a quid and she had a quo.

Mark, I said, I wasn't trying to get anything. I really am sorry, but I really wasn't, not any more than you are.

He closed his eyes and squeezed the bridge of his nose and shook his head and then said, But I am trying to get something.

You know what I mean.

No, he said. I mean literally. She's the coinage of the realm; appearances are a kind of currency. I need someone like her. She's of immense practical value. She's a passport to a portion of society. Unlike you, Mr. Morrison, unlike her, I wasn't born into this world. He sighed. What she does with herself when she's off the clock is her fucking business, but the position carries certain requirements that do not include getting wasted in the dark when there's a company event. So the next time you want to fuck my drunk girlfriend, Morrison, he said, and then he stood up, jumped to his feet, snatched the laptop off my desk, and hurled it past my head and against the wall, where it snapped and fell like a bird against a window, do it on your own fucking time. Understand?

And quite suddenly, I was afraid that I did. I only nodded.

I'll send someone up from IT, he said over his shoulder as he left and slammed the door.

30

That night while I was sitting at home feeling the faint first tug of nausea, I heard the key in the door, and was surprised to see Johnny lumbering through with a huge rucksack and sleeping bag, which he deposited on my living room floor. Morrison, he said; I need to crash here tonight.

When did I give you a key? I asked.

You used to keep a spare in the kitchen.

I still keep a spare in the kitchen.

Not for about three years, he said. I borrowed it.

Johnny, I said, I haven't seen you in months, and why do you need to crash here?

There's someone in my apartment, he said. I think it might be a squatter, but I didn't have the heart to kick him out. He seems to be feeding the cats, anyway. Plus, I'm on my way out of town.

Yes, I said. You appear to be. Where are you going?

The Knotty Pine.

I'm sorry?

It's an old lodge in the state game lands up past Kittanning. One of Dr. Wilhelm's associates owns it. We're planning a happening. You ought to come. Have you got any eggs, by the way? I'm starving.

Yes, I have eggs. I followed him into the kitchen. A happening? I said.

Our own little Bohemian Grove. Art, music, revelry, and satanic rituals.

I'll pass, I said.

You're such a conformo. Where do you keep that faggy salt that I like?

Cupboard to your right. Johnny, what the fuck have you been doing?

I've been exploring the limits of human consciousness. When I died—

I'm sorry, I said, when you what?

When I died, before you found me in the hospital, an angelic being named Calsutmoran appeared to me in a vision and explained to me that I needed to find Winston Pringle and stop him. I told you.

So you've found him.

Yes.

Have you stopped him?

Not yet. I'm, you know, taking temporary advantage of his access to high-quality research chemicals.

Jesus, Johnny.

Just dabbling, he said. This is my life's work, brother. Pringle is dangerous. The Pittsburgh Project—he's not some unwilling patsy; he *is* the project. His whole shtick is a double-fake. I'm on to him. I'm going to stop him before he destroys the world.

You sound crazy, I said.

Don't worry, I've got it all worked out.

Apparently.

You have any beers?

In the fridge.

We sat at the table.

It's good to see you, I said.

I missed you, too, honey pie, he told me.

I may have made some poor professional choices myself, I said.

Morrison, Johnny said, what have I been telling you?

IV. THE TIME BEING

1

You have 1 new friend request from Helen Witold.

2

Birthday dinner with my parents always came after my birthday had passed in order to commemorate, approximately, the date of our release from the hospital and therefore, my mother said, her own contribution to the accomplishment, which was—crunch of an ice cube—significant, you have to admit. So it was the Saturday after my birthday, the week after the party, that Lauren Sara and I met my parents at the Hyeholde, my parents' favorite restaurant, a venerable fieldstone pile in a stand of willows on some farmland out by the airport. The menu consisted principally of creatures harvested from the forests nearby. I'd actually taken Lauren Sara there once before. This was during a period in which she'd rejected veganism as a first-world affectation that was intolerable in a world in which billions subsisted on a calorie-poor diet. She had a medium-rare rack of venison, and I do remember that we did actually have sex that night. Now, however, and despite our recent rounds with Mark and Helen, I suspected that she wouldn't eat meat in front of my parents, which threatened to make the whole evening ridiculous. More ridiculous.

And yet, despite the fact that she could never remember her name, or at least pretended never to remember it, I was convinced that my mother actually liked Lauren Sara, or at any rate felt that she served an instrumental purpose, which was, for Mom, effectively the same sentiment. I always suspected that my mother secretly wanted to ensure that her son not end up like his father, a genial, prosperous goof playing second fiddle to a woman of superior achievements, and that Lauren Sara, unlike the girl who preceded her, seemed likely to fulfill these requirements. The more I considered it, the more certain I was that there had been a tugging fear wrapped up in Mom's ostensible affection for Katherine; she was not, after all, an affectionate woman; and it may have been in part her oddly sentimental approval of that pairing that had nudged me into infidelity. When I'd confessed to my mother that cheating was the cause of Katherine's and my breakup, she'd been less dismayed than I'd anticipated. Had I detected a flicker of pleasure before she composed her face for disapproval? I sometimes thought I'd been manipulated, the appearance of one thing maneuvering me into achieving its opposite and actually desired outcome. In any case, her tolerance for Lauren Sara felt provisional upon her conviction that Lauren Sara was what Lareun Sara appeared to be, and it pleased me to think that this appearance was itself a bit of a concoction.

Fortunately there was trout on the menu for Lauren Sara, and the Pirates were finally winning, which gave my dad something to murmur on about while we made our way through our salads and our first round of cocktails. Lauren Sara was surprisingly conversant, and I said, When did you become such a baseball fan? I've always been a fan, she said. Really? I said. I think Barmes is going to take us into October, said Dad.

I hear you saw your grandmother again, Mom said later on after our main courses had arrived.

Yes, I said. At the party. You were invited.

Your father hates parties, Mom said.

Now, Suzanne, I don't hate parties per se. I enjoyed myself at the Reynoldses', you remember.

Larry's retirement? Mom said. Honey, that was in 2008.

Was it? Yes, I suppose we were talking a lot about the election. Well, nevertheless, I had a good time.

Peter likes parties, Lauren Sara said; there was no reason to think so, but I thought that she meant something else, only I wasn't certain what.

Peter hated parties when he was little, my mother said. He always came home crying.

It's true, I said. I was an exquisitely sensitive youth.

What happened? asked Lauren Sara.

I grew up, I said.

Well, said my mother, I'm not sure that all the evidence is in just yet.

Red or white with our entrées? asked my father from behind the wine list.

And how is Nanette? Mom asked me.

Her foot seems recovered. She was enjoying herself dissing the nouveaux riches.

Is that who you're hanging out with these days?

Peter *is* the nouveau riche, said Lauren Sara. Totally.

Not exactly, I said.

You always had such interesting friends, my dad said. I think I'm going to order the Allegrini, unless someone is having fish.

I'm having fish, said Lauren Sara, but I'm not really a wine drinker.

A woman after my own heart, Mom said.

Well, Dad said, Peter and I will manage, won't we?

Speaking of your interesting friends, said my mother, how's little Johnny doing?

Lauren Sara snorted. Little Johnny?

He used to be, I said.

Whoa, she said. That's hard to imagine.

He's been better, I said.

And what is he doing these days? asked my dad, who was searching the room for our waiter. Wasn't he writing a screenplay?

He's always writing a screenplay, I said. It was true, if not strictly so. Johnny's screenplay was an artifact of our adolescence that he still claimed to be working on even though I knew for a fact that he hadn't written a word in ten years. It was set in a small town in rural West Virginia and had the elements of a murder mystery, a courtroom drama, and a gothic horror. He claimed it was a retelling of the Abraham narrative from the Old Testament, with the role of God played by a bigfoot.

Ah, my father replied. Well, I don't imagine you can rush

THE BEND OF THE WORLD   219

that sort of thing. I always— But he broke off, because the waiter had arrived.

While he and the waiter engaged in a hushed conversation over the list, Mom said, So why isn't he doing so well?

Drugs, said Lauren Sara.

I let my eyes settle on hers for a moment; she pretended not to notice.

He never was a teetotaler, Mom said. But you'd think he'd know better, what with his brother and all.

What about his brother? Lauren Sara asked.

Nothing, I said.

My mother offered me her purest expression of consternation. Really, Peter, she said. It's not as if it's some taboo. He died, she said to Lauren Sara. An overdose.

They don't actually know that it was an overdose, I said.

Everyone knows that's what it was, Mom replied. We agreed to a degree of ambiguity in order to preserve the feelings of their poor grandmother.

Well, anyway, I said. Apparently he doesn't know better. Although I did just see him and he seemed to be doing all right, relatively speaking.

I always liked your friend Johnny, Dad said. A real character. I remember when you two boys first met.

Hey, speaking of which, I said. Who is this William Morrison character that Nana was going on about?

Bill? Dad asked.

No, I said. William. You told me we didn't have any English relatives.

What are you talking about? Mom snapped. I didn't think she meant it to come out as quite such a bark.

Nana, I said, mentioned at the party that we had a cousin in England named William Morrison. And you told me that there was no such person.

Really, Peter, Mom said. She was talking to my father.

He sighed. The waiter arrived with the wine. My father sniffed the cork. My father swirled his glass, smelled, sipped, made the tight-lipped grimace that is a wine drinker's approving expression. He sighed again. Well, buddy, he said, the truth is, and you're certainly old enough to know, there were some related Morrisons in England, including your, well, I guess he'd be your first cousin twice removed, William. But the family is rather . . . embarrassed of that connection, and we generally feel it's best not to mention it.

Oh Jesus, I said.

Well, Dad said, they were . . . I should put this delicately.

They were members of the British Union, my mother said.

Yes, said Dad. And you can imagine, this was a source of some embarrassment for the family after the war, your grandfather in particular.

Why?

I should think it would be obvious, said my mother.

Well, of course, he'd lost most of his money, you know, Dad said, but I wasn't sure which of us he was addressing.

No, I said. I don't know.

Yes, hm, said my dad, and he gulped down half a glass of wine, uncharacteristically, and poured himself another. Well, he got involved in some sort of crackpot scheme with a German inventor by the name of Wilhelm Zollen. Hm, well, interestingly, the person who was always fascinated by this was your friend Johnny's grandfather, who, you know, was always working on that perpetual motion machine invention in his shed. Yes, I suppose that's where Johnny first heard it from.

We know that's where he heard it from, my mother interjected. We had to call him and have a little talk after you came home from school when you boys met.

My father shrugged and sipped his wine again and continued. In any case, Peter, it was all a confidence game. Your grandfather was fortunate to have married your grandmother when he did. She managed to wrangle some money out of the British Morrisons, who had some industrial concerns, and, you know, she really did run the business for all those years. But of course it wasn't very fashionable to admit that your family fortune had been resuscitated by a gang of British sympathizers.

So, what about Zollen? What, you're going to tell me he was some sort of German spy?

A spy? My father chuckled. No, I don't think so. In fact, I don't think he was even really German. The accent was just apparently a put-on, as far as your grandmother can recall. Hm, well, I never met him, of course, but I've seen pictures. He was very fat. No, no. A spy? No, but he did end up in jail. His problem was, well, there's no delicate way to put it, really, was that he was perhaps a little too fond of . . . that is to say—

He was a pedophile, said my mother. Little boys.

Well, my dad said, teenagers.

Really, Peter, said my mother.

3

Jesus fucking Christ, I said on the way home. My family is so weird. And what about this shit? Wihlem Zollen? Can you believe it? Johnny's going to shit himself. Lauren Sara didn't say anything. I glanced at her. What? I said. Nothing, she said. You're being weird, too, I said. Listen, she said, there's something I want to tell you. That doesn't sound good, I said. You have to promise to be cool, she said. Okay, I said. I promise to be cool. Cool, she said. A pause. Then: I'm breaking up with you. I almost ran off the parkway. The wheels hummed on the buzz-strip dividing the lane from the shoulder before I regained control. What? I said. You promised to be cool, she said. That's before I knew what you were going to say, I said. Yeah, that's why I made you promise first, she replied. Jesus fucking Christ, I said, why? You just don't seem to be super into it. What do you mean? I said. I'm totally into it. Aren't we both more into it than ever? Yeah, she said. I don't know. I guess, but it feels like something else. I mean, come on, Peter. I mean, if you were super into it, what's the deal with Helen? What about her? I asked. Well, you fucked her, for one, said Lauren Sara. No, I didn't, I said. Peter, she said. Okay, fine, I said. But whatever. That doesn't have anything to do with anything. No, I mean, I agree, Lauren Sara said, but the thing is, I don't care about the sex part. That's cool. Whatever. I mean, it's just like you don't care that I hook up with Derek sometimes. What it is, is the whole creepy Internet stalker thing. You sleep with Derek? I said. I couldn't believe it. What the fuck! You knew that, she said. No, I didn't, I said. He told

me he told you, Lauren Sara said. Well, he fucking didn't, I
replied. Oh, she said. I hope that's cool. No, I said. It's not
fucking cool. How the fuck would that be fucking cool? And
what the fuck do you mean, Internet stalker? You left your
browser history open the other day, she said. No, I didn't, I
said. Who leaves their browser history open? I don't know, she
said. I stopped by on Thursday last week and it was open on
your computer. You were at work. Oh Christ, I said. Johnny.
What? she said. Fuck, I said. This is such bullshit. I can't
believe you fucked Derek! I can't believe you want to break up.
We'll still be cool, she said. I mean, we can still have sex sometimes, you know, if you're into it. Fuck, I said. Or not, she
said. No, I said. That's not what I mean. We'd reached the top
of Greentree Hill, and we stopped. Traffic went bumper-to-
bumper down the long descent to the Fort Pitt Tunnel. Nothing was moving. The next day, in the paper, we'd learn that a
seal had blown on a gas truck in the tunnel. Everything had to
be diverted out to the West End. It took an hour to cover the
two miles from where we were to the detour, and neither of us
said another word in that time.

4

I had nothing to do. Mark had gone out of town on one of his
vague missions, and there was no work. I sat in my office with
the door closed and went back to reading blogs. I watched an
old animated .gif of the mayor pulling his head off to reveal
a dinosaur skull on Alieyinz in a loop for hours, giggling

uncontrollably as an approximation of tears. I read Facebook updates. Helen's remained unchanged, her most recent post a link to a postdated museum page about Jergen Steinman. I watched animal videos. I tried to call Johnny, but he never answered. In a series of texts, I told him he was an asshole. Then I told him: I believe. He replied to that one: headless lives, he wrote, and he included an address that Google showed me to be somewhere off PA 268 up near East Brady.

Then it was Thursday night. I'd come home to discover that my squirrel had chewed through the screen, chewed into and eaten the rest of a box of granola that I'd left out on the counter, and taken a squirrel shit on the dish towel I'd left beside it. *Et tu*, and all that, I thought. I thought about calling my mother.

I thought, I am thirty years old with no girlfriend and just one close friend, if you can even call him that anymore; my work is purposeless; it isn't even work; it isn't anything; my boss is probably a sociopath, or, if not, an alien from another dimension, because what human, given the option to do otherwise, given the option to do nothing or anything else at all, would willfully choose to do what he did, ranging from one bland office to another, tossing grenades at balance sheets, before jetting off to the next pointless exercise? I thought, Oh God, *I'm* that human. I thought, Maybe I should do something to give some sort of form to my life, because, at last, when the books have been closed and the accounts settled, the bills paid and the paychecks deposited, the promises made and broken, the goods and services bought and sold, the statements reconciled, the tip laid on the counter and the change folded back into the wallet, there is nothing to be saved, there is only one balance, and it only gets smaller, which is this life, and there is only one way to spend it, prudently or in a spree, which is the living of it.

But the world always gives you something better to do than the best thing you could be doing. Someone knocked. I answered the door. Hi, said Helen. She had a six-pack and a bottle of whiskey, which I could already smell on her breath. How did you know where I live? I asked. I don't remember, she said. Well, I said, okay. Come on in.

5

Hey, listen, I said in the morning, what are you doing today?

Oh God, she said. Have you got any Advil?

Probably, I said.

I couldn't sleep, she said. Which was not true. She'd had four of the beers and half of the whiskey before we fell into bed in order to have slapstick, drunken sex that ended with her snoring, one leg uncovered, and me with the spins, sick and unable to sleep myself until just around dawn. But all drunks pretend to be unsound sleepers; thus are hangovers transformed. It was ten-thirty in the morning.

Found some, I said from the bathroom.

Some what?

Aspirin, I said, emerging. Here.

All I need is some vodka to wash it down.

Haha, I said, but I shouldn't have. So listen, I said. What are you doing today?

I was planning on staring at the paintings in my studio for a while and getting stoned enough to take a nap. Why?

Do you want to go somewhere strange with me? I said

A motel in the woods, probably full of freaks and weirdos, I didn't say.

Sounds killer, she said.

6

So we ate some breakfast around lunchtime, or I ate breakfast, and Helen drank a Bloody Mary and picked out the innards of her omelet, then we got gas and bad gas-station coffee, which was the sort of thing that assholes like us considered to be mild transgressions, and headed out 28 toward Kittanning. It had stormed overnight, not hard, but the heat had broken, and it was one of those odd days in Pennsylvania that are sunny and cloudy all at once; the sky as far as you could see enrobed in light gray clouds, their undersides glowing like a Belgian block street in the bright sunlight just after the rain. We drove with the windows down and the radio tuned to an opera broadcast out of Chicago or L.A.; I can't remember, but I remember it was *Lucia*. Helen said, You know, I thought you'd drive a different car.

You've seen my car, I said.

I don't think so.

THE BEND OF THE WORLD

I'm pretty sure.

I expected a BMW.

You're not the only one.

What do you mean?

Nothing. Something someone else said to me. You know, I used to work for a guy who was really into cars, and then I had to fire him.

Do you have any cigarettes?

Glove compartment. There's a lighter in there somewhere, too.

Thanks. You had to fire your old boss?

I didn't exactly fire him. I mean, I wasn't the one who actually did it. It sort of happened in my general vicinity.

That's what you get with him.

Who, Mark? What do you get?

It's hard to say, really. How old are these cigarettes? They taste like a glove compartment.

Old, I said. Emergency only.

Gross, she said, but she kept on smoking. What I mean, she went on, is that around Mark things seem to have a habit of happening without happening. You realize something's changed, but how did it change, and when did it change?

That's true.

I hate it, she said.

How did you two get together? I asked. I mean, did you start dating right after you met?

I don't know, she said. There he was. I realized something had changed.

Oh, I said.

So this is going to be a party? Or what?

To be honest, I don't know. Yes, a party, I think. Or an art show, maybe. With bands? I'm sort of trying to track down my friend. He's gone off the deep end a little. Also, he may have been right about something.

How can you tell?

To be honest, I said, I'm not really sure.

Well, I could use a good party.

I can't promise you that.

She touched my arm. That has its own kind of promise, she said. I felt a thrill mingled with dread that went straight to my dick, even though, in my so-far limited experience, sex with Helen was a less desultory but also less satisfying affair than sex with Lauren Sara, and I was beginning to suspect that it was all the promise of Helen, rather than Helen herself, that had taken me in. I took the wheel with my right arm to break the contact between us, and I was beginning to regret the decision that I'd made, although, to be honest, I wasn't actually sure what, if any, decision that was.

From Kittanning we took 268 for a few miles, two narrow lanes over the hills, the woods on either side, my car sandwiched between two suicidal tanker trunks on their way to or from one of the new gas rigs that had sprung up like monster-movie mushrooms all over that part of the state. Helen had fallen asleep, and I was glad, because I drove with both hands gripping the wheel, leaning forward like my grandmother. We turned off on a county road through the woods. The shoulders were washed out on either side. It wound its way up a hill for another mile or two. Helen was awake. Where are we? she asked.

The cut, I said.

Look, she said. Balloons. And there they were, tied to a post at the end of a driveway like at a child's birthday party or a graduation cookout, a bunch of grocery store Mylar balloons, although, as we passed, I saw that someone had drawn pentagrams on their silver skin in black marker.

The driveway led to a clearing of a few acres. In the middle was an old two-story lodge with an alpine character; a balcony wrapped around the second floor under broad eves. There were already a dozen or so cars parked; one couple, a man and a woman, walked down a path toward the woods on the far side of the field. I pulled off the drive onto the grass and parked beside an old Chrysler. Only by accident I saw its plate as we walked down the drive toward the lodge. WCHY-POO, it read.

7

Ah, the fat man said. Herr Morrison.

It looked like a ski lodge indoors, too. A shitty ski lodge. Partitions had been erected in the main hall, poorly done gallery walls on which hung all manner of drug-inspired art. You know the type. Heads breaking open to expose mandalas and that sort of trash. Tableaux of action figures. Knickknacks strung together with florist wire. There were old couches and chairs here and there; the hall was a sort of atrium in the center of the lodge, lit by skylights, but the glass was dirty, and if the cloudy light outside had a magical undersea quality, in there it was like opening your eyes underneath a murky river. But Pringle didn't disappoint. He was seated on a loveseat, its color somewhere between turd and loam, and, given his bulk— it's hard to express just how fat he really was; he seemed like a creature from some watery planet with a lower gravity—the love seat appeared almost like an armchair beneath him. He was wearing a United States Department of the Interior ball cap and a big white apron stained with some kind of sauce. He looked, I thought, familiar. There were a dozen other people in the room, wandering in the aimless fashion that art of any quality confers on the people who have committed to looking at it, or else lying on the suspect couches, smoking. A few of them were women; the rest appeared to be barely older than boys. Pringle was unattended. I'd half expected to find Johnny doing duty as a human ottoman, but he wasn't around.

Winston Pringle, I presume.

Yes, he said, and I feel thankful that I am here to welcome you. He turned his little dark eyes on Helen. And you, my dear, are not who I was expecting at all.

I'm not, she said. I'm someone else.

This delighted him, and he clapped as he giggled. Indeed! he said. I could not have said it better myself. Won't you have a seat? Would you like a drink?

No, I said.

Yes, Helen said.

Have a drink, Pringle told me. Mandy! he called, and a

petite woman of indeterminate age—her posture suggested
thirty-five, but her face and hair implied another decade or
two—rose from one of the couches after extinguishing a cigarette and came over. Mandy, he said, this is the infamous Peter
Morrison, and his lovely traveling companion.

Helen, Helen said.

Helen, Pringle repeated. The woman who launched a thousand starships.

Hm, I said.

Two cold beers, Pringle said, unless you'd prefer something
stronger.

Beer is fine, I said.

It's a start, Helen said.

You know, I told Pringle, you look awfully familiar.

I could say the same, he replied.

I can't quite place it.

Ah, but I can, he said. You remind me of my dear old dad.

Why does that not surprise me? I said. Cheers.

Don't be too eager to take it as a compliment, he told me.
My father was one of the most powerful men in history, a
deep, devious, and very dangerous man.

Oh yeah? I said. I think Johnny may have mentioned that.
He was going to open the time portal at the Point, right?

A bowdlerized version, said Pringle, but sufficient. And how
about you, mademoiselle? How do you fit into the picture?

Peter and I are having a torrid love affair, she said.

Well, I said.

Oh, delightful, Pringle said. I have always felt that my little
annual gatherings could use a solid infusion of heterosexual-

ity. They tend—he waved vaguely—toward the ephebophilic. I only ask that if you do engage in any such, ahem, predilections, you try to do so in one of the orgone accumulators conveniently located throughout the property.

The what? asked Helen.

Mandy arrived and handed us our beers. What're you going to do with all that orgone? I asked.

No funny stuff, Pringle said. Just a little cloud-busting for the weekend. Wouldn't want rain at the barbecue.

So, I said. Where's Johnny?

Mandy raised an eyebrow at Pringle and gave an almost imperceptible shake of her head. He is, I'm afraid, indisposed at the moment, Pringle said.

He's resting, said Mandy.

Resting, I repeated.

He may, Pringle said, have overindulged ever so slightly over the last few days, but Mandy has him on a strict regimen of rice protein and kombucha. We expect him to be in full working order by the evening.

You know, I said, no offense, but the last thing Johnny needs is more drugs in his life.

I disagree entirely, said Pringle. He's on the verge of something very important, I feel.

He's on the verge of dying, I said.

Potato, potahto, said Pringle. But if you will excuse me, Herr Morrison, I have certain duties to attend to. We'll be dining—your friend included—in my private dining room. Suite twenty-three, haha. I hope you'll join us. I insist you join us. He went to rise but found it difficult to get out of his seated position. He tried to rock forward, but didn't quite make it. Mandy offered her hand, but he pushed it away. Now, now, my dear. I just need to get a little momentum. I stared at him as he repeated the maneuver and hauled himself out of the chair. I stared at him as he waddled across through a door beside the dingy hearth.

No fucking way, I said.

You know, Helen said, I swear to God I've had nightmares about that guy.

Un-fucking-canny, I said.

8

We did not take advantage of the orgone accumulators. They're just boxes, Helen said. Uh-huh, I said, exactly. What the fuck? she said. We did take advantage of the fact that someone always seemed to be asking if you needed a beer when you needed a beer. The cloud cover had resolved itself into a more distant scattering of cumuli, and the breeze had stopped blowing, and there was a stillness in the air that amplified the sounds of insects and birds in the grass and in the woods. We wandered the grounds for a while—dirt and gravel paths wound through the lawn and the fields and the nearer, thinner trees. Other than the plywood accumulators, there were a few old outlying cabins, a few fire pits, an odd collection of lawn chairs and chaise longues sprouting here and there. We found ourselves in a pair of peeling Adirondack chairs at some point. As the afternoon passed, people arrived, filling the upper field with cars. They lugged pieces of dirty art out of their trunks, or brought drum kits and guitars. They were mostly younger than me, although a few middle-aged folks as yet enamored with the romance of rejecting something rolled up as well, unkempt and gray and zany in an entirely unendearing way. It was true that the attendance skewed toward the male and toward the immediate postadolescent and toward the gay, but no more so than any hipster bar, and there were plenty of wide-hipped chicks with pretty boyfriends as well. Some of them brought tents and other accoutrements of camping, although none of them was dressed for camp: their jeans were too tight, or they wore ripped shorts; they wore open-toed shoes or vintage sneakers. These people, I said at one point, would not survive a night in the woods. The panthers would get them. Or the bigfoots. Helen said she didn't take me for such an outdoorsman. I said hardly but I know better than to wear Roman sandals to a campground. She said that do be fair we were hardly outfitted for camping. We're not camping, I said; we're on a rescue operation. Your friend Johnny, she said, whom I've never met. My best friend, I said, since we were kids. What're we rescuing him from? she asked; the clutches of Winston Pringle? He seems like a harmless kook. No, no, I said. From himself. Well, she said. That could be more difficult. It poses some ontological difficulties. I like a woman, I said, who says ontological difficulties. Don't get ahead of yourself, she said. I went to art school. I learned to say a lot of things that I don't understand. She looked toward the forest. I've always wanted to meet a bigfoot, she said. See a bigfoot? I said. Either way, she said.

We walked some more. It is always preferable to attend a party where you know no one and are known by no one. A party where you know and are known has the quality of a dream; it rushes by, unmoored from causation and progression, scene after scene arriving, correlated, somehow, but unconnected; when you don't know anybody, or what you're celebrating, or why you're there, it becomes less a dream and more a dance, less a movie and more an arrangement of bodies in space, a sculpture, a mobile pivoting slowly around you. There were some girls doing yoga in the grass. There were some boys playing guitars. There were some dogs living the pure delight of a few hours of unbelonging. Everyone had their phones and took a lot of pictures. There was a crew putting together a wooden scaffold of some kind. It's an owl, one of them said when we asked. Like at the real Bohemian Grove. It doesn't look like an owl, I said. It looks like a horse, said Helen. Guys, the guy said, these guys say it looks like a horse. No way, dude, said another guy. It's a fucking owl. I don't know, said the first guy. He rubbed his face and lit a cigarette. It does have a horsey quality. Fuck that shit, said a third guy, who, upon closer inspection, was a girl. It's a fucking owl. Use your imagination.

Someone was shooting bottle rockets. Someone was riding a unicycle. A group of girls were smoking a joint and making fun of the guy on the unicycle. A guy told one of the yoga girls that he'd like to do her downward-facing-doggy-style and laughed. The girl started to cry. Someone called him an asshole. Two young dudes made out in an orgone accumulator. It had gotten very hot. The sun was high. Maybe there's some-

thing to this cloud-busting shit after all, I said. I love all this
bad art, Lauren Sara said. But, no, I was with Helen. Helen
said that. Peter Morrison, someone said. I turned around.
My weed dealer? Scooty? I said. What are you doing here?
We shook hands like business colleagues. Drumming up biz,
he said. I come to this shit every year. He looked at Helen.
You smoke weed? he asked. I drink, she said. He laughed. I
gotta make the rounds, he said. You let me know if you need
anything. I like this party, Helen said. Really? I asked. Why? I
haven't done anything like this since college, she said. I'm not
sure that recommends it, I said. Peter Morrison, she said, resting her hand lightly and briefly on my neck, her fingers in the
curls of my hair, you are such a buzz kill.

Someone said, Oh my God I was down at the river with
Tom he has the biggest dick ever. Someone said, Have you
seen Mandy she was supposed to meet us? Someone said, He's
a fucking pervert. Someone said, I left it in my car, maybe.
Someone said, They used to date, I guess, but he was more
into his Tumblr. Someone said, I worked at the co-op for a
while but then they were all, like, we need you to come in an
hour earlier and I was all, like, fuck that shit. Someone said,
He's definitely got a problem but I don't want to say anything because he'd probably just tell me that I do a lot, too,
but that's totally not the point and he knows it. Someone said,
Fucking mosquitoes. Someone said, There's never any food
here we should drive down to the gas station who's coming?
Someone said, Who's Winston Pringle? Someone said, I saw
them making out in one of those boxes. Someone said, Last
year they lit the whole thing on fire like at Burning Man but I

guess maybe it caught someone's car on fire, too, so this year they're just doing a regular bonfire. Someone said, This weed sucks have you see Scooty? Someone said, Where the fuck is Mandy? Someone said, I've got a job interview there tomorrow but I told them I was going to probably be late or maybe have to miss it and they were all, like, Well, if you miss it you don't get the job and I just think that's such bullshit because I have a life, too, you know. Someone said, No, if you wait long enough he'll definitely show you his dick. Someone said, Does anyone know who that dude is with the hot girl? Someone said, if you can't find Mandy you should ask Johnny? Someone said, Who's Johnny. Someone said, He's just a fucking junkie but he hangs out with Dr. Wilhelm and usually has some stuff. Someone said, Who's Dr. Wilhelm? Someone said, It's Pringle. Someone said, Wait, who? Someone said, Yeah, he's a real pervert, but it's so cheap it's worth it. Someone said, Peeeter Moooooorison!

We turned toward the house. Johnny was on the second floor. He appeared to be wearing a bathrobe. He called again across the yard. Come eat yer dinner!

9

The private dining room was in fact just another of the lodge's guest rooms emptied of beds and nightstands with a rough picnic table in the middle. Pringle didn't sit at the table, but reclined in a nestlike rattan chair with his various plates and bowls of food balanced on his belly as they arrived and

departed. Helen and I sat on one side; Johnny, freshly showered and dressed in a familiar uniform of shorts and a hunting
vest, sat across from us. To old friends and new, Pringle said,
and raised a plastic cup to us. Here here, said Mandy. Her big
dog had stalked around the exterior of the room and then
curled into a ball in the corner.

We were eating corn and barbecue on paper plates. Pringle
was asking me about the flying saucers. Helen and I described
them. Yes, he said, those are most likely emissions from a
future iteration of Project Pittsburgh. We have yet to actually
make contact with them. We believe that they're returning to
the past in order to complete some necessary task that would
otherwise be overlooked, thus dooming the Project to failure.
Having achieved our ultimate goal, which is total probabalis-
tic determination, or TPD, they are able to move up and down
the time spiral, self-editing their own history. It's very interesting that you saw them when you did. Typically, they don't
arrive until summer.

Perennials, I said.

Pringle either didn't get or didn't care that I was making
fun. Yes, he said. Very astute. They are actually associated
with the harvest, particularly in ancient Egypt. We presume
they are also associated with the dog-headed god Anubis.

Mandy's dog raised his head and gave an approving woof.

Distant relative? Helen said.

That's his name, actually, said Mandy. She pulled off a rib
and tossed it to the beast. Stinky, she said. Yummy-yums.

So straight through the stargate, huh? I said.

Of course, we have no idea what they were doing that far

back, Pringle replied. Interestingly, we've discovered that FTL and transtemporal navigation is closer in form and fact to the Guild Navigators from Frank Herbert's *Dune* series. Among other sources of inspiration, it was the early recovery and medical examination of pilots from UFO crashes that first sent us down the path of pharmaco-temporal manipulation. The Russians got to it at Tunguska. We suspect, but cannot prove, that Rasputin was able to isolate certain compounds from the alien's body that became the principal source of his power and apparent imperviousness to ordinary physical harm, but the chaos of the Revolution significantly impeded their progress in such research. The Germans of course believed otherwise, which ultimately led to Hitler's ill-conceived invasion of Russia. We—the Americans, I mean—were never especially concerned; not until we figured out that the Germans and the Russians had been after it. Then of course came Roswell, and we quickly moved into similar lines of research. As with the Manhattan Project, the core of our team consisted of former Germans with a few Russians and Poles.

I thought they were extradimensional, I said. But now you say they're aliens.

A term of art, really, said Pringle. Recall they emanate from the distant future. We have no idea what sort of physiological evolution they may have undergone. They may have even directed their own evolution. An intriguing possibility that we are investigating. After all, how likely is it that actual extraterrestrials, evolving in an entirely alien biosphere under completely different planetary conditions, would end up looking

like little gray men? Whereas, if human evolution were to continue. Well, you can imagine.

So let me ask you this, I said. If this whole shebang is such
a goddamn secret, how come you can write a bunch of books
about it?

Ah, said Pringle. Fortunately, in a parallel time track, I
have been able to convince my compatriots on the Project that
the Winston Pringle self-modality who is writing the books
is engaging in a necessary kind of disinformation. By telling
a truth so strange it appears to be fiction, the true truth is
obscured.

The true truth, Helen said.

The best kind, said Johnny.

That's what I was thinking, Helen said.

I like this new girlfriend of yours, Johnny told me.

She's not my girlfriend, I said.

I'm his boss's girlfriend, she said.

No shit, said Mandy. I thought you were a fag. No offense.

None taken.

That's what I've been telling him for years, said Johnny. He
positively reeks of sexual deviancy.

You haven't been telling me that for years. You once accused
me of an aggressive heterosexuality that resembles American
imperialism.

Did I say that? said Johnny. I'm very quotable, aren't I?

The point being, haha, said Pringle, that if you view higher
dimensionality from a calculitic perspective, the difference
between time travel and space travel becomes extremely vague.

So, I said, what's their deal? The UFOs. What are they doing in Pittsburgh, uh, out of season?

Presumably, Pringle said, still ignoring my tone, they are drawn by the psycho-temporal distortions in the local time field caused by the Project as it nears its completion.

Is it near completion? Helen asked. She pressed her knee against mine. Our eyes met. She grinned privately, just for me.

Oh, very. December, or thereabouts. They don't know that I plan to preempt them.

They? I said.

The Project, he said.

Including you? I mean, aren't you part of the Project?

Possibly including me. Possibly including *you*. He turned to Helen. Very possibly including you, my dear.

Me? she said. I just moved here.

Time tracks can be tricky, Pringle said. And, of course, none of us can be sure if we are or are not involved. But I have a strong feeling about you. I've seen you, you know.

Oh yeah? she said.

Yes, Pringle said. In dreamtime. I very clearly recall seeing you enter the main Time Chamber with a reptiloid humanoid.

Haha, I said. Maybe it was Mark.

Maybe it was, she said. She didn't laugh.

I'm kidding, I said.

Me, too, she said.

So where's the Time Chamber?

Directly under the fountain at Point State Park, Johnny said.

For real? I gave him a look that held the promise of mutual understanding if he'd just give me some sign that he found this whole deal as much a trip as I did, but he only raised an eyebrow at me, and I admit that, despite all my efforts to the contrary, I began to wonder what was really going on.

Of course, Pringle said, it's on a separate time track.

Of course, I said.

You're very dismissive, Mandy said.

What's *your* deal? I said.

Merchandising, she replied.

You know, Pringle said, we're not so different, you and I. He fixed me in his unblinking Murine gaze.

I'd probably beg to differ, I said.

Children of privilege he said. Scions of a powerful family.

I'm not sure I'd call my family powerful, I said.

Bearing the burdens of a past fascism, seeking amends.

No, I said. I don't think I'd agree with that characterization, precisely.

Your grandfather, you know, was involved heavily in the Westinghouse empire.

Did Johnny tell you that? I asked. Johnny shrugged. In fact, my grandfather wasn't much of a businessman after all.

Regardless, Pringle said, I can see you have yet to cut the cord.

Oh no? I said.

Verily, Pringle said.

Amen, I said.

Well, ahem, Pringle said. Dessert?

I could use another drink, said Helen.

I'm sure you could, Johnny said.

She glared at him.

I was thinking, Pringle said, more along the lines of a pick-me-up.

I've got a little coke, said Helen. I tilted my head. A girl's gotta be prepared, she said.

Thank you, no, dear. I propose we instead imbibe in something altogether more potent.

No, thanks, I said.

Live a little, Johnny told me.

I intend to, I said.

Fear of death is an animal emotion, Johnny responded.

Well, then me and Anubis over there will be dancing partners for the evening.

The dog, hearing his name, gave a pleased, throaty little bark and slapped his tail a few times against the floor.

10

But I was steadfast in my refusal to take any of Pringle's weird concoction, and after a bit of cajoling and the offer of a complimentary hand scan, the dinner party broke up. Some young, smoother, more attractive boys than Johnny or me required his product and his attention; Mandy and the dog went off to continue the distribution of the sacraments; a band was playing out by the bonfire. A crowd was smoking and drinking and dancing under the crooked wooden horse. Helen had had one too many and told me she was going to go do a few

bumps to sober up. It seemed like an offer of sex, but when I
looked at her, her hair falling across her face, a slight redness
to her eyes, that brittle, careful timbre returning to her voice, I
got depressed; I thought, Lauren Sara never looked like that; I
said, No, thanks, and maybe Helen understood something else
in it, because she frowned furiously before she walked away. I
was at last alone with Johnny on the balcony looking out over
the field. You've got a real way with women, Morrison. Maybe
you *are* a fag.

I wish, I said.

You look like shit, he told me.

It's been a weird couple of days.

You know, your new employer is implicated in the Pittsburgh Project.

I'm not surprised.

I'm thinking of doing a significant exposé, Johnny said. On
my blog.

Come on, I said. I thought you'd quit blogging.

It is possible, Johnny said, that I may still blog a bit here
and there.

You ought to watch it, I said. Everyone's still pissed off
about that Alieyinz shit.

I have no idea what you're talking about

Whatever. Derek told me that Jonah Kantsky is looking for
the perp.

Kantsky? Did you know he's ex-Mossad?

That's the rumor, I said.

How is Derek? Still doing the dirty work of the corporate
surveillance state global gulag?

He's fine, I said. Except that he fucked Lauren Sara.

So? Johnny said. Didn't they used to date?

Recently, I said.

Oh. He shrugged. Want me to kill him? Mandy can dispose of the body.

I hope you're joking.

We'll lure him up here, sacrifice him to that buffalo, and dump him in the river.

What buffalo? The horse?

It's supposed to be an owl. Like—

The Bohemian Grove, I said.

I've missed you, Johnny said.

What the fuck are you doing out here? I said.

It'll all be finished soon.

Johnny, I said.

Seriously. Trust me. This is nothing permanent. It's just something I'm working on for the time being.

For the time being? I said.

Just for the time being, he said.

I hope so, I said.

Helen returned, looking both more awake and more miserable. What's wrong? I said.

I want to go, she said.

I'm too drunk, I said. We're stuck.

Fuck that, she said. The cocaine, or something, had made her angry. This is fucking boring. I want to go. She was tired, suddenly, with that ironic, exhausted look that comes after too many visits with stimulants in too short a span, and for the first time I considered her age and realized that she must

actually be nearly forty, a discomfiting thought, because
while thirty seems the far rim of a yawning canyon all
through your twenties, right up to the very last second of your
twenty-ninth-year, the moment you cross into that fourth
decade of your life, forty rushes at you as inevitably as the
ground when you've leapt from a cliff. There was a suggestive dampness around her nostrils. I thought back to that first
night we'd met. I thought of Mark saying, She gets a little
crazy, and then felt badly for thinking it.

You said you liked it.

I don't anymore. I'll drive.

Oh no, I said. You're not driving.

Fuck you, Mark, she said. I can drive.

Who? I said.

Whatever, she said. Give me the keys.

No, no, no, I said. I tried to laugh, as if we were all having a
good time. She stuck out her lip and turned to Johnny.

Fine. Then I want to do the time drug.

He winked at me. I think it's counterindicated with your
other little what-have-you, he said.

I dropped the rest in the toilet, she said. Let's do the other
thing.

Helen, I said.

Who the fuck are you? she said. Fuck off.

Johnny, I said.

Sorry, buddy, he told me. It's the libertarian thing to do.
Don't tread on me. Do what thou wilt and that shall be the
whole of the law. Who is John Galt?

Huh? said Helen.

Follow me, beautiful, Johnny said.

And I, reluctantly, but less reluctantly than I made it appear, followed as well.

11

What's her fucking problem?

We were waiting for the drugs to come up. They were not coming up. Dissociatives were the most infuriating of all psychopharmacological playthings. They messed with your sense of time even before they messed with your sense of time. The ductile moment of anticipation elongated and thinned and became a gossamer thread that caught the breeze and carried your excitement away like a baby spider on its own silk. It was replaced by anxiety and annoyance. It wasn't going to work. The drugs were bogus. Your mind had adapted. Your metabolism had changed. An hour had passed. Fuck it. You got another beer. We were drinking some beers.

I shrugged. Beats me, I said. She dropped the coke in the can.

We were sitting on the edge of the woods. The bands were still playing up by the lodge. The fire was still going strong. It was bright, but not as bright as the city, and you could see the stars overhead.

You can see Canis Major, said Johnny.

Yeah, thanks, Edwin Hubble.

Copernicus.

Tycho Brahe.

Oh, good one. Georges-Henri Lemaître.

Jan Hendrik Oort, motherfucker.

Kip Thorne.

I concede, I said.

Helen was sitting apart from us in the grass and playing with her phone. Thorne, Johnny said, was instrumental in the development of black hole cosmology. Pringle thinks he was involved in the Project back in the seventies.

Was anyone not involved?

Shit goes deep, Johnny said.

Do you really believe this shit? I asked him. I meant, Should I believe it?

I believe everything, he said. A man who believes in everything is surprised by nothing. All eventualities ultimately obtain. The best of all possible worlds is the possibility of all possible worlds.

I think it's starting to work.

No, Johnny said. I'm not feeling it.

She's probably texting Mark, I said. I get the feeling she got a nastygram.

A what?

Oh, God, sorry. Something a coworker used to say. Fortunately, we fired her. Well, she quit.

Fortunately? Johnny turned enough to look at me. How is that fortunate? Fortunate for whom?

She didn't do anything, I said.

Do anything? he said. Jesus fucking Christ. And you think I'm the dangerous one.

I never said that.

No, he said, you didn't.

Helen, I called, are you okay?

I'm getting a drink, she said. She sighed. Want anything?

I'm good, I said.

I've got to make a call, she said. I'll be back.

To who?

She bit her lip with displeasure, seemed about to answer, and then walked away toward the house.

Morrison, Johnny said, you are one smooth motherfucker. How do you keep fooling these chicks into liking you?

Let's take a walk, I said.

12

We walked around the perimeter of the party, but something compelled us to go into the woods. Our fondest memories of each other involved the woods, the acreage north of Johnny's grandparents' house or the other times when Pappy would take us to Raccoon Creek and Ohiopyle and Linn Run. We had been fortunate to be neither very popular nor very unpopular in school; attainment of the former state required a swift, early, and brutal self-amputation of the better part of imagination, the substitution of sarcasm for irreverence, and the acquisition of all the fucked up values of adulthood that adults try to disclaim when they compare the office or the PTA or the neighborhood association to a high school, their cliquey, backbiting colleagues to teenagers. The office and the other women at the gym and the social committee at the church are not like high school, not like teenagers—rather, the opposite. Rather, the young acquire all their most iniquitous habits from the grown-ups in their lives. Meanwhile, the truly unpopular, beset constantly by the depredations of the sociopathic socially adept, had no time for imagination, being too busy simply seeking to avoid attention. But to the slim middle, those of us who were rich enough or self-possessed enough or weird and resilient enough to glide through like distant relatives at a wedding or a funeral, it was possible to cultivate some wonder at the world, and the woods, because they were essentially private, permitted us the expression of it.

13

We were somewhere near the river—we could smell it—when we heard the first shot. I wasn't sure when we'd stopped hearing music, but we had, and then something like a distant thunderclap, but muffled, as if heard through a thick curtain. Did you hear that? I asked Johnny. Huh? he said. He was walking with his head tilted back, his mouth hanging open, staring through the leaves to the stars overhead. What I love about the country, he said, is that you can really see the stars. You're fucked up, I said. Sober as the day is long, he replied. I swear I just heard a gunshot, I told him. Yeah? said Johnny. What's the upshot? Fuck you, I said. Then I felt the pressure change beside my ear and a trunk beside us popped with splinters. This time the report was clearer. Holy shit! I said. Run! Huh?

said Johnny. Run! I grabbed his arm and pulled him after me. It was dark. We took two steps and tripped down a muddy embankment and slid thirty feet into a leaf-choked trickle of a stream. The muck and loam smelled sweet and yeasty. Johnny was on top of me. Fuck, you weigh a ton, I said, but he was giggling and wouldn't move. What's so funny? I said. You have a boner. That's my phone, you asshole. Get off of me. Someone just shot at us.

Oh, I don't know, Johnny said. It's dark. Probably a case of mistaken identity.

We've got to get out of the woods, I said.

No, don't worry, Johnny said. I have excellent night vision. He started laughing again.

Come on, I said, and I pulled him to his feet, and we set off through the mud beside the stream.

But I was feeling pretty high myself, and as my awareness swam into a moment of adrenal lucidity, it occurred to me that we were walking very, very slowly. Johnny was saying something about the time he ran a campaign on the Western Front. We need to find the Fist of Odin, he said.

The what?

The Fist of Odin, dude. It looks sort of like a rock.

Why?

Beats me.

I think we need to find a fucking phone, I said.

Use your boner.

What? Oh, asshole. Yeah. I'd forgotten. I pulled the phone from my pocket, but it was soaked, cracked, ruined. Well, so much for that, I said.

What we need is a good old-fashioned field radio, Johnny said.

Yeah, well, if we happen to stumble across one. We were getting closer to the river. The creek bed was getting rockier, and I could smell the muddy water.

I think we've lost them, Johnny said.

Keep walking.

We're having an adventure! He put his big arm around my shoulder and gave me a sideways hug. Fuck, yeah.

Yeah, I said. We are.

It's a fucking stupid adventure. My pants are all wet.

Mine, too.

I have something to confess, Johnny said.

Oh yeah?

It's possible that I may have been stealing money and, you know, drugs from Pringle.

He delivered the line soberly; he was nonchalant. I shrugged off his arm and pushed him away. Fuck, Johnny! You think maybe that's why someone just took a shot at us?

Whoa, no reason to get pissed at *me*!

Fuck.

You said that already.

We've got to get back to the city, I said. We've got to find my car.

No need! We turned. Pringle stood outlined against the sky like a boulder on a stone outcropping about six feet above us. He was dressed in something like a cross between a paratrooper and a school janitor's uniform.

Behold me and despair! Pringle declaimed.

Shit, we said. He was holding a rifle. It had the look of an antique, and I wondered if it was real, but I didn't know anything about guns, and it looked real enough.

You boys have gone far enough.

Listen, I said. I held up my hands. There's no reason to be crazy. I can pay you. I can cover whatever he took. I make good money. My family's rich.

Oh, you'll pay, all right. You'll pay, Herr Morrison. I've come to balance the accounts.

Johnny tried to step in front of me, arms extended, but he was so stoned that he slipped and fell on his ass in the water. Leave him, he yelled. Take me!

Johnny, Jesus, I said. Get up.

Both of you shut up! Pringle screamed. Then he fired a shot above our heads. The gun was unbearably loud this time, and I realized in some distant, dimly functioning portion of my mind, the cold corner of my consciousness that could see and record and remain disinterested, that I was afraid.

It's Morrison that I want, Pringle said. It's always been Morrison.

What did I do?

Your grandfather, Morrison. He ruined me. He ruined me and took the Project from me. For I *am* Wilhelm Zollen!

My grandfather? You've, uh, aged well, if that's the case.

Olive oil, said Johnny. Is that your secret?

You guys are assholes, said Pringle, now petulant. He seemed as if he were about to leap from the rock, but instead he slung the rifle over his shoulder and sat and dangled his legs over like he was going to ease himself into a swimming

254 J A C O B   B A C H A R A C H

pool, and then he sort of slowly shuffled around and hung by
his arms, his huge ass toward us, and then he dropped the last
couple of feet to the ground. He righted himself slowly and
panted. I guess if we'd been sober, if it had been daylight, if
either of us had been a different sort of person, we might have
taken the opportunity to jump him and take the gun, or to run
away, but Johnny just sat there in the stream, and I just stood
there, and Pringle caught his breath and cried, I am his son! So
you're not him, I said. You're his son.

I am both him and his son.

Johnny also did a very good Faye Dunaway: I'm both him
and his son!

You're so gay, I said.

You're so gay, he said.

Both of you are so gay, Pringle bellowed.

But what do you want with me? said Johnny, now a bit petulant himself as he realized that he might not be at the center
of this little plot.

You? It was never about you, you fool! You patsy! You . . .
homo! You were never more than the bait in the trap, the lure
on the fishing line, the, uh . . .

Salt lick, I suggested.

Chum, said Johnny.

Will you two fucking cut it out!

I think we're getting to him, I said.

Yeah, said Johnny. By the way, Pringle, your drugs fucking
suck. I'm not even high.

For real, I said.

My plan— began Pringle.

Yeah, I said. We're not really interested.

Nope, said Johnny.

My plan! said Pringle. Was always to draw you here and incapacitate you, Mr. Morrison. Of course, I knew I could never reach you directly. Your crass, arrogant materialism would never permit a real interest in the deep occult. You were never more than a dilettante.

He's got you there, said Johnny.

Stop talking! yelled Pringle. I drew your friend in, tantalizing him with secret knowledge, dangling the possibility that he might join me in my Great Working, for I knew that your concern for your foolish friend would ultimately drive you into my arms. And here you are. Helpless.

Um, I said, what's to stop us from just running away from your fat ass? You probably have terrible aim.

Yeah, said Johnny.

I am. Mandy stepped from the shadows, the vast dog, bigger even than I'd remembered it, at her side. She was holding a gun. Don't even think about it, she said.

You should have kept an eye out, hot dogs, said the dog.

Whoa, I said.

Pringle glowered at me. My father was going to transform the Project, turn it into something for the betterment of all mankind. He was a great inventor. And your fascist reptilian grandfather took it all away, had him framed for terrible crimes!

Wait a minute, I said. I thought your father was deep, devious, and powerful.

Based on your grandfather, obviously! The *real* secret master. The real Bonesman!

The way I hear it, your dear old fucking dad was a hustler who conned my family out of millions of dollars.

Precisely what a reptiloid yuppie monster would say, said Pringle. Well, it's too late now. Any hope of warding off the nightmare has vanished. Any hope of turning the tide has disappeared like the spring dew. The Project now requires a sacrifice, and only a true ancient bloodline will do. What an irony that *your* sacrifice will consecrate it.

Wait a minute, I said. What about Mark and Helen?

Who? said Pringle.

Peter's fancy new yuppie friends, said Johnny. Helen's the coke slut he brought tonight.

She's not a coke slut, I said. Actually, I think she's really unhappy. It sort of seems like an abusive relationship.

That's real after-school of you, Johnny said.

It's all irrelevant! Pringle screamed.

Don't bag the groceries, said the dog.

What? Johnny and I said.

Hey, uh, sorry. A pretty young man in a tank top and painted-on jeans walked toward us. Do any of you guys have a light? He didn't appear to notice the firearms.

Oh, I don't think so. Uh, let me check. Oh, maybe, we all said. Mandy found a little plastic lighter in her pocket. The guy lit his smoke and handed it back. Thanks, he said. What's your name? Johnny said. Johnny, I said. What? he said. Do you guys know when Presumption of Innocence is supposed to go on? the guy asked. Who? I said. They're, like, a band, the guy said. Soon, I think, said Mandy. After Butt Machine. Cool, said the guy; well, thanks.

He was into me, said Johnny.

Both of you. Mandy gestured with the gun, and the dog growled. Walk.

14

We came to the bank of the river. There was no moon. The arm of the Milky Way rolled overhead. Far to our left, I caught sight of a solitary figure beside the water. Look, I said to Johnny. A river spirit. Ooooohhhh, he said. Coooool. There's no such thing as river spirits, said Pringle. Right, said Mandy. We walked along the river. It felt like miles. Where are you taking us? I asked. A hired boat will convey you back to the city, said Pringle. There, you will be bound in the Time Chamber to await my return, at which point we will release your lifeblood directly into the sensory deprivation tank from which the psychoperator will draw the sacrificial-orgonic magical energies necessary to collapse the quantum borders between realities and begin reordering the quantum genome of the multiversal reality matrix.

Simple enough, I said.

Can you reorder it so that they don't replace Michael O'Hare with Bruce Boxleitner in B5? Johnny asked. It really fucked up the whole arc.

You'll regret your irreverence, said Pringle.

You know, I said to Johnny, I think I should apologize to Lauren Sara.

Oh God, he said. You're such a fag.

We came around a long bend in the shore and saw a small boat bobbing along a small dock. Well, I said, Johnny, it's been a pleasure serving with you.

But as we reached the boat, there was a humming overhead that resolved itself into immense mechanical whirring. Oh shit, said Johnny. Oh, AWESOME! There it was above us, liquid and silver, its skin reflective and luminous, the air around it shimmering like the air above the thousandth foot of highway on a hot day.

No, said Pringle. No! They always interfere! And he started firing wildly into the air, but it was no action movie, and after just a second or two of flashing and reporting, the magazine was empty.

The dog whimpered and dropped its belly to the ground.

A shaft of brilliant light dropped from the ship and surrounded us.

A voice with the smooth cadence and hushed sibilants of a public radio host seemed to come from the ship. *Waffe Weg. Hände hoch!*

Johnny, I hissed, run!

And while they were dazzled we stomped back into the woods.

15

Johnny, I said. We'd lost Pringle and Mandy and that goddamn wolfhound with no trouble. I'm sorry. What for? he said. Well, apparently this is all my fault. They wanted me.

Johnny stopped and considered it, then slapped my shoulder. Nah, he said. I still think he was pissed that I was dipping into his stash. I mean, I probably stole a thousand bucks' worth of heroin, not to mention all the ketamine. But hey, man, what did I tell you about that fascist family of yours? I believe the phrase you used was big Jews, I said. Yeah, he said, well, tomato tomahto. How long have we been out here? I asked. I feel like we've been out here for a couple of years. No, he said, maybe, like, fifteen minutes. I think it's been longer than that, I told him. Possibly, he said. Do you think maybe the drugs are altering our sense of time? I asked him. I'm perfectly sober, he said. Well, other than the beers and such. Me, too, I said. We should find Helen, I said. Who? he asked. Helen, I answered. Helen, the girl I came with. Fuck her, said Johnny. She was a downer. I'm telling you, I said, I think that she just has a shitty relationship. I think that Mark is, like, controlling her mind or some shit. Controlling her nose is more like it, Johnny said. Controlling her bank account. Well, yeah, I agreed. That, too. My point, Johnny said, is that bad relationships are made by mutual consent. I don't know, I said. I don't know if I agree about that. Look at you and Lauren Sara, he said. We didn't have a bad relationship, I argued. We were great. I mean, good, anyway. Yeah, Johnny said. A real pair of paragons. There may have been some communication issues, I admitted. Morrison, he said, how come the minute I admit you're not a fucking boring Stepford dude, you come back at me with communications issues? Sorry, I said. I love you anyway, he said. You're the brother I never had. You did have a brother, I reminded him. You are the midseason replacement casting choice for the brother who was offered a better gig, Johnny told me. Jesus, I said. That's an interesting way of looking at death. Is there another way? asked Johnny.

16

We kept thinking we heard the party; we kept thinking we saw other guests in the woods, taking a stroll or smoking a joint or looking for a place to lay down a blanket and fuck, but as soon as we approached any of them, they revealed themselves to be insubstantial, melting back into the darkness between the trees, and the sounds of music were night birds, or just the wind in the branches, and the light was just the moon. Johnny, I said, is the moon out?

No, he said. There's no moon.

I think I see the moon.

Beats me, he said.

Do you smell something? I asked him.

Like what? he said.

It smells like piss, I said.

Maybe, he said.

We're lost, I said.

Yes, you are. The voice boomed from above us. It had a certain Eeyoreish quality to it, gloomy, all in the head, fairly gay. We started and looked up. Two bright eyes glinted out of a shaggy form in the leaves. It dropped, grabbing branches here and there, swinging on its huge hairy arms like an orangutan.

Oh, fuck, said Johnny. A fucking Sasquatch!

It landed gracefully in front of us, hardly a sound but the slight settling of leaves under its weight. It was huge, hundreds of pounds at least, though it held itself on four legs like a gorilla, and its eyes were at our level. Its huge canines gleamed. Nonsense, it said. I am Targivad, the Wise Monkey of the Forest.

No fucking way, we said.

I bring tidings from the Time Being.

I'm sorry, I said. What?

The Time Being, said the ape. He had, I decided, a regal bearing. I glanced at Johnny, who seemed absolutely stupefied. Out of the primordial No-Thing-Ness, the Time Being came into being for the time being. His being is the forward motion of time and being.

Dude, said Johnny, do you know Calsutmoran?

Who? I said.

He's in the Ein Soph Department, said Targivad. We usually bump into each other at the Christmas party.

Well, said Johnny, if you see him, tell him that I know he took my Seventh Guest CD-ROM. That shit is a collector's item.

Your pizza deliveryman took it, along with a twenty-dollar bill and three Pabsts from your refrigerator.

Shit, said Johnny.

You should do less drugs, said Targivad.

No fucking kidding, I said.

Shut it down, said Johnny.

You hot dogs, said Targivad, have not kept an eye out.

That's probably true, I said.

The Time Being commands me to say unto you that, verily, thou art a pair of major fuckups.

Hey, I said. Tell that to this guy. I pointed a thumb at Johnny. I'm a fucking young professional.

Oh, fine, said Johnny. Throw me under the bus.

Get it together, said Targivad.

Yeah, whatever, I said.

The promise of your youth is wasted on your adult lives, Targivad replied. You cling to youth but not its promise; you are seeds that have sprouted into vines that bear no fruit.

Johnny bears fruit, I said.

Oh, ha ha, said Johnny.

Boys, Targivad snapped. You only get one life. Your account is full of time. There is only one way to spend it, which is in the living of it.

Huh, I said.

Boys, said Targivad.

Yes? we said.

Keep an eye out.

He leapt away and swung back into the trees. Then the forest was pierced with light, bright beams like the beam that had trapped Pringle. We heard the humming again overhead, but it was louder, more insistent, metronomic, a thump-thumping. Luftwaffe, Johnny said. UFOs! We ran again, smashing blindly through the brush. We'd been on the edge of the clearing all along. There was the lodge. There was the bonfire. There were the rest of the party guests, running in every direction, screaming, terror overtaking them. Huge beings moved among us, their faces obscured. They seemed to be wearing some sort of mechanized armor. They emitted shouts and bursts of static. We were caught in the human tide. We surged this way and that but were driven ever tighter. Johnny! I called. Johnny! Morrison! he cried. One of the beings had caught hold of my arm. I screamed and struggled. I tried to break free, but its grip was superhumanly strong. I kicked at it. It touched my chest with some sort of energy weapon. My whole body seized. My muscles froze. One spasm after another pulsed through me. I thought I was going to lose control of my bowels. I felt it in my eyes. I felt it crackling around my brain. I wanted to move, but the effort only induced more agony and only made me tremble harder. I wanted to scream, but I could only manage a dull moan. I tried to say, Why are you doing this? I must have said it, because the creature looked at me through its big glass eye, its whole face, and it said, in English, oddly enough, Resisting arrest. Then it used the weapon on me again. Well, huh. I found myself feeling unexpectedly sober. Oh shit, I thought. Maybe those drugs *did* work. I found my jaw moving again. Helen? I said. We'll find your girlfriend, said the creature. Oh, it was a cop. I lolled in his grip. There was a helicopter overhead. She's not my girlfriend, I said. She's my boss's girlfriend. Kid, said the cop. Shut up. You have the right to remain silent and so forth. He was dragging me toward the lodge, which was surrounded by cars and wagons, their lights swirling. I saw Johnny being dragged along as well. Johnny! I called once more. We were thrown against the side of a van, side by side. Hey, man, I said. Yo, he said. Shut the fuck up, a cop said. They were zip-tying our wrists. My cheek was pressed to the side panel. I saw, a few cars down, Winston Pringle on the ground, bucking wildly like some kind of enraged walrus. Police state! he shouted in his avian voice. Police state! One of the cops looked at another. He shrugged. Resisting arrest? he said. Looks like it to me, said the other. The first baton fell, then the rest, then Johnny and me and half a dozen others were snatched up harshly and tossed into the back of a different van and taken to jail.

V. LOCKS AND DAMS

1

I recall falling asleep on a bench with my arm under my ear. I recall waking during the night because my arm had fallen asleep. I recall peering through one squinting, open eye at one of my cellmates, a skinny boy with knotted hair, and asking about my car. What car, man? he asked. Can you, like, describe the car? I said a little VW, small dent on the front quarterpanel, gray. Oh yeah, he said. Your girl took it. Mm, I said.

2

The Morrisons of Sewickley, Pennsylvania, had several lawyers, but they were not the sort of lawyers that drove out to Armstrong County to spring you from the lockup, so I called Cousin Bill, the closest thing I knew to a criminal, a man who I knew for a fact had spent a night or two in the tank himself, and as I'd hoped he would he laughed, his squeaky, wheezing little voice trilling with pure delight, and said he was sending Ben David posthaste. He said it as if I should know who Ben David was. Who's Ben David? I asked. David Ben David, he said. He's the swingingest-dicked Jew in Pittsburgh, bar none. I thought the mayor's man was the swingingest-dicked Jew in Pittsburgh, I said. The sheriff's deputy in the room looked up from his cell phone. I shrugged. He shook his head. Kantsky? said Bill. He's not Jewish. I mean, maybe his dad was. His mom was Italian. A DiBella, if I remember right. We went to Allderdice together. He's a goddamn Knight of Columbus. For real? I said. Far as I know, said Bill. Anyway, Ben David is a fucking shark. He'll chomp chomp chomp those oakie fucks up there. Just don't mention the Palestinians. Why the fuck would I mention the Palestinians? I'm just saying, said Bill. He's ex-Mossad. Not. A. Fan. Okay, I said. So I should just sit tight? Exactly, said Bill. By the way, my recommendation is to take a shit, if possible. No one'll mess with you if they know you just took a shit. Yeah, thanks, I said. Kidding, he said. I'm proud of you, little cuz. Seriously, try not to get fucked in the ass.

3

I spent a night with some miscellaneous hippies from the party and a few pacing meth heads who may or may not have been from the party. After we'd been unloaded from the van, I'd been hauled one way and Johnny another. We'd passed each other, and he'd offered me a grin so extraordinary and out of place that I thought I must still be hallucinating. Hot dogs, he'd said, and he'd laughed as they dragged him away. He'd never arrived in my cell. Then in the morning I was free. Ben David was waiting for me with my phone and wallet. I looked carefully at my phone. It was undamaged. I checked the contacts. It was definitely mine. He wore a shiny golf shirt, pleated khakis, and suede driving shoes. He had broad shoulders, gray hair that looked as if it belonged to a European orchestra conductor, and the barest suggestion of a paunch behind his braided belt. Peter, he said. His big hand gripped mine. He had the last, ineradicable trace of an Israeli accent. A pleasure to meet you. Bill sends his regards. I told the lawyer I was really grateful. Don't worry, he said. I know the sheriff up here; I do a lot of drug cases up here. Meth, you know, mostly. A little heroin. Trailed off a lot since the gas companies came in. A good economy is bad for a criminal defense practice. We walked outside. It was a bright, cool morning. Shit, I said. What about my car? Impounded, probably, he said. Sorry. I'm working on that. Seizures—he lowered his voice—are the biggest cop scam of all. I'm seeing what I can do. You know what, I said. Forget it. It isn't worth anything anyway. Ben David said reverently, *Okeir beitoo bo'tsayah bat'sa v'shonay matanot yich'yeh.*

4

I'm sorry? I said. The greedy for gain brings trouble to his home, but he who hates bribes shall live, said Ben David.

5

That's an interesting attitude for a lawyer, isn't it? I said. We walked down a slight incline toward the far parking lot, where Ben David's long, late-model Cadillac glinted in the sun.

Beyond it, a line of trees and a muddy creek. Not at all, said
Ben David. Bribes are the province of officials. There are no
bribes among criminals. All exchanges among the lawless are
legitimate. The law itself is a precondition for corruption. This
is why I went into defense. Well, that and the money. He smiled
and offered my shoulder an avuncular slap. Everyone is guilty,
you see. You're a Catholic; you should understand. But rarely
is anyone guilty of what they're accused of. Hey, I said. What
about Johnny? Ah, said Ben David. Your friend. I inquired. He
was transferred to Allegheny this morning. The phrase "other
charges" was used. I didn't press it. Apparently there was a warrant. Since all they had up here was public intox and resisting
arrest, they sent him down right away. A warrant? I said. For
what? Don't know, said Ben David. I made some calls. We'll see.
Let me ask you this—we stood beside his car—do you think that
he might have been mixed up with this Wilhelm Zollen character? Pringle? I said. Sure, said Ben David. Whatever his name is.
Yes, I said. Yes, unfortunately, I do. Well then, Ben David said,
he's probably fucked in the short term. But like I said, I'll see
what I can do. Thanks, I said. We got into the car. Oh, I said.
Also, did my cousin mention Helen Witold when he talked to
you. Yeah, said Ben David. Is she the artist? He told you she
was an artist? No, said Ben David. No. I know her name. One
of my partners at the firm has a piece by her. Got it as a part of
a payment in a divorce thing for some museum person or other.
No shit, I said. Yes shit, he said. Anyway, no, nothing about her.
According to the cops, everyone who didn't get arrested dis-
persed. Most of them were from Pittsburgh, presumably. I'm
sure she got a ride. Hm, I said. I dialed her and went straight to

voice mail. Then I realized I didn't have my keys. Did they have keys with my other shit? I asked. No, he told me. Why? Did you have keys? I must have given them to Helen, I said, although I could not recall having given them to Helen. She must have taken the car. I called her again, and this time I left a message. Helen, I said. I'm going to need my car back.

6

On the ride home, Ben David asked me, So what do you do exactly? I was watching the trees swing past the highway. A deer looked up as we passed. Exactly? I said. Good question. Bill says you work for Global Solutions. Oh, I said. You've heard of us. One of my partners, Ben David said, just started working on a wrongful termination suit. Ah, I said. Well, I guess you could say I wrongfully terminate. Ah, said Ben David. Actually, there is no more Global Solutions. We are now Vandevoort IRCM WorldSolv. As of earlier this month. Jesus, said Ben David. Vandevoort, said Ben David. The Dutch company? They were collaborators, you know. Really? I said. One of the few foreign companies that kept supplying Speer in the last year or so of the war, he said. Huh, I said. Did you learn about it in Mossad? Mossad? said Ben David. He laughed. Who told you that, Bill? He's a real joker. So you weren't in Mossad, I said. He didn't answer, but he shook his head and seemed amused. Instead, he said, So, do you like firing people? No, I said. Bill told me he once asked you to come into the business. That's true, I said. When I'd first moved into the apartment, he'd asked if I wanted to work with him. I was right out of school and just starting to interview for corporate jobs. I could use a hand, he'd told me. I've got three new buildings, and I need someone to keep track of my Mexicans. I'd declined. Well, he said, if you ever change your mind, it beats working. And he'd purred away in his fast Mercedes. Never considered it? Ben David asked. Not really, I said. Why not? he asked. To be honest, I said, I always liked Bill, but he sort of seems like a slumlord. Perhaps, said Ben David. He gave me a sidelong look. His mouth had the suggestion of a grin. I wouldn't be so quick to grasp at the pejorative. And anyway, doesn't a slumlord serve an actual and essential function in the world you people are making?

7

Ben David promised to call me on Monday and let me know what he found out about Johnny. I asked him if I owed him anything. Like what? he said. I don't know, I said. Like money. He laughed. His fingers tapped the wheel. Gratis, he said. Tell your uncle he owes me one. He's my cousin, actually, I said. Once removed. Well, tell your cousin, then. And stay out of trouble. I will, I said sincerely. Hell, kid, Ben David said. I was *kidding*.

8

I took a long shower. I considered the past twenty-four hours and wondered how exactly I ought to separate the actual from the unreal; what should I believe and what shouldn't I believe; what was true and what had been false; what, if true, was the true truth, and what its mere facsimile? I remembered the woods with a clarity that was unusual after a serious dissociative trip; the particulars of those experiences—and it had been years since I'd had those trips with anything like regularity—were usually like the particulars of a dream: the more you tried to hold them firmly in your memory, the more swiftly they receded into a general impression, leaving only that impression along with a few disconcertingly precise but seemingly disparate, disconnected details in your mind. Now, of course, it seemed to me that I could match at least some of the experiences to the refraction of a bright, external reality through the weird prism of those drugs, whatever they'd been, and yet it also seemed to me that some of what I remembered had to have, in some way or other, happened. It seemed to me that Pringle must have appeared in the woods, that his minion Mandy must have threatened us, whether or not with an actual gun. But I was sure it had been an actual gun. And I was sure that Pringle had been exactly that grandiose. Or, anyway, I was fairly convinced. I was fairly convinced that he bought into that bullshit just enough really to try to kidnap us, and he might really have tried to kill us, but for the intervention of that UFO, unless that had been the police helicopter—but I had seen identical UFOs before, and they'd not been helicopters. And, also, I was mindful that dissociative drugs didn't generally cause the mind to manufacture hallucinations; they were confabulatory; they autotuned outside stimuli to the harmonics of a user's imagination. Or anyway, that was what I thought that I thought. Then the water was cold, and I dried myself and lay down in bed. The windows were open. Had I opened them? It had begun to rain. I had the sense that I had something to do with the rain. No, I thought; that must be an aftereffect. You got that sometimes. I thought about Johnny, who was probably in jail. Then I thought about my dad. I'm not sure why. I thought about him in his study at home, listening to the Pirates on the radio, because, he always said, he preferred it to TV, while my mother read in the other room and waited for some or other call that would send her back to the hospital; I thought of all the years between myself in that moment and him in his moment, and it occurred to me, suddenly and without warning, that my inevitable regret was not for the last night, the night before, or any day or night before that; the memories I regretted were for a remembered future, an intimation of a life that ended up in a similar study in a similar house on a similar street in a similar overmoneyed town; everything I'd ever done to the contrary was an affectation, if not exactly the affectation that Johnny, half jokingly, had always accused me of. Everyone is guilty of something, just not necessarily what they're accused of, I thought. It occurred to me that, without knowing what it was that I wanted, I wanted something worlds away from what I had.

9

There are several appendices to *Fourth River, Fifth Dimension*, and after the last appendix (Appendix F: An Electronics

Hobbyist's Guide to Time Chamber Construction), there is a brief authorial afterward. Of course I can understand, Pringle writes, if you find the preceding material hard to believe. It is full of both what you might call the true truth, which is empirically verifiable with documents and so forth, and the unclear truth, which is the gray area you run into when you begin messing with the time stream. If you prefer to treat it as speculative fiction to increase your enjoyment of the subject matter, I would encourage you to do so. You won't offend me! My only goal is to open your mind to different modalities of thought and consciousness, although I would also encourage you to dig more deeply into the goings-on in Pittsburgh, Pennsylvania, and even to write your congressman or other government officials to let them know about your concerns. This bit of civic boosterism seems a little bit absurd, but I guess if you believe, why not? Anyway, Pringle goes on to say that political solutions are probably insignificant nevertheless, since they can always be deleted out of the self-editing timelike feedback loop. In the end, I think, the Project is, or was, very sad; being generally godless, I would have wanted flying saucers to be a kind of miracle, not just a red pen applied by our timid descendants to all the flawed self-creations that preceded them.

10

Mark, I said. I quit. You can't quit, he said. You're fired. He produced a document that said as much. It was dated that Monday, and since he already had it, it obviously predated my announcement. Oh, Jesus fucking Christ, I said. He can't help you, said Mark. No, I said. I suppose not. I would also, Mark said, like to know what you've done with my girlfriend. What? I said. Nothing. What do you mean? Look, Mark said, I know you took her to that confab of degenerates. We left separately, I said. Don't tell me you let her take your car? Mark grinned, that swift, wolfish baring of his canines that I'd come to recognize as the pleasure he took from another's error. So? I said. She's probably in flames on the side of a highway, Mark said. Never let Helen drive. I was sort of indisposed at the time, I said. Yes, said Mark. Apparently so. Well, I said. Well, Mark said. He was sitting behind my desk. I was standing just inside of the doorway. Well, look, he said. You were never really cut out for this. I still don't know what this is, I said. No, said Mark. I don't imagine you do. You have a tendency to look at things through a frustratingly human lens. Is there another lens? I asked. Mark tapped a pen on the desk, watching me, his eyes moving as if the eyelids were closed and they were tracing the rapid paths of a dream. He sighed. Go see Karla, he said. There will be a modest severance. And Pete, he said. Yes? I said. Keep an eye out.

11

Mystery Man, said Karla. I guess you didn't make it after all. I guess I didn't, I said. You're better off, she told me. Am I? I said. She smiled, and she shrugged. She fingered one of her big copper earrings. Think about what we do with resources,

Mystery Man, she said, and then she explained how our last mutual act, the company's and mine, would be for them to buy, and me to sell, my silence. I would like to tell you that I said fuck it and threw the money, or the promise of it, back in her face, but I didn't, and I won't. Instead, I left the building and tried to have a smoke, but it tasted like a mouthful of dirt, and I couldn't swallow. I wandered down to a filthy cop-and-lawyer bar near the river and had a couple of shots and beers with some off-duty cops and public defender types. I eavesdropped. So she says, one of the cops was saying, she says, Don't arrest him. If you arrest him, how'm I gonna *kill his ass*? Another one laughed. You should've let her take a few swings, he said. No way; this was your classic skinny guy/fat girl domestic situation. She'd have killed him for real. Skinny guy/fat girl black, or skinny guy/fat girl white? asked one of the lawyers. White, said the black cop. Ooh, said the lawyer. The worst. Definitely the worst, the cop agreed. You think? Another lawyer. Oh yeah, the cop said. Skinny dude/fat girl black is a sex thing ninety percent of the time. He chuckled. He was pretty skinny himself. You know how we do. But for whites it's a she-got-fat-after-a-couple-of-babies-and-he-does-a-lot-of-crank thing. Yeah, one of the lawyers said. So listen to this shit, said the other lawyer. He was young, just my age or thereabouts, although his hairline had already retreated into a W across his pale scalp; his suit was too big, and his delicate wrists were too small for his cuffs. Listen to this shit: I got one this morning who says he saved the world. I didn't look, but tilted my head to hear them better. Oh yeah, a cop said, laughing. What from? The aliens, said the other cop. More or less, said the young lawyer. What's the charges? asked another cop who'd just then leaned into the conversation. Plagiarism, cracked the other lawyer. They laughed. No, said the skinny lawyer. A bunch of drug shit. Hoofing it for some fat fuck down in the Mon Valley. Winston Pringle, I said. They turned and stared down the bar, their cop eyes and lawyer eyes looking through my suit, which was probably worth more than all the rest of the suits in that bar combined, and finding underneath a man who, by their expressions alone, I could see they assessed as being worth something somewhat less.

12

The lawyer's name was Mike Kelly. He wasn't a public defender, he said. The public defender's office, he said, is bogged down in seventeen kinds of shit and doesn't have time for this sort of trial work. Oh Jesus, I said, are they going to prosecute Johnny? I had sketched out, with as little self-implication as possible, what had transpired the weekend past and what I knew about the Pringle gang. They're going to threaten to, Kelly told me. Christ, I hate prosecutors. Your buddy thinks he's an expert on Nazis, wait till he meets the asshole assigned to this one. He even looks like a fucking Nazi. Blond and blue-eyed. The works. The Fourth Reich, he said. You and Johnny, I said, are going to get along. Kelly raised an eyebrow. You know, he said, I'm sure we will. Your friend is fucking crazy, but he's a charmer. That'll probably be to his advantage. Anyway, look: He's already indicated his willingness to become a cooperating witness. To, I quote, end Wilhelm Zollen's reign of evil will and subjugation on this earth forevermore. He cleared his throat. As we move, uh, forward in the process, I am going to suggest to him that all interests might be better served if we dial back on the grandiloquence. Of course, Drake isn't really inclined to deal too generously, since those incompetent rednecks up in Armstrong lost the girl. The girl? I said. Yeah, said Kelly. The main accomplice. The partner, or whatever. Mandy, I said. Right, Kelly said. Not really her name, but not really relevant. Yeah. Fucking idiot deputies. Once they'd rounded up anyone obviously using or possessing, they just let the rest go. In her case, Jesus Christ. She walks right up to one of them and she says, You guys arrested my asshole boyfriend and he had the keys. Asshole boyfriend. Kelly shook his head. Nice touch, right? So they *give her some poor jagoff's keys*, and she fucking splits in his car.

13

Helen.

14

Johnny was sitting in something resembling a half lotus when they let me into the little meeting room to see him. He had his index fingers to his thumbs and the backs of his hands resting on his knees. Jesus Christ, Johnny, get off the floor, I said.

What are you doing? I'm at peace, he said. You're in a shitload
of trouble, I told him. Brother, he said, you sure are swift to
swing to the moral opprobrium. I have achieved my life's purpose. Getting thrown in the clink? I said. Very funny, he said.
No. I've set things right. I've broken the cycle. I've let the tide
turn of its own accord. Come on, I said, get up. He did, reluctantly, and I hugged him. He smelled like jail, but I didn't want
to let him go. He held me in his big arms, too. It's okay, buddy,
he said. It's going to be okay. You're going to go to prison, I
said. We sat down at the plain table. Probably. He shrugged.
For a little while, anyway. But that's part of the plan. The plan?
I said. Jesus, Johnny. Don't worry, Rabbi Mustafah Elijah and
I have discussed it extensively. The Universal Synagogue must
grow, and I intend to become its chief evangelist on the inside,
spreading the gospel of mental discipline, sobriety, and Gnos-
tic self-programming. Oh, Johnny, I said. You met my lawyer,
said Johnny. Poor kid. He's terrified of the prosecutor. Did he
tell you who's prosecuting Pringle? Maybe, I said. I'm not sure.
Who? Billy Drake! said Pringle. William, now. Can you fucking
believe it? Do you remember that kid? I do, I said. He looks
like a goddamn *Bel Ami* model these days, Johnny said. I told
him he ought to quit persecuting poor innocent criminals and
go into porn. He didn't think that was very funny. He claims
not to remember me, but I can tell he's never forgotten our
night of passion. Wearing a wedding ring, though, so I'll play
it DL for now. Johnny, I said, you're incredible. You're really
going to prison? Seriously, kiddo, he said. The tough-guy thing
is all an act. He does keep telling poor Mike that I've managed to offend all the wrong people. Your blog, I said. Yeah,

he said. I guess someone figured it out. I told him I'd offended all the *right* people, but you know how lawyers think. Johnny, I said, what if I found you a, you know, better lawyer? Aw, said Johnny, I like Mike Kelly. He's sweet. Could stand to eat a pie or two, but sweet. Yeah, I said, but why don't you save all that charitable sentiment for your ministry? Hm, said, Johnny. Well, what's your lawyer's name? David Ben David, I said. Whoa, said Johnny. Sounds like a big Jew. The biggest, I said. Ex-Mossad.

15

I can tell you where I was when they found Helen. I was at the gym. I'd been playing racquetball with Julian, who seemed to be the only unincarcerated nonrelative whom I could call. He and Tom had broken up after Accounting had noticed some irregularities in his expense reconciliations and he'd discovered that Tom had spent a few thousand dollars on bars and clothes with Julian's corporate card. Julian kept making lame jokes about our being two single dudes on the hunt, and I pretended to laugh, because I needed someone to hang out with. It had been a few weeks since Johnny and I had gone into the woods. It had become August; you could see the end of August already. It was still hot during the day, but at night you wanted to open the windows, and the leaves, although they were still green, had started to dry in anticipation of the fall and sounded like paper when the breeze moved them. I'd spent a week doing absolutely nothing, walking aimlessly around the apartment or the neighborhood, watching TV, buying wild ingredients and attempting to cook elaborate meals for myself that kept ending in failure and Chinese. Then Cousin Bill called and said, with no preamble, Peter, Cuz, listen, I've got some Mexicans coming by to drywall one of the units. Keep an eye on them for me, will you? I gotta do a thing. What do you mean, keep an eye on them? I said. I mean, he said, point them at 3A and say, *Trabayho a key*. I can do that, I said, and, in effect, I did.

16

So somehow these little projects were popping up every couple of days in the neighborhood, and Bill kept calling, and I'd even said to him, I see what you're trying to do. Thank God, he'd said. I was beginning to think you were as dumb as your old man.

17

So I was at the gym. Julian had beaten me again, always a step faster, his swing that much harder, his aim that much better. But because he played hard, had no natural inclination to play to anyone's level but his own, I had no choice but to run harder and faster than I might otherwise be inclined, and while it hurt at the time, it felt, far from frustrating, freeing, renewing, and clean. Then afterward, after we'd showered and changed, after he'd gone back to work—after, by the way, he'd asked me if I'd ever had any interest in finance, because, given my background, he thought he could probably find something right in my wheelhouse, an expression that I found as unbearable and off-putting as an overripe and under-emptied kitchen garbage can, to which I must have reacted visibly in kind, because he grinned and slapped my shoulder companionably and jogged off toward the exit—after all that, I was standing at the stupid hippie juice bar at the gym drinking the sort of concoction that I'd have theretofore scoffed at as the purest sort of bullshit but which, lately, having finally tried, I found that I rather enjoyed—I was standing there with a glass full of greenish liquid in my hand watching the muted TV when something about the local reporter standing beside the big concrete bathtub beside the river with the drizzly sky behind her caught my eye, and then the closed captioning read, I'm Katie Bologna reporting from Lock Number Nine on the Allegheny River just outside of Harmarville, where this morning a local technician discovered a body floating . . . And though the body had not yet been identified, had been in the water for weeks, had bloated and swollen and begun to rot beyond easy recognition, they knew that it was a woman, and I knew, I just knew, that it was Helen, and that the Allegheny and its currents had conspired to bring her body back to us.

18

It was her. They used dental records. It was reported in the paper. I nearly called Mark, but couldn't. There was an obit.

There would be a funeral and burial in two days, a service at Rodef Shalom, and internment at Homewood Cemetery.

19

In the immediate aftermath of her death two things happened: she was suddenly a famous artist again, and I was suddenly the last person who'd seen her alive. Two detectives came to my house and asked me a series of leading questions; I broke into a sweat and said I'd better call my lawyer. The detectives exchanged glances. You're not a suspect, one of them said. We just want to know, Was she distraught? Well, yeah, I said, I guess. Do you know of anyone who'd want to harm her? Yes, I thought. Why? I said. So we can rule out homicide, said the other detective. You think somebody killed her? I asked. No; we think she jumped in the drink. She had more drugs in her than a pharmacy. To *rule out*, they said. No, I said. No.

20

An up-and-coming artist. The potential to rescue abstraction from its post-seventies dead end. The best hope for representational painting. A savagely insightful mind that exploded the old categories. A sort of visionary and mystic. A darling of the scene. A favorite of important collectors. A significant force in contemporary painting. An Audubon of the post-natural, post-human age. The Philip K. Dick of visual arts, who'd bridged the gap between science and science fiction and fine art. A major player. A critical darling. An articulate spokeswoman. An articulate spokes*person*. A back-to-basics painter. A genius, really. Yes, absolutely. An immense loss to the American art community. A once-in-a-lifetime talent. Always underappreciated by the commercial galleries. No, no, never valued highly enough by the museums and institutional collectors. The next so-and-so. The next this. The next that. And this was just what the Internet had to say. She hadn't, I knew, had a significant show in years. But the valedictory virus was already multiplying out of control. For whatever reason, it was this more than anything else that made me decide to go to her funeral.

21

The service and burial were in the evening. I'd tried to call Mark, but he'd never called back. Not that I'd expected otherwise. I woke up early. I'd wrapped myself in the blanket during the night. The window was open. It was cool. It smelled like the fall. The air was dry. I could hear dogs out on morning walks yipping with pleasure after the long summer they'd endured. I heard the beep of a truck backing up. I heard a distant helicopter, an ambulance, the sigh of a passing bus. I made myself coffee and sat in the kitchen for a long time. Then I got dressed and caught a bus downtown and walked through the suits and ties along the glass and brownstone corridor of Grant Street, past the Federal courts and the Federal Reserve and the Steel Building and the Frick Building and the little church tucked between skyscrapers and the courthouse and across the Boulevard of the Allies and down under the rusting frame of the Liberty Bridge approach along Second Avenue past the squat public works building and the bail bondsmen's offices to the county jail. I stood in line with the wives and girlfriends and the occasional parent and the occasional husband and the many children and the few friends and the lawyers. I forfeited my wallet and phone and sat on a bench for a while. Then I went in to see Johnny. He'd lost some weight over the last few weeks, but he didn't look sick this time. I almost regret to say that it suited him. His features were more pronounced; his jaw looked stronger; his eyes more deeply set. Morrison, he said. Johnny, I said. How's Ben David working out for you? I don't know where you found that guy, brother, said Johnny, but he's the goddamn moshiach as far as I'm concerned. Well, good, I said. I'm going to be a star witness, he said. He announced it as if he'd said he was starring in a film. That's great, I said. Pringle is fucked. Well and truly fucked. We're going to pin his ass to the wall like a fat fucking butterfly. That's great, I said. Really. Reb Elijah says I shouldn't take so much pleasure in another man's downfall, but I have to admit I'm enjoying myself. Uh-huh, I said. So, what about you? What's the deal? A year, Johnny said. Then probation. The powers that be—he lowered his voice—are highly displeased by this outcome. Oh yeah? I said. Yeah. Apparently, certain insinuations contained on Alieyinz.com hit a little too close to home for a certain elected official. Hm, I said, so the mayor's really an alien? No, Johnny said, his face drawn and serious. No, a *homo*. Oh yeah? I said. Apparently, Johnny told me, he and his whole inner circle are a gang of utter pervs. I mean, boy-butt sex orgies at the Duquesne Club, the works. You have this on good authority, I said. Common knowledge on the inside, Johnny told me. Well, I said, I guess that would explain why Kantsky was so pissed about the whole deal. I was joking, but Johnny said, Exactly. *Exactly*. A classic lady-doth-protest-too-much situation.

22

We talked for a while longer, and Johnny filled me in on the secret homosexual underground directing the politics of the city of Pittsburgh. I told him it was a shame he'd never been invited to participate. He insinuated that certain, uh, overtures had been made. When were these overtures made? I said. What overtures? Just overtures, he said. I'm afraid that I need to remain hazy on the details, for the safety of all involved. He grinned. I could not tell if he was shitting me. I asked him if he'd really been selling for Pringle. He shrugged. Nah, he said. The sales end never really appealed to me. Mostly, I was helping him out with the Internet. The Internet? I said. For a guy who built the fucking time portal and the psychic chamber and cetera, Johnny said, you'd think he could hook up a wireless router. Are you shitting me? I said. When have I ever shit you? Johnny replied. I gave him that look. Don't give me that look, he said. I'm not, I said. You are, he told me. On the plus side, he said, I got to see a UFO. I'm pretty sure that was just a helicopter, I said. Fuck, no, he told me. Helicopters can't make directional changes like that. That was a goddamn UFO. Sirian, by the looks of it. Definitely extraterrestrial. I'd stake my reputation on it.

23

By the way, I said, do you know about Helen? Ben David told me, he replied. What a fucking shame. And how about fucking Mandy? I can't believe that bitch took your car. I don't care about the car, I said. Do you know I think the whole thing is Mark's fault? What whole thing? asked Johnny. Helen, I said. That thing. That was him on the phone, for sure, texting her and shit. I'm sure it was him when she said she had to make a call. You know she fucking jumped in the river. Whoa, whoa, said Johnny, that's a pretty wild tale without any evidence. Seriously? I said.

24

I cried when they took him back to his cell. Not much. But I had to blink it away. I had to touch my face with hand, a thumb beneath one eye, my forefinger beneath the other. Then I went back out under the empty sky.

25

I caught a different bus home, and on the walk from Liberty Avenue up to my apartment, I passed a neat Queen Anne with a for sale sign. I stopped to look. There were six mailboxes; it was divided into apartments. The roof over the front porch sagged a little, but I could see where a crew could replace some rotted wood and shore it up without tearing the whole thing down. You could replace the buzzer on the front door. You could get rid of those shitty, seventies-era crank casement windows and knock out the original openings in the exterior walls, put sash windows in. The roof needed shingling, but it looked fine structurally. I could not recall when I'd begun to think this way. I pulled out my phone and entered the listing number from the sign on the real estate company's website. It occurred to me that I had, or I would soon have, enough money to buy the place. Six units, I thought. You could turn that into income. The Mexicans could do the whole thing for twenty, thirty K. And not a shitty job. But still, a reasonable price point. Mid-level. Appropriate for a medical resident or an arts admin or something. An actual and essential function for the world I'd made.

26

After lunch, I met Julian at his other gym in East Liberty and we played racquetball for an hour. I'd considered canceling;

it seemed absurd to play before going to a funeral; but then, phone in hand, finger about to tap Julian's number, I thought, Well, what the fuck, it would be even weirder to cancel because of a funeral, as if a dead woman could be insulted that your attention was elsewhere and otherwise, as if an as-yet-unascended soul could be fooled by the artifice of grieving in excess of the grief one actually felt, as if, having already spent the morning in a jail and contemplating a future livelihood bought with my blood money bribe, it would be anything less than entirely absurd to sit in my apartment trying to be, of all things, appropriate. So I went, and we played, and I was glad that I went and glad that we played, because the *thwack* of the ball against the raquets, the *thock* of the ball against the walls and floor, the whine of our shoes as we sidestepped and pivoted, the drops and then rivulets of sweat, the pulse, the breath—they conspired to take my mind out of itself. I couldn't remember running quite so fast or swinging quite so hard. I felt, as we went into the third game, the beginning of a strangely familiar separation from myself, a sense of seeing my own body move from the outside, an abiding calmness, a weird pleasure in sensing my own self move in spite of me, a thin figure moving toward the ball as the ball moved toward it, right arm back, left arm angled slightly out, the wrist cocked, the shoulder pivoting, and as my left foot planted and my torso turned slowly toward the little blue onrushing globe, I swear to you I saw my head open up like a flower in the morning; out of the bright cavity erupted a mandala with a thousand petals; then Julian had his hand on my back, and we were both bent over; my hands were on my knees. Finally, he said. Finally what? I said. You won, asshole, he said. About fucking time.

27

Julian was meeting Tom. I thought you guys broke up, I said. Yeah, we did, but you know, Julian replied. He's making me go to some funeral, he said. We were getting dressed. Helen's funeral? I said. I guess, he answered. That artist. Whatever. Did you guys know her? I asked. Not me, said Julian. Tom did. Well, Tom says he did. And he smiled at me, the conspiratorial smile that men share when discussing the women in their lives, which I imagine women also share when discussing their men, and which, in an era and in a scene where half the men date men and the women, women, probably ought to have been a relic but persisted—among some of us, anyway—and said more about those of us who used it than it did about the absent boyfriends and girlfriends. Anyway, I responded in kind. And Julian said, I think she was more someone that Tom thought we ought to know. And I'd like to tell you that it had a profound effect on me, his referring to her in the past tense, but it didn't, because I suppose I'd always thought of her in the past tense anyway.

28

Tom was waiting for us at the coffee shop across the parking lot from the gym, looking as always as if something, or every-

thing, were a great inconvenience to him. Lauren Sara was
with him. Her hair was shorter. I didn't think I liked it. Hey,
I said. Hey, she said. What's happenin? Not much, I said. You
cut your hair. Patra cut my hair, she said. I hate it. I look like
a dyke. A little, I said. She smiled at me, and I smiled back.
We're going to be late, Tom said, ostensibly to Julian. I heard
my own voice coming out of his mouth. I looked at Lauren
Sara, and she at me, and we both laughed at the same time.
What? said Tom. Nothing, I said. Late for what? He sighed,
exasperated. Helen Witold's funeral, he said. Oh, I said. Are
you going? Everyone's going, said Tom. Oh, I said. Everyone.
She was an important artist, said Tom. It's fucking tragic.
All coincidences converge on the inevitable, I said. Huh? said
Tom. Nothing, I said. Just something someone said to me
once. It's a good definition of tragedy. Hm, said Julian, swing-
ing his bag from one shoulder to the other. I always thought
it was just shit that's sad. Really, Jules, said Tom. Well, I said.
I've got to go to the whatnot as well, so I've got to run home.
Are you going? I asked Lauren Sara. Yeah, no, she said. Funer-
als are weird. Yeah, I said. Well, see you around. Yeah, said
Lauren Sara. I'll be, you know, around.

29

I thought I'd arrived early, but I was late. The sanctuary was
already full, and the temple staff were folding back the rear
wall and clanging folding chairs into rows and aisles in the big
room beyond.

30

It occurred to me—it only then occurred to me—that I didn't know these people. Oh, I mean, I knew some of the guests. I knew Arlene Arnovich, and I knew Tom, who was worming his way toward the front with a sheepish Julian in tow, and I recognized David Hoffman; I recognized some of Nana's friends and peers; I recognized some people who knew my father; I recognized some Vandevoort and Global Solutions types; I recognized some people from the Warhol Museum and CMU; I saw David Ben David in a bespoke blue suit among the blacks and charcoals, who saw me and raised an eyebrow that said, How about this shit, huh? I saw some artists whom I'd seen around when I'd dated Lauren Sara, and I saw a lot of New York–looking fools looking very deliberately New York; I saw a party planner I knew and a florist everyone knew and I even recognized the rabbi—I do not mean Johnny's rabbi, for the record—who'd been much in the news protesting transit cuts lately. What I mean is that I couldn't have told you which of the expensive people in the front few rows were Helen's relatives, her parents or brothers or sisters or cousins or college friends; I didn't know if she had living parents or aunts and uncles or siblings or friends; I didn't know where she'd been born; I'd always assumed New York, but what did I know? I hadn't even known she was Jewish. I didn't know how she'd grown up, in what sort of home, with what sort of food served on holidays; which relatives she was close to; which relatives her parents disdained at the dinner table; which real friends of the family; which social acquaintances; where she'd gone to school; where she'd gone to camp; or if not camp, what sports; or if not sports, what instrument; or when she'd learned to paint; or where she'd sold her first piece; or where she'd gotten her undergraduate degree; or what boyfriends she'd had before Mark; nothing; nothing at all. I found a folding chair and sat down. I wondered if I ought to be wearing a yarmulke. All the other men were. I couldn't worry about it. A piano was playing. The rabbi was walking down the front row shaking hands, kissing a few women on the cheek. I saw Mark for the first time, leaning toward the rabbi, their right hands locked, their left hands on each other's elbow, saying something into his ear, the rabbi nodding once, then nodding again. The distracting sound of more chairs being unstacked and set up behind me. A phone going off. A disapproving murmur. The piano playing again. The rabbi leading a song in Hebrew whose melody was sad and familiar. The rabbi saying, It is always deeply vexing to think that we must celebrate the life of someone who passed out of it with so much life left. The rabbi reading lines from a Galway Kinnell poem, the one about his dead brother. The sound of a sob. Another song or hymn or whatever. Someone—a relative?—saying a prayer. It was all quite lovely. Then the whole train went right the fuck off the goddamn rails and tumbled down the steep embankment into the river below.

31

My grandmother once told me that she'd stopped believing in the Church as soon as they started speaking English.

I thought, she said, *that's* what they've been saying all along? It was very disappointing. I remember saying, But Nana, you still go to church. Well, of course I *go* to church, she'd said. What's that got to do with anything?

32

So anyway, it would have been fair to say that the spirit of the thing was already somewhat straining against its earthly form; in the pace and organization, I detected Mark's influence. He was sitting alone in the front, separated from everyone by the sanctuary's one conspicuously unoccupied seat. Through the first part of the proceedings, his chin had rested on his thumb, his fingers over his mouth, his elbow on the armrest, his face betraying no human emotion, being instead composed like one single lens behind which some fractal algorithm aggregated and interpreted an infinity of data. You could sense, I thought, in the officiants, a certain inclination toward the freewheeling or the holistic or the organic or what have you that I felt certain Mark would have, and must have, vetoed, and you could sense, or I could, in Mark, despite his preternatural composure, a certain impatience at, for instance, the poetry. So when the rabbi invited Helen's stepmother up to speak—her stepmother?—I detected a palpable relief among some of the mourners and a twitch, a tremor, a slight quickening of his pulse that I swear to you I could detect from Mark from a hundred feet away. He moved his head from his left to his right hand. A rather florid woman with close black hair and a vaguely Etruscan necklace that sat like a piece of ancient armor on an operatically excessive chest wandered up to the microphone. Her torn black ribbon had been awkwardly pinned in precisely the spot one would expect to find her left nipple. Oh, Helen, she said, and she immediately began to weep. This in and of itself did not strike me as unusual; it's unfair to generalize based on body type, but she looked like a crier, and the crying seemed natural; but then the crying went on. She stood up on the Bimah gripping the podium in both hands and cried and cried. There was something formulaic about it. She could have been speaking in a monotone with a PowerPoint going in the background. She looked out at the audience, eyes bubbling, chest heaving, and it was as if the crying were itself some form of speech, some otherworldly language like a whale call, a song in an ancient, indecipherable syntax. We all sat politely. If this was the fucking stepmother, I thought, just the stepmother, how many more were in store? She kept on crying. Several minutes had now passed. I glanced toward Mark. His hands now gripped each other, fingers intertwined; his lips were thinly drawn. The rabbi walked to the woman and put his hand on her back, a gentle shepherd's crook, possibly, to draw her offstage, but she wouldn't let go of the podium; she didn't move. The crowd began to rustle. Then someone said, Oh, Jesus Christ, Janet. The voice was so like Helen's you'd have thought it came from the casket. Janet froze. Blinked her big eyes. We all murmured. Another woman walked to the podium. Helen's mother. Obviously. The same body. The same face. Her hair drawn severely away from her face. A narrow line of gold around her neck. Diamonds in her ears. Moved purposefully. Put a hand on Janet's elbow. Go on, she said. Sit down.

33

They told me, the mother said, to be short, but Helen was my daughter, so I'll say just as much as I want to. Her voice had slight tremor. It appeared to me that she might be slightly drunk. She had her daughter's overage of control; her performance had the sound of being sight-read. Helen, she said again, was my daughter. Helen, she said, was *my* daughter. More movement among the mourners, a shifting in the chairs. None of you, she said, none of you really knew her. She was looking at Mark now. I was surprised to find that he was avoiding her gaze. You saw that she was beautiful, you saw that she was talented, you saw all of those things on the outside. But what did you know? A mother knows. She was never really happy. Even as a little girl. There was something unhappy about her. There was something that saw what a lot of *shit* it all is. What a lot of *shit*. She was cynical. We're not supposed to be cynical. Women aren't supposed to be cynical. We're supposed to be, I don't know. We're supposed to be optimists. We're supposed to see the bright side. We're not supposed to see the shit. She was an artist because she saw the shit. She made such beautiful things, but she was never happy. What I wanted for her more than anything was to live long enough to be happy. It takes your whole life to be happy. I never figured it out, but I wanted for her to figure it out. You all, she said,

but she was only talking to Mark, you all didn't care about her
soul. You wondered why she even had a soul. You looked at
her and thought, Why would you put a soul in one of those?
But she had a soul, and it was better than your soul.

34

Then the mother sat down. The rabbi looked like a dog-walker
who finds he forgot the plastic bags as his dog squats at the
edge of the neighbor's yard. He was halfway between his seat
by the ark and the podium. He looked toward Mark, and he
looked toward the family. I thought, and felt badly for thinking, that the biggest tragedy was that I couldn't text Johnny. I
eased my phone from my pocket. I texted Lauren Sara: funeral
is fucked. She replied right away: where's tom? up front, I
replied. LOL, she said: figurz.

35

David Hoffman tried to save it. Tried to apply the brake. Tried
to step into the breach. I didn't imagine he was scheduled
to speak, but he rose before anyone else could and made his
broad-shouldered way to the microphone. He looked like an
architect with that buzzed gray hair and those little glasses.
He said, I did not know Helen Witold well, but I knew her
work. She was that rare artist whose work remained personal
even as it became more widely known and admired. Personal

is a word that often damns with faint praise in our art world. I say our art world because it belonged to Helen as much as any of us. Personal is a word we use, often when describing a woman's work, to imply that it lacks some essential ambition. Ambition is a word we use, often when describing a man's work, that suggests we should forgive its weak grasp because of its broad reach. Don't look too closely at the trees; we propose a forest. There is nothing wrong, perhaps, with ambition, but our art has become so intently focused on *saying* something that it has largely stopped *being* something. I found Helen's work expressed a purity of being that is largely absent these days. I remember the first time I saw one of her paintings at Daniel's gallery—he gestured toward a man who must have been the other Arnovich, who, Jesus Christ, raised his hand in reciprocation as if being introduced on a panel of speakers at some convention somewhere—and I said, Daniel, what is *that*? And Daniel replied, *That*, he said, is Helen Witold. And I said, Is it any good? (Relieved laughter in the audience. The first joke.) Because I couldn't tell. It was like seeing poetry in a language you don't understand. (Oh, come the fuck on, I heard someone mutter a row or two behind me.) And Daniel said, I don't know, either, but she's going to be a hit at the parties. (Laughter again, this time less comfortable.) That's a joke. If there is a human soul—he gestured with an offhanded, patrician magnanimity in the general direction of Helen's mother—then we need more poets who speak its untranslatable language. (For real? The same mutterer as before.) Yes. Poets of that ineffable dialect. (Throats clearing.) We have lost a poet of the soul, he said.

36

This all struck me as the purest horseshit, but as it was more within the tradition of an overchoreographed memorial service, it took a little edge off. I texted Lauren Sara: we have lost a poet of the soul. Haha, she said.

37

And yet it made me sad, the whole thing; it made me wish I could stand up and spout some horseshit myself, find a well of extemporaneous platitude to toss like a beach ball to the expectant, anxious crowd. Her poor, drunk mother had been right, mostly, if a bit, well, infelicitous in her expression of it.

38

Then Mark went up and recited the Ninety-first Psalm. He was wearing the same suit as the first day I'd met him and Helen, the same gray tie. No disaster will befall you; no calamity will come near your tent, he said. He was holding a copy of the psalm in his hands. His hands were shaking. I construed it as guilt. You will tread down lions and snakes, he said. Young lions and serpents, you will trample them underfoot. His voice was flat. He saw me. I saw him see me. I saw the corners of his mouth move. I tried to stare back at him, but, as had always been the case, I had to look away first.

Because he loves me, I will rescue him, he said to me. Because he knows my name, I will protect him. He will call on me, and I will answer him. I will be with him when he is in trouble. I will extricate him and bring him honor. I will satisfy him with long life and show him my salvation.

39

Helen's father said, When she was about ten, Helen decided that she was going to be a famous artist, and since most of you know me, you know I told her never take less than 60 percent on a painting. The New Yorkers laughed. Tom laughed loudly enough for them to notice him laughing. Well, my Helen was just getting started. She had a future. A real future. A real future. But it isn't so real anymore. I wonder, if I could go back in time, would I have made that joke? Or would I have said, Honey, don't be an artist. Artists die young. The good ones anyway. Oh, hell, I don't know, he said. He shook his head. I just don't know. He was short and fat and his hair exploded in every direction. I just don't know, he said.

40

Then the rabbi said, O Lord, what is man that You recognize him, the son of a human that You think of him? Man is like a breath; his days are like a passing shadow. In the morning it blossoms and grows, in the evening it fades and withers. Teach us to count our days, and we shall acquire a heart of wisdom. Guard the innocent and watch the upright, for the destiny of man is peace. But God will ransom my soul from the grave, for He will surely take me. My flesh and my heart yearn— rock of my heart and my portion is God, forever. The dust returns to the dust as it was, but the spirit returns to God who gave it. Then he said, *El male rachamim.* Then we all filed out gratefully to the cool evening to wait for the family, whom we would follow to the cemetery.

41

I waited with Tom and Julian. Well, I said. Well, Julian said. I thought that David Hoffman was amazing, said Tom. Tom, I said, you are one crass motherfucker. Whatever, said Tom. You didn't even know her. Come on, Tom, said Julian. No, I said. That's true. Are you going to the cemetery? asked Tom. I think so, I said. You? Yeah, he said. It's impolite not to go. Really? I said. According to whom? It just is, said Tom. Well, I said, I'll need a ride. You can ride with me, said Ben David, who was walking past. Come on. Catch you dudes later, I said, and I followed Ben David. So, he said, you never found your car. We were sitting in his, waiting for the procession. It was stolen, I said. How about all that shit? he said, meaning the funeral. Not precisely what I was expecting, I said. I thought the poor husband, or fiancé or whatever, was going to have a goddamn aneurism, said Ben David. Yeah, I said. Mark. He's a little, uh, he can be controlling. Well, that sort of freak show will do it.

So you knew her pretty well? he asked, and I could sense that he was asking something else, so I answered with a question: What are you doing here, anyway? Technically, he said, I'm part of the *chevra kaddisha*. Her relatives were all from out of town, and she wasn't exactly *active* in the Jewish community. Rabbi Blum called and said, be a good boy, so here I am. As an attorney, I try to do whatever service to HaShem and the congregation that I can fit in around the billable hours. Hedging my bets, and so forth. Anyway, you feel bad for the poor thing. Look at that family! And that goon of a boyfriend. Yeah, I said. He probably killed her. Ben David arched an eyebrow. Oh yeah? he said. Not, like, literally, I said. I actually think she probably killed herself. But it was his fault. Say no more, said Ben David. I know the type. *Nifter-shmifter, a leben macht er?* my mother, may the Lord keep her away from the telephone, would say, but I never trust these squirrely corporate lawyer types. Hm, I said. How'd you know he's a lawyer? Oh, hell, just look at him. Spot them a mile away. Corporations only hire lawyers when they want to do something illegal. Well—I smiled—like criminals. No, no, said Ben David. Criminals are charmingly naïve about the whole thing. They hire lawyers *after* they do something illegal. The corporate guys are the ones who use legal prophylaxis in the whorehouse. Assholes. Anyway, I'm sure that poor little rich girl got hooked up with him and thought he was just great, some young buck on the make. No old-money, fratboy simp; no probably-a-homosexual backslapping Whiffenpoof; a real, honest-to-God Fordham type. Made a bunch of money together, partied all through their twenties, then found herself in her thirties

married or close enough to a soulless hatchet man who kept
her around for social cred. Am I close here? Shockingly, I said.
You can tell that just by looking? I can tell that just by looking, he said. So, what? he said. You took her up to that little
shindig. You were fucking her, right? Don't answer. I don't
need to know. He figures out she's stepping out on him. It's
a goddamn inconvenience to him in some way or other. He
says a bunch of nasty shit. She's drunk enough or depressed
enough to toss herself in the drink. Jesus, I said. Sorry, he
said. I tend to look at these things with a clinical eye. Personally, it seems like a goddamn shame. Oh, okay, here we go.
We pulled out into the procession of black cars. Anyway, he
said, look, I don't want to get into the sex part, but you've got
to put her out of your mind. Listen, this is legal advice. Take
a moment at the cemetery. Put some dirt on the coffin. Say
whatever prayers you pagan Catholics say. Then forget about
her. You've got a better, closer friend who's going to go to jail,
and you're sure as rain in Pittsburgh going to get called to
testify or at least get deposed at some point or other, and I do
not need you showing up with a dead mistress around your
neck—and neither does your pal Johnny. *Capiche?* Yes, I said.
I understand.

42

Speaking of your pal Johnny, Ben David said, any chance you
can get him to ease up on the weirdo quotient just for the time
being? I'm happy that he's committed to sobriety or whatever,

but he seriously pissed off the wrong people with that idiot blog he was running, and they're leaning on that faggot prosecutor to drive a hard deal. I'll do what I can, I said, but I can't promise anything. Fucking Pittsburgh Democrats, he said. The worst. Yeah, I said. You don't strike me as a GOP type, though. Ben David snorted. Republican? he said. Not likely. I'm a libertarian. Since before there *were* Libertarians. I voted for Hospers and Nathan in '72. Tonie Nathan, he said. Now, that was a woman with balls.

43

We went through the iron gates and past the gothic gatehouse and through the row of gingkoes that were turning golden already and past the mausoleums of millionaires' row, the alternatingly reserved and gaudy tombs of all those Fricks and Browns and Benedums and Wilkinses and Morrisons and so on and over the rolling hills and lawns between the sycamores and beeches and horse chestnuts and buckeyes and the few big cedars and the fields of ordinary graves through the several hundred acres until we came to the Jewish section on the far eastern edge where the cemetery turns over a slow hillside into the thick trees of Frick Park. And we all got out of our cars. But there were so many of us that it took quite a while for all the cars to pull up and park and for all the guests and mourners to make their way to the graveside. The sun was getting low in the sky. It really was almost the fall. It was cool. A breeze lifted men's ties and women's shawls. I didn't get too near to

the grave. I didn't want to get too near to Mark. I didn't want
to be there, really. I wanted to go home and pour myself one
glass of red wine, to stand in the kitchen at the window and
let the night come, to drink that one glass of wine and go
to sleep. I wanted to feel the cool night coming through the
screens while I fell asleep. I wanted to wrap myself in a blanket against the breeze again. I wanted to dream about Winston
Pringle one more time and tell his fat ass to fuck off. I wanted
to wake up with nothing to do but determine what it was that
I ought to do next. One of the New Yorkers was saying quietly
to another, Definitely going to drive up the value, and there's
not that much work to begin with. There was the sound of
a distant lawn mower. Tom was whispering something in
Julian's ear. Both Arnoviches were playing indiscreetly with
their cell phones on opposite ends of the casket. Beyond the
crowd, along the road where the cars were parked, I could have
sworn I saw Lauren Sara with a couple of prominent-looking
older people beside a long dark Mercedes, but then some people got in the way, and when they moved again, the car was
driving off, and she was gone. The rabbi was saying again, O
God, full of mercy, Who dwells on high, grant proper rest on
the wings of the Divine Presence, in the lofty levels of the holy
and the pure ones, who shine like the glow of the firmament,
for the soul of Helen Witold, daughter of Joel and Marion
Witold, stepdaughter of Barbara Witold, who has gone on to
His world. May her resting place be in the Garden of Eden;
therefore may the Master of Mercy shelter her in the shelter of
His wings for Eternity, and may He bind her soul in the Bond
of Life. Adonai is her heritage, and may she repose in peace

on her resting place. Now let us say: Amen. Then everyone was pushing forward, a gang of the criminally well dressed, even falling in some cases like fools to their knees in order to get their own handful of turned earth, as if it were in limited supply, as if there weren't enough dirt to cover every one of us.

44

I wandered off. I sat in the grass at the edge of the cemetery. The sun was going down behind me. I could hear a few evening birds calling in the woods in the park. I thought, I'd been wrong. We would not end as a ruin. Well, in a thousand years we might. In ten thousand, there wouldn't be any ruins. There would be trees and birds and insects. A brief heartbeat of the world. Long enough to heal itself of all of us. Let the aliens arrive then, and see how little the sparrows and the earthworms and the squirrels and the field mice care. Then I saw that Mark was standing next to me. You are one sneaky fucker, I said. You said it, he said. Well, I said, condolences and so forth. Yeah, he said. Thanks and back at ya. So, I said. So, he said. He sat in the grass beside me. So what's so interesting in there? he asked, looking toward the trees. I was just thinking about global solutions, I answered. Oh yeah? he said. Yeah, I said. Long-term, strategic solutions. Your next career, he said. Another life, I said. There is no other life, he said. So I'm told, I told him. How about that funeral? he asked. I let myself look at him. He seemed smaller, softer, as if he'd just shed his skin and hadn't quite firmed up yet. Can I ask you something? I asked. Other than that? he answered. What did you say to her? I said. When? he said. Over the phone, I said. That night, I said. Nothing she hadn't heard before, he said. You know, I told him, I've come to the conclusion that you're a real asshole. He stood up. He brushed some grass from his pants. You've come to that conclusion? he said. You've examined the evidence, arrayed the facts, done the regression analysis. Fuck off, I said. You know, Peter, he said. It was, I think, the first time he'd ever called me Peter. What? I said. Actually, he said. Nothing. Nothing. Yeah, I said. Me, too.

Then he put his hands into his pockets. He whistled tunelessly, a few high notes that seemed intended to answer the whistling birds. It was almost dark. He didn't look at me. He walked in a straight line through the grass toward the tree line. He paused there briefly, and I thought he might turn around, but he didn't. He walked right into the woods, right into the shadows between the trees. I stared after him for a while. And then I thought I saw a light in the woods. Something glowing. Something that moved. Maybe I saw it rise toward the treetops. Maybe I saw it fade as it reached the last daylight above them. But you know, if there was something there, then it was not so bright, nor was I so sure that I'd seen it as I'd been six months ago.

ACKNOWLEDGMENTS

First, thanks to Will Menaker, my editor, who saw this book drinking alone at the far end of a dingy bar and sidled up to it and bought it a drink and took it home, and then to everybody else at Liveright and W. W. Norton who welcomed it into the family despite its appalling lack of pedigree. Thanks to my agent, Gail Hochman, who not only took me up for no good reason but also worries whether anyone is meeeting me for dinner when I'm visiting New York. My parents, who still ask me, "Are you writing?" Thanks to Josh, Nate, Alex. and the other residents and transients of the apartment above the satanic daycare, who both read and inspired the early drafts of this book. Last and most, to John Allen, without whose friendship and insatiable interest in everything weird and appalling and otherworldy I never would have written this at all.

ABOUT THE AUTHOR

Jacob Bacharach is a writer and nonprofit administrator living in Pittsburgh, Pennsylvania. He has a BA in English and creative writing from Oberlin College and an MBA from the University of Pittsburgh. He is not, to the best of our knowledge, a shape-shifting reptiloid or a descendent of the Merovingian dynasty. In his spare time, he cooks, rides bikes, and occasionally plays the violin badly. He prefers "experiencer" to "abductee." This is his first novel.